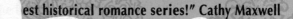

"...est historical romance series!" Cathy Maxwell

Kinley MacGregor

USA Today bestselling author of
A Dark Champion

Return
OF THE
Warrior

BROTHERHOOD OF THE SWORD

*Enter a world of passion,
danger, and incomparable love
with the remarkable*

Kinley MacGregor

BROTHERHOOD OF THE SWORD

And don't miss these sensational masterworks of romance:

TAMING THE SCOTSMAN

BORN IN SIN

CLAIMING
THE HIGHLANDER

MASTER OF DESIRE

MASTER OF SEDUCTION

A PIRATE OF HER OWN

"Are you Christian of Acre?"

He stiffened at the question, especially since he had recently come from Hexham, where assassins for him and his brothers-in-arms had abounded. And some of those assassins had been female.

"Who seeks him?"

The woman moved forward and boldly pulled at the thin gold chain around Christian's neck, where his mother's royal emblem had rested since the hour of his birth. "Aye," she said, letting it fall back to his chest on the outside of his black monk's robes. "You are indeed the one I seek."

"And you are?"

Her elegant hands came out of the dark folds of her cloak to unclasp the catch. Before he could even draw a breath, she let the whole of it fall to the floor with a rush of wind and a heavy thud.

Christian's jaw went slack as he saw her standing there with not a single stitch adorning her dark, pale beauty. Long black hair cascaded over her shoulders, obscuring her breasts. She was beautiful and his body reacted wildly to her brash nudity.

"Who am I?" she asked in that wickedly erotic voice. "I'm your wife and I'm here to claim you."

**"Humor and passion are the trademarks
of any Kinley MacGregor book."**
Christina Dodd

Books by
Kinley MacGregor

KNIGHT OF DARKNESS
SWORD OF DARKNESS
RETURN OF THE WARRIOR
A DARK CHAMPION
TAMING THE SCOTSMAN
BORN IN SIN
CLAIMING THE HIGHLANDER
MASTER OF DESIRE
MASTER OF SEDUCTION
A PIRATE OF HER OWN

Kinley MacGregor

Return of the Warrior

AVON BOOKS

An Imprint of HarperCollinsPublishers

This is a work of fiction. Names, characters, places, and incidents are products of the author's imagination or are used fictitiously and are not to be construed as real. Any resemblance to actual events, locales, organizations, or persons, living or dead, is entirely coincidental.

AVON BOOKS
An Imprint of HarperCollins*Publishers*
10 East 53rd Street
New York, New York 10022-5299

First Avon Books paperback printing: May 2005

Avon Trademark Reg. U.S. Pat. Off. and in Other Countries, Marca Registrada, Hecho en U.S.A.
HarperCollins® is a registered trademark of HarperCollins Publishers Inc.

Printed in the U.S.A.

10   9   8

To my fans, who have been so incredibly wonderful and supportive. You guys are the best! For the RBL women, who are always there when I need a pick-me-up. To my loop members, who fill my life with laughter and caring. God bless you all.

For May, Lyssa and Nancy, who work so tirelessly to make every book the best it can be. I don't know what I'd do without you guys and I never want to find out. To my husband and boys, for filling my life with love and for making it complete.

But most of all for my mother, who really wanted to read Christian's story. I'm only sorry I didn't get it done sooner, Mom. I miss you more than I would have ever thought possible and I hope that you were right and that heaven is filled to the brim with all the books you loved so much.

There are three acts in a man's life which no one should advise him either to do or not to do. The first is to get married, the second is to go to the wars and the third is to go to the Holy Land. These things are all good in themselves, but they may turn out ill, in which case he who gave the advice will be blamed as if he were the cause of it.

—EBERHARD OF WÜRTTEMBERG

BROTHERHOOD OF THE SWORD

Prologue

Taagaria
A small kingdom adjoining Byzantium

"Well?" Queen Adara asked in nervous anticipation as her senior advisor drew near her throne.

Xerus had been her father's most trusted man. At almost three score years in age, he still held the sharpness of a man in the prime of his life. His once-black hair was now streaked with gray and his beard was whiter than the stone walls that surrounded their capital city, Garzi.

Since her father's death two years past, Adara had turned to Xerus for everything. There was no one alive she trusted more, which didn't say much, since, as a queen, her first lesson had been that spies and traitors abounded in her court. Most thought that a woman had no business as the leader of their small kingdom.

Adara had other thoughts on that matter. As her father's only surviving child, she refused to see anyone not of their royal bloodline on this throne. Her family had held the royal seat since before the time of Moses.

No one would take her precious Taagaria from her. Not so long as she breathed.

Xerus shook his head and sighed wearily. "Nay, my queen, they refuse to allow you to divorce their prince. In their minds you are married and should you try to sever ties to their throne by divorce or annulment they will attack with the sanction of the Church. After all, in their eyes they already own our kingdom. In fact, Selwyn thinks it best that you move into his custody for your own welfare so that they can protect you . . . as their queen."

Adara clenched her fists in frustration.

Xerus glanced over his shoulder toward her two guards who flanked her door before he drew closer to her throne so that he could whisper privately into her ear.

Lutian, her fool, crept nearer to them as well and angled his head so that he wouldn't miss a single word. He even cupped his ear forward.

Xerus glared at the fool.

Dropping his hand, Lutian glared back. A short, lean man, Lutian had straight brown hair and wore a well-trimmed beard. Possessed of average looks, his face was pleasant enough, but it was his kind brown eyes that endeared him to her.

"Speak openly," she said to her advisor. "There is no one I trust more than Lutian."

"He's a half-wit, my queen."

Lutian snorted. "Half-wit, whole-wit, I have enough of them to know to keep silent. So speak, good counselor, and let the queen judge which of the two of us is the greater fool present."

Adara pressed her lips together to keep from smiling at Lutian. Two years younger than she, Lutian had been seriously injured as a youth when he'd tumbled from their walls and landed on his head. Ever since that day, she had watched over him and kept him close lest anyone make his life even more difficult.

She placed a hand on his shoulder to silence him. Xerus couldn't abide being made fun of. Unlike her, he didn't value Lutian's friendship and service.

With a warning glare to the fool, Xerus finally spoke. "Their prince-regent said that if you would finally like to declare Prince Christian dead, then he might be persuaded toward your cause . . . at a price."

Closing her eyes, she ground her teeth furiously. The Elgederion regent had made his position on that matter more than clear. Selwyn wanted her in his son's bed as his bride to secure their tenuous claim to the throne, and the devil would freeze solid before she ever gave herself over to him and allowed those soulless men to rule her people.

How she wished she commanded a larger nation with enough soldiers to pound the arrogant prince-regent into nothing more than a bad memory. Unfortunately, a war would be far too costly to her people and her kingdom. They couldn't fight the Elgederions alone and none of their other allies would help, since to them it was a family squabble between her and her husband's kingdom.

If only her husband would return home and claim his throne, but every time they had sent a man for him, the messenger was slain. To her knowledge none of them had ever reached Christian and she was tired of sending men to their deaths.

Nay, 'twas time to see this matter closed once and for all.

"Send for Thera," she whispered to Xerus.

He scowled at her. "For what purpose?"

"I intend to take a lengthy trip and I can't afford to let anyone know that I am not here to guard my throne."

"Your cousin is not you, Your Grace. Should anyone learn—"

"I trust you alone to keep her and my crown safe until I return. Have her confined to my quarters and tell everyone that I am ill."

Xerus looked even more confused by her orders. "Where are you going?"

"To find my wayward husband and bring him home."

One

Withernsea, England

Christian of Acre sat in the aleroom of the town's only inn, finishing his supper in solitude while the rest of the inn's occupants ate and drank noisily around him. It was dark inside, with most of the light coming from the fireplace, on the hearth, where a portly stout woman roasted venison and pork.

He'd been here for the last four days, waiting for Pagan and Lochlan MacAllister to meet him. The plan was for them to join forces.

They were all on the trail of a friend's murderer who was said to have headed this way with his brothers. If Lysander's killer was anywhere nearby, Christian would find him and make him pay for what he had taken from them. And if Lochlan happened to learn anything helpful about his missing brother Kieran MacAllister, then Christian would rejoice even more.

But at the end of the day, the only thing that mattered to him was putting Lysander's soul to rest. The man had been a good one, and as a member of the Brotherhood he had been invaluable. His murder sat ill with all of them. The Brotherhood members hadn't survived hell to return home and be slain over nothing more than sheer meanness.

Drinking the last of his ale, Christian left money on the table, then got up to go to his rented room.

Times like this, he almost hated that he traveled alone. Especially since Nassir and Zenobia were newly departed from his company. They had left just the day before, on their way back to Outremer.

But then, Christian had chosen of his own free will to live his life alone.

It was better this way.

He had lived for almost six years sequestered in a monastery cell where the brothers forbade any chatter at all. They had used their hands to speak to each other. Never their mouths. So silence and solitude were nothing new to him.

After living with the monks, Christian had spent another six years imprisoned in the squalid twenty-foot cell of his enemies. He had no desire to ever again be chained down by anyone or anything.

For the first time in his life he was free, and he fully intended to stay that way.

If solitude and loneliness were the price of his freedom, so be it. It was only a trifle compared to the blood and bone he'd paid for far lesser things.

Christian reached his room at the end of the

hallway and pushed open the door. He pulled up short as he caught sight of the lone figure waiting there beside a small table where an oil lamp flickered brightly.

Slight of stature, the unknown person was robed in a long black cloak that gave him no indication of gender or nationality.

"Did you perchance enter the wrong room?" he asked, thinking maybe it was another traveler who had lost his way.

The figure turned toward him.

"That depends," she said, her voice smooth and erotic, and tinged with an accent he couldn't place. "Are you Christian of Acre?"

He stiffened at the question, especially since he had recently come from Hexham, where assassins looking for him and his brothers-in-arms had abounded.

And some of those assassins had been female . . .

"Who seeks him?"

The woman moved forward and boldly pulled at the thin gold chain around Christian's neck where his mother's royal emblem had rested since the hour of his birth. She turned it over to see on the back another engraving of a crest of a kingdom he'd only visited once as a small child.

"Aye," she said, letting it fall back to his chest on the outside of his black monk's robes. "You are indeed the one I seek."

"And you are?"

Her elegant hands came out of the dark folds of

her cloak to unclasp the catch. Before he could even draw a breath, she let the whole of it fall to the floor with a rush of wind and a heavy thud.

Christian's jaw went slack as he saw her standing there with not a single stitch adorning her dark beauty. Long black hair cascaded over her shoulders, obscuring her breasts as the ends of it tickled the dark triangle at the juncture of her thighs.

She was beautiful and his body reacted wildly to her brash nudity.

"Who am I?" she asked in that wickedly erotic voice. "I'm your wife and I'm here to claim you."

Completely stunned by the unexpected words, Christian felt his jaw go slack as she reached for him.

He stepped back immediately. "I beg your pardon. I have no wife."

She stared up at him with dark soulful eyes from under her long black lashes. "How I wish it true, but alas, my lord, you most certainly do, and I have no intention of leaving your side."

Christian forced himself to close his gaping mouth. 'Twas obvious the woman was mad. He retrieved her cloak from the floor and quickly wrapped it around her nude body, even though part of him screamed out that he was an utter fool to turn her away.

How often did a man find a woman like this offering herself to him in such a bold manner?

It definitely wasn't often enough.

"My lady, you ap—"

"Adara," she said, interrupting him. "Remember me now?"

Christian opened his mouth to deny it, but before he could, an image went through his mind of a young girl from his childhood. All he remembered of her were two large brown eyes that had reminded him of a gentle fawn as they studied him with great curiosity. She'd been shy and quiet, certainly not the type who as a woman would bare herself to a complete stranger.

But those large brown eyes . . .

They were the same and every bit as enchanting now as they had been then. More so, point of fact.

"I can see that you do." Her exotic voice whipped through him with power. "And I remember you as well."

Adara grew quiet as the memory of the boy Christian went through her. The first time she had seen him, she had been entranced by his fair coloring. In her kingdom, blondes were exceedingly rare. Handsome ones even more so.

He'd come to their palace on their wedding day wearing the finest of silk, which had floated around his body like a dark blue cloud. Barely seven years of age, she had stared at him from her window, curious about the fairness of the eight-year-old boy who was to be her husband.

Now she was enthralled by the man before her. Extremely tall and handsome, he was well muscled and had the bearing of a man well used to commanding everyone around him. He was exactly what she sought. A man who could send his usurper scurrying away from their kingdoms with his tail tucked firmly between his legs.

Not to mention he was far kinder on her eyes than she had ever dared to hope.

His long golden hair hung just past his shoulders and he had a small, well-trimmed goatee that added a fierce air of masculinity to him. His blue eyes were searing and intelligent. He held the kind of face that was compelling in its manly beauty, the kind of face that a woman couldn't help but stare at in awe and with desire.

"We were only betrothed," he said in a deep, resonating voice that somehow managed to send a small shiver through her every time he spoke.

"Nay, Christian, we were married that day. I have the papers to prove it."

"Show me."

Ignoring the challenge of his tone, Adara refastened her cloak to her before she moved to the corner where she had left her small parcel that contained two simple gowns and enough gold to see her safely home again. In the bottom was the leather pouch that held the proof she needed.

She pulled it out, then handed it to the doubting man whose regal presence seemed to fill the entire room. This was not going the way she'd planned at all. Lutian had assured her that the instant she bared herself to her husband he would fall down on his knees in gratitude, then consummate their marriage immediately.

As she watched Christian, she doubted anything on this earth could make a man this proud fall down onto his knees.

It would certainly take more than a mere woman's nudity.

Christian's eyes narrowed as he opened, then read the document he could barely recall from his childhood. It had been a warm summer day not long before his parents' deaths. Adara hadn't spoken a single word to him as her father had led her into the throne room so that the two of them could meet before they signed the betrothal contract.

She had merely glanced up at him, blushed, then signed the vellum document and ran away, not to be seen again during his two-day stay at her palace.

Now, as he scanned the Latin words and their childish handwriting, his vision turned dark. Deadly. The queen was right. This was no betrothal. It was indeed a contract for marriage.

"I was duped," he snarled. Nay, not entirely true. Had he studied Latin more strenuously as a child and been more attentive, he would have been able to read it then and protest its contents.

Even as a child, he should have known better than to trust another human being with his future.

No one could ever be trusted.

Sadness and confusion mixed on her brow, gifting her face with a somber expression that was somehow no less lovely. "I see," she said quietly. "But that changes nothing. We are legally married and I need you to come home with me and be crowned king."

He shook his head in denial. "I will have this contract dissolved immediately."

"Nay," she snarled at him. "You will not."

He scowled at her insistence on the impossible. "Are you mad, woman? I have no intention of going to Elgedera. Ever."

She straightened. Her dark eyes snapped fire at him as her cheeks mottled in anger. "And I have no intention of allowing you your freedom while I need you to be husband. I am virgin still, but if you walk from this room, I shall find myself the nearest willing male and swear by all that is holy that you were the only man I have ever known and I will drag you home in chains if need be."

He saw red at her threat. Truly her audacity knew no limits. "You would jeopardize your immortal soul to keep me bound to you?"

"Nay, but I will sell my soul to the devil himself to keep my people free from the cloying hands of your cousin, and if bearing false witness is the only way to save my kingdom, then aye. I shall do whatever is necessary."

Christian couldn't breathe as he stared at her. She was unbelievable. "You don't even know me."

"Since when are men so discriminating? Can you honestly say that you have never taken a woman to your bed that you barely knew? I am your wife and our union needs to be consummated."

Christian didn't answer her question. He refused to.

Her gaze drifted over his body and the robes of a Benedictine monk that he wore. Her face turned completely pale. "Have you taken holy vows? Oh, please tell me that I didn't just bare my body to a monk! I'll burn in eternal torment for it, surely."

It was on the tip of his tongue to say aye, but he couldn't bear to lie. He had suffered the lies of others far too many times in his life to ever deal that to another human being.

Even an insane one.

"Nay. I have not."

Her face and tone softened and a smile played at the edge of her well-shaped lips. "You are indeed a good man, Christian of Acre, not to lie to me about this."

He narrowed his gaze at her. "Make no mistake, my lady, I am never a good man and I have no intention of seeing this marriage met."

His words cut through her. Nay, this was not what she'd planned. She'd expected her husband to be more cooperative.

And deep inside, in a place where she dare not look, was disappointment that he hadn't remembered her at all, while there had never been a day since their marriage that she hadn't thought of him and wondered where he'd been, fretted for his welfare.

But that was something she would never let him

know. A pining, sentimental buffoon she might be inwardly, but outwardly she was still queen with a heavy burden to bear. She might not have much, but she did have her dignity.

"It is not a marriage I want from you, either. I only want a few weeks of your time to secure my borders. After that, you shall be free to live out your life in any manner you choose."

He cocked his head at her untoward words. "What say you?"

She took a deep breath before she spoke to him in a calm, even tone that belied the maelstrom of anger, desire, and fear she felt. "I have no need of a husband to rule my lands. I am more than capable of seeing to my people. I need only your presence so as to appease your people so that your usurper cannot force himself upon me any longer."

"My usurper?"

"Aye. Basilli. Do you remember him at all?"

He shook his head. "I know no one by that name."

"Do you at least recall his father Selwyn, then?"

Christian recalled the man's hawkish features quite well. A cold, unfeeling man, Selwyn had been the one to tell him about the death of his parents when he was a boy. Selwyn had been callous and vicious as he told him to stop crying and be a man. *Life is tragedy, boy, you might as well accept it and grow accustomed to it.*

Little had Christian known at the time just how true those words were.

"Aye, I remember him."

"Then you might want to know that he is a snake out to claim not just your throne, but mine as well. He and his son must be stopped at any and all costs."

Christian frowned. "If that is true and his son wishes to marry you, then why has Selwyn been writing to me to come home and see our betrothal met?"

She scoffed at that. "Begging you home to murder you, most like, my lord. As they would murder me if I were ever foolish enough to wed Basilli."

"You lie."

She gave him an arch look. "Think you so? Tell me, have you ever once thought about how odd it is that your parents died together in a fire while you were safely tucked away? That they hid you so as to save you from their fate?"

Christian struggled to breathe as her accusation ran through his mind. Could there possibly be any truth to it?

As a child, he'd been too torn apart by grief to think of it. As a man, he'd done his best never to dwell on the past at all.

"For that matter, haven't you ever wondered why your inconsequential monastery in Acre was attacked and destroyed by thieves, and why no one from your own family ever came to see if you lived? You're the sole heir to an important throne and yet they left you to rot. Why would no one ever try to find you? Could it be because you were supposed to have died with the rest of the monks and that is what they told everyone?"

Christian paused at her words. To his knowledge no one had ever checked into his welfare while he had been imprisoned. He had been the one to send a letter home to tell them of his fate once he was freed.

Selwyn had written back immediately to beg him home while Christian had recuperated from his injuries in an Italian monastery. Christian had refused, then made his way to France with several other Brotherhood members. In the years since, he and his uncle had passed brief letters through designated monasteries a few times every year.

"Selwyn has known for years that I live and he knows where I travel."

And over those years, there had been countless attempts on his life . . .

Her dark, sincere stare burned him. "Selwyn dares more than you know. He is an evil man who rules your people as a tyrant. Unlike you, I will not allow my people to suffer while I do nothing to help them."

Her words rang in his ears and ignited his temper. He had lived the whole of his adulthood on a quest to help the downtrodden, and now this woman dared to tell him his own people suffered while he did nothing to help them?

It was preposterous.

Wasn't it?

"How do I know *you're* not lying?" he asked.

"I am here, aren't I? Why else would I have traversed hostile lands to come to a country so far from my own unannounced?"

"And how is it you found me?"

"A hired tracker."

Christian was surprised by her words, though why that should surprise him, given the rest of her ludicrous accusations, he couldn't imagine. "A tracker? How could a tracker find me when you have no idea who or what I am? For that matter, you had no idea what I looked like."

She hesitated, then looked uncertain. "My younger advisor found him for me and the tracker said that he knew who you were and that you should be near the Withernsea Abbey in England this time of year."

Adara paused as a bad feeling settled over her. She'd been so focused on finding her wayward spouse that those questions had never entered her mind.

Indeed, the tracker hadn't even asked for a description of Christian.

And before that thought could complete itself, the door to the room crashed open.

Adara looked past Christian to find five soldiers rushing into the room with swords drawn.

Two

 The men paused in the doorway as they surveyed her in the cloak and Christian in his monk's black robes.

Adara felt ill that she had allowed herself to be so easily duped. "Where are my men?" she asked the tracker. Most importantly, where was Lutian?

"Dead. All of them." Her tracker laughed as he looked at her and Christian. "An unarmed queen and a monk to kill." He tsked as he moved closer. "This'll be the easiest money I've ever earned."

Adara grabbed her parcel as Christian drew a sword from beneath his monk's robes. He whirled toward her and handed her their marriage contract.

"Excuse me," he said politely before he placed himself between her and their attackers.

The eyes of the shortest of the men widened as he saw Christian swing his sword to ready it.

"Sierus," he said with a gulp, "I don't think he's a monk."

Her heart hammering, she watched as Christian engaged the men with a skill that was deadly and precise.

It was a beautiful, macabre dance as the five men sought to kill Christian and he deflected their blows with a manly grace and ease. She'd never seen anything like it. The sound of steel echoed loudly in her ears while they each fought for their lives.

Suddenly one of the attackers took notice of her. He lunged.

Adara jumped back an instant before Christian whirled and caught the man with a blow to his back. As the man fell, three more came through the door.

They were doomed!

Christian grabbed his bed and flipped it over, toward the men. He whirled around, kicked open the window, threw his sword out, then grabbed her up in his arms.

"What are you doing?" she asked, clutching her bag even tighter.

He said nothing.

Two rapid heartbeats later she found out as he jumped from the window with her firmly cradled in his arms.

Adara gasped as they fell, then landed in a haystack down below. His weight was crushing, as was the pain of her body from being slammed into the hay.

It was all she could do to breathe from the agony of it.

Christian didn't hesitate before he sheathed his sword, then grabbed her hand and hauled her toward the stable that was just across the way.

She blushed profusely as she realized what she must look like as her cloak kept parting to expose her naked body.

Why had she thought to play Cleopatra to his Caesar and meet her husband this way?

But then how was she to know her hired men would try to kill them? In the future, she would never make either mistake again.

Provided she had a future, anyway.

Christian entered the stable, where she saw the bodies of her two guardsmen lying dead in the first stall they reached. Grief tore her heart asunder as Christian moved to the next stall and was confronted by another knight.

"Lutian?" she called, knowing he, too, must be dead. But without his body being there, she thought mayhap he'd escaped somehow. Her fool could be most wily at times.

But Lutian didn't answer her.

Consumed by guilt and anger over the senselessness of his death, Adara picked up a pitchfork and launched it at the knight, who tried to dodge it while he fought her husband.

It caught him in the shin. He yelped as Christian parried his sword stroke.

She seized the pitchfork and went for the knight again, only to have Christian kill him before she could. Still she lunged for the fallen knight.

"My lady, he's already dead."

"Not dead enough!" she sobbed. "He killed my men. And . . . and . . . poor, helpless Lutian."

"Hello?"

Adara couldn't breathe at the sound of the wonderfully familiar voice. To her immediate relief, Lutian stuck his head up from a pile of hay. Pieces of straw were stuck and tangled in the brown locks of his hair, even in his beard.

It was the most precious sight she'd ever beheld. "Oh, thank the Lord and His saints for their mercy!" she cried as she ran to him and embraced him without decorum. "You're alive!"

"Only a fool would be fighting them, my queen, and though I am a fool, I'm not that foolish."

Before she could speak, Christian seized her from Lutian's arms, then swung her up onto the back of a solid black horse. "This is no time for chatter," he growled at them.

She barely had time to cover herself and settle her bag before he joined her.

He looked at Lutian. "Grab a horse if you're able and keep up."

Christian spurred the horse from the stable.

"You can't leave Lutian!" she snapped an imperious tone. "Go back for him. Now."

"Death waits for no one, Adara." Even so,

Christian wheeled the horse back toward the stable until they saw Lutian headed out behind them on her brown mare.

Adara was impressed by Lutian's abilities. Normally Lutian rode an ass. 'Twas the first time she'd ever seen him on a horse, and he rode with remarkable skill.

Christian reversed direction again. They flew through the small town, while people scurried to get out of their way. By the time they reached the edge of town, arrows began to whiz past them.

"Stay low," Christian said in her ear as he wrapped himself around her to protect her.

Adara didn't argue. "Stay down, Lutian," she called to her friend she could no longer see. "Don't fall behind."

She latched on to the horse's neck and kept herself huddled there while Christian's heavy breathing filled her ears. She prayed that they all made it to safety. Terror pounded through her veins. How could this be happening?

But then, she should have known. What better way to take her throne than to kill both of them together? Then there would be no one left to contest Basilli's rule.

Perhaps she should change places with Lutian and let him rule her kingdom. Surely he wouldn't be so blind or stupid.

They rode onward until her entire body was cramped from her uncomfortable position. The bag bit harshly into her stomach, but she didn't move. She wasn't sure if anyone still followed them or not. However, she didn't dare look. Better she should be huddled over for eternity than dead.

Christian glanced behind to see no one in pursuit. He slowed his horse ever so slightly as he tried to hear something other than the horse's hooves and his own heavy heartbeat.

"I think we lost them," he said, slowing even more.

Lutian kept pace with them as he looked behind as well.

Adara lifted herself up with a small groan. "I'm sure by now you must have guessed that the first man through the door was the tracker who led me to you."

"No doubt paid to put us together so that we could be murdered," Christian said with a disgusted breath.

"Aye," Lutian concurred. "I was fetching a nice leg of lamb in the inn when I saw the Elgederion soldiers enter the stable. Even before I went to the stable to find your men dead, I knew them for villains."

"Oh, and what made you think that?" Christian asked sarcastically. "The swords in their hands?"

Adara ignored him. She was grateful that at least Lutian had survived. "You hid?"

"Not at first. I started back to the inn to tell you what they'd done, but they were headed to your room and I had hoped your prince would be prince enough to champion you. If not, I was going to chop them up in the stable when they returned for their horses, which I let loose out the back."

"That would hardly have helped her had they slain her in the room," Christian growled.

Adara grimaced at him. "Christian, please be kind to him. Lutian isn't quite right."

"Quite right, how?"

Lutian knocked a fist against his skull. "Not right in the noggin. I took a tumble in my youth and scrambled my brains."

Christian frowned. "Is he right enough to know how many men are after us?"

"Aye," Lutian said. "I can count with the best of them. There were half a score of men who came to the stable, but I overheard them speaking and there is a full garrison of them who have been following us since we left Taagaria. The tracker was apparently leaving them signs to let them know which way we were heading until the two of you were together."

Adara rubbed her head to alleviate some of the pain that was beginning to throb just over her brow. "I can't believe I was so stupid as to trust that tracker. Why didn't I stop and think that it was unlikely he would find you so soon? My poor guardsmen. I can't believe I was such a fool."

"You had other things on your mind." Christian's charitable response surprised her, especially since he, more than anyone else, had plenty of reason to agree that she was a nitwit in this matter.

"Perhaps," she said as she adjusted her cloak to conceal her body more effectively. "But I should have known better. My court is riddled with spies."

"And my life is ever riddled with enemies."

Christian's bland tone told her much about his life and his view of it. It didn't appear that enemies concerned him much.

But they definitely concerned her.

"So what are we to do now?" she asked.

Christian turned his horse north. Lutian followed suit, riding just behind them.

"First we need to find quarter and then think with clear heads." Christian passed a look over his shoulder to Lutian.

"No clear head here. See?" He knocked against his skull again. "This one is thoroughly dense."

"Lutian," she said gently. "Please give us a few minutes to talk." She looked at Christian after Lutian rode up ahead. "I doubt any place is safe now that they know we're together."

"The Scot will see us safe. No one has ever breached his castle's walls."

She frowned. "The Scot?"

"An old friend."

Adara fell silent as the horse picked its way through the dense forest. She still couldn't believe this had happened to her. How could Selwyn have known what she planned?

And if he knew she was leaving . . .

"Oh, Lord," she breathed. "He must know I'm not on my throne."

Christian's arms tightened around her. "Easy, Adara. There is nothing you can do."

Still her panic swelled as she twisted to look back at him. "But what if he's harmed my cousin Thera? I left her there to pose as me until my return. Think you he's killed her as well?"

"I don't know, but I doubt that he would. Killing her would serve no purpose until he's certain you are dead."

"How do you figure?"

"Who is next in line after you?"

"Thera."

"And if she dies?"

"There is no one to take the throne."

"Then why would he kill her if he could rule the throne through her?"

She settled down a bit at that, hoping he was right. "So you think she's safe?"

"As long as you live, aye."

"It's true," Lutian chimed in. "He would not dare harm her until he's sure of your fate or lack thereof. To kill her would make everyone mad, especially the lady Thera. She would be most put out to find herself dead by their hands."

It was a small hope, but one she seized gratefully. "Are you completely certain?"

It was Christian who answered. "Nay, not truly. But if he intends her harm, there's no way to get to her in time. We can only hope for the best."

Adara wanted to cry as pain engulfed her. She

loved Thera and had never intended to put her in harm's way.

Damn Basilli and Selwyn for this. And damn herself for being so foolish. When she returned home, she would make certain the beasts paid dearly for their treachery.

Provided she made it home again . . .

"Thank you, Christian," she said quietly.

"For what?"

"Saving my life."

Christian inclined his head to her, but didn't speak.

As they rode, Adara glanced down to his hand that held the horse's reins. Tanned and scarred, it was a large, strong hand, well-shaped and masculine. It was obvious his weren't the hands of a courtier or prince. They were the hands of a capable warrior who was unused to pampering or mollycoddling. And yet the sight of that hand warmed her greatly, far more than any soft, gentle hand that she had seen on other noblemen.

His was the hand of a rugged man.

He turned his hand slightly so that she could see the back of it. Adara frowned at the sight of what appeared to be a crescent moon and scimitar branded into his tanned flesh.

Without thinking, she reached out and touched the raised mark. "What is this?"

Christian couldn't speak as bitter agony assailed him. He glanced down to his hand where the permanent reminder of his past mocked him daily, just as his enemies had intended.

" 'Tis nothing," he said, unwilling to share that horror with a stranger. Even if that stranger was his wife.

What had gone on during his captivity was no one's business except his and those friends who had escaped with him.

There in the deepest pit of the Holy Land, he and his friends had banded together to survive the unimaginable and return home.

Then again, not everyone had gone home. Some had been unable to face those they'd left behind. Since their escape, like him, they wandered constantly, trying to outrun the demons of their past.

But then, it wasn't that *he* couldn't face his past, his cousin, or his people. It was more that having lived in hell, he'd only wanted to save others like himself. Something he couldn't do while enslaved to a throne.

Kings and princes were never free to do as they pleased. They were politicians who must curry favor and make treaties.

The only treaty Christian wanted was the one he had with his sword. If someone got in his way, he removed him. He owed no one anything and he lived only to serve his brothers-in-arms.

As a king, one wrong step wouldn't just endanger his own life, but the lives of everyone in his kingdom. It was a burden he'd never wanted.

He'd spent the whole of his youth in captivity

being told when to speak, where he could go and how to live. Those days were long past. His life was now his own and he intended to keep it that way.

Adara tried a few times to engage Christian in conversation, but he made it readily apparent that he wasn't willing to speak as they traveled through the foreign countryside.

By nightfall, she was exhausted. Christian refused to stop.

"Your horse is tired, my lord, as am I."

"We will reach a village within the hour."

For the first time since their mad dash from the inn, she felt a modicum of relief. "Will we stay there this night?"

"Nay. I will leave you and your fool to eat something while I trade my horse for another, and then we shall continue onward."

"With no rest?"

He shrugged. "I have no desire to give our enemies time to catch up to us. Do you?"

"We can't fight them if we're exhausted."

"You'd be amazed, my lady, at what you can survive and how hard you can fight with no sleep whatsoever."

Adara hesitated at his dour tone of voice. There was something in it. A hidden piece that she could sense he didn't want to retread. "And what have you survived, to feel so confident?"

"Life, my lady. Sooner or later, it does make beggars and pawns of us all."

Lutian applauded. "Spoken quite well, my prince. Quite well."

Adara opened her mouth to contradict him, then caught herself. He was right. Here she was, a queen of great renown, far from home and being hunted like a frightened rabbit, and all because of one man's lust for power.

She *was* a pawn . . .

And a fool.

"You have a wise prince, my queen," Lutian said from beside them. "I would give him my fool's scepter, except that I no longer have one, since I left it at home so that no one would know I was a fool." He pulled a piece of lint from his tunic and held it out to Christian. "Take this as a token of my esteem."

She half expected Christian to scoff and mock Lutian, as most people did.

Instead, he took the lint, thanked him for it, then put it on his shoulder as if it were some kind of prize.

She smiled at his actions, which made him even more handsome to her. And he was a handsome man who held her. One who made every feminine part of her feel alive and on edge.

"How long have you been on your own, Christian?" she asked him.

He didn't respond.

Nay, he was a man of few words. A brave man who had left behind everything he'd ever known to travel about for reasons she could only guess at.

It must be awful to be a stranger in foreign lands.

"I can still feel the sting of my father's death," she said, confiding in him what she had seldom confided in anyone else. "He was a good man. A competent, merciful king who always placed his people first and lived his life in service to them. There is not a day that goes by that I don't think of him and wish I had his guidance and strength. I cannot imagine losing both parents so young as you di—"

"Enough," he said, cutting off her words. "I don't care for idle chatter, my lady. It plagues me."

It was the underlying hurt she heard in his voice that kept her from being stung by his sharp tone.

"You travel alone?" Lutian asked.

"I have my horse."

Adara sank her hand in the coarse black mane of the beast that carried them effortlessly. "Hardly a fitting companion for a prince."

"True, he would be more fitting for a king or emperor."

She smiled at that and was struck by the thought that she was currently traveling with her husband. A man she had spent countless nights trying to imagine.

But the prince holding her was so much more than the pale, gallant man she'd envisioned in her mind. She had imagined him as a polite, courtly youth like the ones in her palace. A man of poetry and culture.

This one was real. He was hard and serious. Deadly. Rugged.

Dangerous.

Christian of Acre was nothing like the other nobles she'd known who were pampered and frail. He lived his life like a pauper. Denied himself the luxuries he could have at home.

And yet he still carried himself with all the commanding presence of a king.

"Do you ever miss Elgedera?" she asked him.

He clenched his teeth before looking down at her. "Why do you persist in asking me questions?"

"Because I'm curious about you."

"Why?"

"You fascinate me. I can think of no other noble who would refuse his destiny or a throne. Most men spend their entire lives trying to gain the very things you shun . . . You've never been home, have you?"

Christian focused his attention on the road ahead of them as old memories sifted through his mind.

In truth, he'd never had a home to go to. His parents had chosen to be pilgrims who traveled about. Before their deaths, the most he'd ever spent in one place was six months. Everywhere they went, his parents were always careful to let no one know their identities.

He'd never been to his mother's home of Elgedera. He knew nothing of her half of his family except for his uncle Selwyn, who had come to tell him of his parents' deaths.

Only a child, he hadn't understood why the man had hated him so. Selwyn had shown up unexpectedly at the monastery in Acre where his parents had left him while they went to meet a friend.

"The boy is mad," Selwyn told the ancient abbot after the abbot had refused to allow Christian to leave. In the event of their deaths, his parents had granted a trust to the monastery that would only be paid so long as he was a resident there. "He thinks himself a prince, but he's just a Norman by-blow."

"Have no fear, my lord. We brook no liars in a place of God." The old abbot who proved himself true to his words. If Christian ever spoke of his parents or their heritage, he was beaten for it.

Then again, any time he spoke, he was beaten for it. So in time, he'd learned not to speak at all.

But it hadn't been all bad. Brother Angelus, one of the Templar knights, had taken him under his wing and had taught Christian much. He'd been a good friend, and he had died trying to keep the Saracens from killing Christian.

"Nay," Christian said at last to his "wife." "I've never been to my mother's homeland."

"Not even when we were wed?"

He shook his head.

"But you were so close."

"And my mother said there was too much political turmoil in her house. She didn't want any of us there until it was resolved."

Adara nodded her head as if she knew exactly what he was talking about. "The *Latraimo*. Your mother must have sensed it was coming."

He scowled at the unfamiliar word. "The what?"

Lutian answered him. "It is an Elgederion term for bloodbath, my prince, and it has become synonymous with Selwyn's rise to power."

"I don't understand."

"I was just a girl," she said quietly as her hand brushed against his while she stroked his horse's mane. Christian tried not to notice the softness of her cool hand touching his skin, or the gentle, feminine smell of her that filled his head. It had been far too long since he'd last had the pleasure of holding a woman for any length of time.

This one in particular was incredibly soft.

Not to mention, she was completely naked beneath her cloak . . .

That thought alone made him hard and aching. Especially since he knew she was more than eager to give herself to him for his pleasure. All he needed to do was push back the soft fabric a bit and he could touch the bare flesh of her stomach.

Move his hand lower and he could brush his fingers through the soft triangle of hair so that he could stroke her . . .

His groin jerked at the thought.

"I remember my family evacuating our palace in fear that the Elgederion hostilities would spill over onto us," she said, oblivious to the painful havoc she caused him. "For reasons no one knows, your uncle Tristoph killed your grandfather late one night. In a rage, his brothers drew swords against him and slew him before they turned on each other. In the course of a year, every royal member of their house, save you, was dead."

"Dead and gone," Lutian repeated. "The Elgederions need more than a king, they need a warrior-hero to release them from their tyrant."

Ignoring the fool, Christian was confused by her words. Not all of his family was dead. "What of Selwyn? He's my uncle, too."

"Nay," Adara said, "he calls himself that, but he is really only a distant relation who was a grand marshal to your grandfather. His only claim to the throne is that he married your grandfather's third cousin, who died shortly after Basilli's birth. There is no royal blood in him which is why he is trying to place his son on the throne. Only Basilli carries a blood tie, and it's faint at best. After your parents' murders, Selwyn came forward as regent, saying you were too young to be king, but that he was seeing you well schooled and trained for your future duties."

Christian frowned at what she was telling him. "My parents weren't murdered. They died in a fire."

Her dark gaze burned him as she looked up at him. "Your parents were murdered by your youngest uncle, who was then slain by Selwyn."

He couldn't breathe as those words echoed in his ears. "Are you certain?"

She nodded. "It is well known by all what happened. Or at least Selwyn's version of it, since he was there. Truthfully, I wonder if he didn't kill all three of them at once and just claim that he was trying to defend your parents when he slew Carian."

Christian's head swam at what she was telling him. "Why did no one tell me?"

"Have no fear, my prince, they never tell me anything, either. Of course, I am simple and they fear I will forget it. Are you simple, too?"

"Nay, Lutian," she said kindly before she looked back at Christian. "You never came home, my lord. When I was ten-and-four, Selwyn said that he had sent for you, only to find your monastery in ruins. Everyone thought you were dead."

"Then why are we still married?"

"I refused to believe it without proof, especially since Selwyn immediately suggested that I marry his son to maintain our border and treaty. Somehow, I knew you were alive, so my father stirred up your people and demanded they present him with your body and with proof that the body was you. Selwyn couldn't produce a body with your necklace and so our marriage stood.

"As your wife, I was to be accorded due respect, which kept them from invading our kingdom. Not to mention that as long as your people believe you are alive, neither Selwyn nor Basilli can formally ascend the throne or take control of the military.

By ancient law, only the rightful king, not his regent, can command the Elgederion troops. When the letter of your survival came a few years back, it was intercepted by an Elgederion steward, who made it known to all. My father and I had our proof that you lived."

"For that we will always thank you," Lutian said. "Otherwise my queen would be married to the beast and I'd be skewered on a pike for his pleasure, since he hates me."

Part of Christian could understand that sentiment, since Lutian did seem to ramble on about nothing, and yet his words were harmless enough.

He turned his thoughts back to Adara. "If the army will only follow me, how is it that you are in danger of invasion?"

"Some grow weary of waiting for their prince to return and be crowned king. They are the ones who listen to Basilli. Unlike his father, he is charismatic and persuasive. He is slowly convincing your people that you should be abandoned and that a true, full-blooded Elgederion should be on their throne. Meanwhile, he is pressuring me to declare you dead so that he can, in turn, marry me."

He scoffed at that. "And now you want me to return to a homeland I have never seen and depose him?"

"Aye."

Christian was aghast at her simple logic. "Have you really thought this through, my lady?"

"Of course."

Christian shook his head as he tried not to mock her plan. "So you propose that I just walk into the Elgederion throne room and demand my kingdom back?"

"Well, nay, it won't be *that* easy."

"It won't be easy at all," Christian said. "I have found in my life that no one gives up a throne willingly."

"No one except you," Lutian said.

Keep that up, fool, and there'll be a wringing of your neck soon enough.

Christian cleared his throat. "Aside from me, most are more than willing to fight unto the bitter death for their powers. It would take an army."

Adara's brown eyes burned into him with her fiery passion and unyielding belief in her rightness. If only he shared her beliefs. "The Elgederion army will ride to your side, Christian, when you return. It is the law of your people."

He snorted at that. "I assume it is also the law of my people that their royal family not murder each other so that a distant cousin can be regent, and yet that is what has transpired."

"He has a point with that one, my queen."

She directed a glare at her fool. "Fine, then. If you've no wish to be king, then give me an heir."

Christian actually sputtered at her unexpected words. Did he hear that correctly? Surely she hadn't just said what he thought she did. "Pardon?"

"If you refuse to be king, then allow me an heir

to take your place. Someone that the Elgederions will be forced to accept and follow."

"And what makes you think for one instant that I will agree to hand my child over to you?"

"Because it is the right thing to do."

Christian was aghast. "You think so?"

She didn't respond to his question as she glared at him. When she spoke, her voice carried the full weight of her royal status that was used to commanding those around her. "You have to decide, my lord. Either you return and be king or you give me an heir to rule in your stead."

"Nay, lady, I have a third choice. I do neither."

"That is not an option in this matter."

"Aye, but it is, and if you think for one moment that I would allow you to carry my child off into that nest of vipers, you are sadly mistaken."

She glared at him. "I *need* your heir."

"And that, Adara, is one thing I will *never* give you."

Three

Adara stared at the man who held her. "I'm not asking you to be a father, Christian, nor am I asking you to be a king. I ask you for nothing more than a few nights of passion, which I am sure you have given any willing female who has offered herself to you."

A tic started in his jaw. "You know me not, Your Majesty, to draw any such conclusion about my character."

It was true, she didn't. Still, she had to make him see reason. She had to do this to save her people. A child would guarantee that Selwyn and Basilli would never be able to threaten Taagaria again.

It was a new and perfect plan.

She hoped.

"Please, Christian. You may not care for your people, but I care for mine, and I cannot allow them to be conquered by a man who lacks all mercy. An heir will solve both our problems."

He shook his head as if aghast at her proposition. "This is a child we are talking about, Adara. Flesh and blood. *Our* flesh and blood. Not once in my life did my parents ever call me their heir. They called me their son."

His pale stare pierced her as he continued to rant. "And how long do you think such a man as Selwyn would suffer our child to live? You just told me how every member of my family was killed by another. How my own parents were murdered and your cousin Thera could very well end up paying the price for helping you. I will not see my child dead over something so senseless."

Why was he being so obstinate? He had to yield on some matter. Too many lives were at stake.

"I understand and I know that we are talking about *our* child. I would *never* allow my child to die. Believe me. I would protect him at all costs."

His eyes mocked her. "Are you some Amazon, then? Some warrior queen to take up a sword against your enemies?"

"Nay, but—"

"There are no buts, my lady. My father was one of the finest knights of his age and if they could kill him as you claim . . . This is a chance I will not take."

She turned in the saddle until she faced him. His handsome features were rigid, unyielding.

Still, she tried to argue her cause. "Then once

you return with me, stay there to protect our child."

"Return to what?" he asked angrily. "A kingdom that never wanted me? One that has tried repeatedly to kill me? I have obligations here."

"What obligations?"

"They are no concern of yours, but I take them most seriously."

"Christian," she tried again. "Please be reasonable. Our child would rule two prominent kingdoms that lie between Tripoli and Antioch. Think of the riches and respect. The power he would command."

"And what good does it for a man to gain the world if he loses his immortal soul? There is much in this world that is cruel and harsh. Better my child be a simple smith who wants nothing more than his forge, than one who is constantly pursued by those out to kill him for what he possesses."

"And it is the king and his justice that protects your smith and allows him his forge," she argued. "If the king is corrupt, then villains will overrun his shire and imprison him wrongfully. He will have no forge, no dignity. It is our destiny to defend them."

He was just as quick with his retort. "A king sits on his throne far away from the shire and has no knowledge of what happens there. But I know because I am in the shire, and so long as I am there, no one will ever hurt the smith."

She let out a long, tired sigh. "You are indeed a

politician, whether you wish it or not. Few men can argue better than you."

"You know, my queen," Lutian said thoughtfully, "there is another solution that I see."

She turned to look at Lutian, who was riding just behind them. "And that is?"

"All you truly need for proof is Prince Christian's heraldic emblem. Return home pregnant, with it, and they will have no choice except to accept your word for the baby's father."

Christian was even more aghast at that proposition than he'd been at Adara's. "And just who would be the father of her unborn child that she would pass off as mine?"

Lutian straightened up in the saddle. "I humbly submit myself to Her Grace's will to use my meek and virile body in any manner she sees fit."

Adara squelched a laugh at his kind offer. Leave it to Lutian to come up with such a solution.

But if looks could kill, Lutian would be severed in twain by Christian's heated glare. "I beg your pardon, fool?"

Adara was almost amused by the anger in Christian's tone. It would be nice if she could attribute it to jealousy, but she knew better.

"Aye," she said, wanting to nettle her husband even more. "It just might work."

Christian gaped at her. "You would bed the village idiot?"

Lutian snorted at that. "Pray tell who is the greater idiot? The man who would see his son king or the one who is holding a beautiful woman in his lap, with full matrimonial rites to her, who refuses her, a throne, and a wealthy kingdom full of people to do his every bidding? I think, in the grand scheme of this, I am by far the wisest man here."

Lutian kicked his horse abreast of theirs and bowed low in his saddle to Adara. "Take me, my queen, and I will give you your heir. I will gladly lay myself down for your pleasure."

Christian's nostrils flared in warning. "You lay yourself down for her pleasure, fool, and you won't be getting back up. Ever."

Lutian went pale as he reined his horse away from them . . . out of Christian's direct reach. "Very good, then, my prince." He shifted his gaze to Adara. "My apologies, my queen, but you're on your own."

"Lutian," she cried in feigned outrage. "What about my problem?"

Her fool took it good-naturedly. "Well, my lady, 'tis *your* problem. Sorry. I . . . um . . . I intend to live a long and *fruitful* life."

"Fruitful?" Christian asked with a gimlet stare.

Lutian twisted up his face as he contemplated his choice of words. "Did I say fruit*ful*? Methinks I spoke too soon. Suddenly I fear I may be impotent. Truly, I can no longer rise to *any* occasion. I shall be old and fruit*less*. My fruit is shriveling even as we speak."

Adara turned to glare at her husband and his

untoward reaction to Lutian's plan. "This I don't understand. Moments ago you couldn't care less about Elgedera or my people, so what do you care now who sits on the throne?"

Christian fell silent.

"Answer my question."

He turned that angry stare to her. "I am not one of your subjects, Majesty. I suggest you take a kinder tone to me."

"I am sorry," she said sincerely. "But I would like to know why you won't allow this."

His gaze burned into her, but beneath the anger she saw something else. Something she couldn't place or name.

"First, my necklace is the last piece of my mother that I have in my possession. I have guarded it in the deepest pits of hell to make sure that no one stole it from me. Therefore I have no intention of letting it go now for any reason other than death. Second, for my beloved parents' memory alone, I cannot allow the offspring of the village idiot to take my mother's family throne."

Lutian gasped. "On behalf of village idiots everywhere, I take offense to that."

Christian cut him a murderous look.

"Well, my queen, he does have a point. It is on his head, but still he has one."

She felt Christian tense as if catching himself before he lunged at poor Lutian, who immediately rode out of reach.

They fell silent as Adara grappled with the sense of failure and struggled to think up a new plan of action.

Not even Lutian spoke. He merely rode quietly as if fearful of pushing Christian past his limit.

None of this was going the way she had planned it.

How simple it had all seemed to come to this land, consummate her marriage, then return home with her husband to present to his people as their king.

Now she would be lucky to return home at all.

Still, she was undaunted. So long as she breathed, she had hope, and so long as she had hope, Basilli would not defeat her. She would find some way around Christian's defenses and make him see the truth of what she offered.

But in the meantime, they had to get to safety.

Her heart stilled as she looked down and realized she was still naked beneath her cloak. This wouldn't do!

Adara placed her hands over Christian's on the reins. "Can we stop for a moment?"

"Why?"

"If we are to enter a village, then I wish to dress."

Christian's breath caught as an image of Adara's bare body whipped unbidden through his mind. During their argument, he'd forgotten her state of undress, though how he'd managed that, he couldn't imagine.

Lutian made a cry of surprise as he covered his eyes with one hand. "My queen is naked beneath her clothes? I should go blind should I glimpse her fair beauty." He split his fingers apart over his eyes to look at her. "Or will I? Mayhap we should test this theory."

"Lutian," Christian said solemnly. "All people are naked beneath their clothes, and if you glimpse Adara's flesh, then it is quite possible that you will become blind when I poke out both of your eyes for the affront."

Lutian gave a devilish grin at that as he dropped his hand from his face. "No matter what he says, your prince is jealous of you, my queen. 'Tis a good sign."

Christian scoffed. "I'm not jealous."

"He sounded jealous to me," Lutian said loudly from behind his hand. "*Very* jealous."

Christian let out a growl that reminded her of a ferocious bear as he glared at Lutian, who took his surly mood in stride.

Reining his horse, Christian stopped before a small copse of trees while Lutian rode a little farther away from them. Christian dismounted first, then helped her down.

As she slid down beside him, her cloak opened, showing him a glimpse of her lean, beautiful body.

Christian hardened even more at the small glimpse of heaven that she gifted him with.

Adara paused as if she knew what it was she did

to him. "Are you sure I can't interest you in a quick consummation, my lord?"

In truth, he hungered greatly for her. How sweet she would be lying in his arms, her body wrapped around his. But this wasn't about his baser urges. This was about getting her to safety and extracting himself from a most unwanted position.

"Do you tempt every man you meet this way?"

"Nay. Only my husband."

Christian's stomach jerked at the reminder. By law and right, she was technically his to do with as he pleased. That knowledge was most potent against his will.

She reached up and placed one silken palm to his cheek. "You are even more handsome than I thought you would be . . . and far more stubborn as well. I should have known that you would be much more than the boy of faint memory."

As she spoke, he couldn't seem to tear his gaze from her well-curved, tempting mouth. It was all he could do not to pull her into his arms and taste her lips. They were red and inviting. No doubt they would be even softer than her hands . . .

Luckily Lutian started singing an off-key harmony that reminded him they weren't alone and that they weren't free for even a few minutes.

"We have people after us, my lady," Christian said, as much for his own benefit as hers. "I would caution you to haste."

She nodded before she withdrew from him.

Still her sweet, jasmine scent clung to his body.

He couldn't help but wonder how much more pleasant she would smell if he buried his face into that wealth of midnight hair.

How warm her body would be lying beneath his while he spent himself deep inside her . . .

Turning his back and grinding his teeth to force that image aside, he went to tend his horse before he let his errant thoughts lead him down a pathway he'd best not venture.

Adara watched her husband through the trees while she struggled to lace her gown. He tended his horse with a gentle touch and a high regard even while Lutian was annoying him with questions and comments.

"I don't think your horse likes you to stroke him there," Lutian said while Christian rubbed it down. He bent over and picked up two clumps of grass similar to the ones Christian was using, then studied them closely.

Christian continued without pause. "I've owned this horse a long time and I know what he likes."

"Aye, but how do you *know* he likes that? Has he ever told you so?"

"He's not kicking me. I take that as a good sign."

"I'm not kicking you, either, but that doesn't mean I like you or that I'd be grateful for your rubbing clumps of dirt over my body." Lutian held one of the grass clumps to his cheek and rubbed it against his skin. "Hmmm . . . although, it could be pleasurable, perhaps . . ."

Lutian turned around and poked his rear toward Christian. "Here, rub some on my flank and let me judge."

Christian looked horrified by the mere thought. "I'd most certainly rather not." He indicated with a tilt of his chin a small clearing where wild seed grew. "Why don't you go over there and pick something for the horses to eat? Not much, lest it make them sick, but enough to keep their strength up."

Lutian dropped the clumps of grass he held and went to do Christian's bidding.

Adara smiled as Christian let out an extremely audible sigh of relief, though to be honest, he'd been far more patient with Lutian than any other man she'd ever known. Which was why she'd allowed Lutian to come with her. Xerus and the others were prone to pick on the poor man from time to time, and without her there to watch over him, she was afraid they might intentionally hurt his feelings.

Or finally make good their threats to see him dead for his nettling.

But Lutian didn't mean anything by it. He was a tender soul with a great heart, and he had been her one true friend in life. He alone had comforted her after the death of her brother and her father. No matter how badly she felt or what happened to her, he could always make her smile or laugh.

Her father had always said a person could tell

much about a man by the way he dealt with ani-
mals, simpletons, and children.

She had yet to see her husband interact with
children, but given his treatment of Lutian and his
horse, she could only imagine he would be
equally kind to them.

"Christian?" she called as she left the trees behind. "Could you please assist me?"

He paused as she drew near him. His gaze
dropped to her loose bodice that dipped low between her breasts. She saw the heat come into his
pale eyes as he stared at her like a hungry man before a banquet.

He might push her aside, but he did desire her,
and so long as he did, she stood a chance at seduc-
ing him to her bed and changing his mind about
being king.

Clearing his throat, he averted his gaze and
moved around her so that he could lace the back of
her gown. She closed her eyes and savored the
heat of his hands as they brushed against the flesh
of her back. He did indeed have a gentle touch that
made her ache with need.

Virgin she might be, but she knew well what
went on between husband and wife. When she
had turned ten-and-four, her father had seen to it
that her nurse instructed her well on what duties a
wife should perform. They had expected Christian to come home that year.

He hadn't.

Instead, they had received word of the destruction of his monastery and Selwyn's letter stating his death.

Poor Christian, to be so hated. Jealousy and greed had stolen everything from her husband . . . just as it had taken much from her. Maybe Christian was right. There were times when the cost of her crown was far too high.

"What happened to you after the Saracens attacked your monastery?" she asked him.

"You don't ever want an answer to that question."

The anger and hatred in his tone gave her pause. There was much he kept hidden. Much he didn't speak of.

She remembered the brand on his hand. It was a Saracen mark. "Were you held captive? A slave?"

He moved away from her without answering.

She followed him. "My mother always said that burdens weigh much less when they are shared with another person."

He scoffed at that. "I have no desire to think of the past in any manner. It's gone and dead. What we should focus on is the challenges before us."

Adara paused.

What had they done to him that was so horrible he couldn't even bear to think on it?

He led his horse to her, then helped her to remount. "Lutian," he called out to her fool, who was feeding her mare grass. " 'Tis time to leave."

A breath later, Christian was behind her in the

saddle and they were on their way again, with Lutian trailing behind them.

"Christian?" she asked.

"Aye?"

"Would you answer one question for me?"

"If I do, will you swear to ask no more of me?"

"That would be impossible."

"Then you have your answer."

Deciding to give them both a reprieve, she didn't speak anymore until they were in the village and he deposited her and Lutian before a hostel.

"Would you care for anything to eat?" she asked Christian before he departed.

"Nay. There's not enough time. You two should eat quickly, then be ready to ride again."

She frowned at him as he left her and headed toward the stable at the edge of town.

"Your husband is a peculiar man, my queen. There is much sadness inside him."

"Aye, Lutian, I have noticed."

"Perhaps we should drop him on his head, and then when he awakens in your arms he would be as charmed by you as I was."

She smiled at that. "Were you charmed?"

"Aye, my queen. I still am. There is nothing in life that I cherish more than your smile and laughter. I live and breathe for them both. I only wish your husband felt toward them the same way as I do."

Even though her father would have frowned at her action, she gave her fool a quick hug. Would that Lutian were her husband. He might not be dashing and handsome, but they got along famously. Yet for all his good nature and sweetness, Lutian could never rule a kingdom. To be a successful king took a great deal of confidence and intelligence. Not to mention a sternness that he completely lacked.

Adara turned toward the small cottage behind them to find a large, buxom woman opening the door to welcome them inside. A few years older than she, the woman had long straight brown hair and friendly green eyes.

"Good evening," the woman said, smiling brightly. "Do you be needing a room for the night?"

"Nay, just a bit of food for us and my husband."

The woman looked down toward where Christian was headed. "You married a priest?"

Adara felt her face flush with color as she realized that Christian still wore his monk's black robes. "Nay, we've been on pilgrimage," she lied.

"Ah," the woman said, stepping aside so that Adara and Lutian could enter. "My brother went to Rome wearing a friar's frock, horsehair tunic, and walking the whole way on his knees. Men, I wonder at times what goes through their heads."

Adara didn't respond as the woman led them to a large hearth on the opposite side of the cottage. "We have leek and sausage soup, mincemeat pies, roasted lamb and chicken. What have you?"

Adara had no idea what Christian might like, so

she decided on what would be easiest to carry with them. "Three pies, please, and two skins of ale." She looked at Lutian. "What of you?"

He stroked his beard thoughtfully. "I should like one maid to take with us."

Adara's eyes widened as the woman squeaked in horror. Covering Lutian's mouth with her hand, she cleared her throat. "He was but jesting, good-wife. He would like two pies and a skin as well."

The woman narrowed her eyes in warning before she left them to gather their items.

"Lutian!" Adara snapped. "Shame on you."

He only grinned devilishly as he scanned the clean but old room, which was empty save for two little girls who were playing dolls in one corner.

She smiled as she watched them giggling and chattering about nothing of consequence, and yet it was significantly important to them. How she loved children. She'd always wanted her own, even when she was a girl. She'd played endlessly with dolls in expectation of the day when she would be a mother.

And she had waited far too many years for a husband who held no desire to grant her the one thing she wanted most.

She felt her smile falter as sadness consumed her. If she were wise, she would annul this marriage and find a husband who would do his duty.

However, that was even harder than convincing her wayward spouse to return with her. What man would jeopardize his life by being her consort while they were on the brink of war with a kingdom that was determined to annex her own?

"Go on, my queen," Lutian whispered in her ear. "No one here knows you are royal. Go and play with your children."

"It's not proper."

"Neither is befriending a simpkin."

Adara squeezed his arm. "You are far wiser than you let on, Lutian."

"And everyone, even a queen, needs a day of play." He indicated the children with a jerk of his chin. "Lay on, my queen, and have a bit of fun."

Before she could think twice, Adara crossed the room so that she could kneel beside them.

"Greetings, little ones," she said to the girls, while Lutian stayed by the hearth, waiting on the woman to return. "What are you two playing?"

"Merry Marge," the older girl, who was probably around the age of six, said as she brandished a doll that was made from brown homespun. The doll's hair was coarse black horsehair and two black stitched X's formed her eyes. The little girl herself had the woman's bright green eyes and blond hair. "She's been really naughty and let the beggar steal her shoes." She held up the doll's bare feet to show her.

"Naughty, naughty!" the other girl, who was obviously her sister and who was probably no older than four, cried as she bounced a similar doll up and down on her lap.

* * *

Christian traded his horse and Lutian's for three others. None of the three were anywhere near the quality of his rounsey, but he paid the avener a small fortune to hold Titan here until he could return for him.

He left the stable and headed for the hostel where he'd left Adara and Lutian. It was getting late and he should most likely stay here for the night. But he wouldn't chance it. He didn't like towns, to begin with. They were too confining and held too many sounds that could mask the telltale noises of someone trying to sneak up on him.

He tied the horses outside, then opened the hostel door and paused as he saw his royal wife on the floor with two small peasant girls who were laughing at her. The sight shocked him. That a woman of her station would do such a thing was unthinkable.

Adara held two dolls in her hands and was dancing them together. She sang a song in a language he had all but forgotten. And in that instant, he flashed back to his own childhood. To the last time in his life he had felt truly safe.

Loved.

I love you, little Christian, his mother's voice echoed in his mind as she kissed his brow and rocked him in her arms. *I always will.*

He couldn't count the times his mother sang to him when he was a child. But even so, her voice was no match for the beauty of Adara's.

Lutian cleared his throat as if to warn them of his presence.

The older of the girls straightened up as she caught sight of him watching them. "Are we doing something wrong, brother?" she asked him.

Adara stopped midsong as she turned to face him. God's blood, but she was a striking woman. Her wealth of black hair fell freely around her like a mantle of sable. And those eyes . . .

A man could lose all sanity while staring at those kind, sweet eyes.

Surely no queen should look so guileless and innocent. Especially not one who had traversed an entire continent just to seduce him to her bed.

"Nay," Christian said quietly. "And I'm not a monk."

The little girl cocked her head at that.

"He's playing dress-up," Adara said. "Like Marge." She handed the dolls back to the girls, then stood up and joined him.

"Did you not eat?" he asked.

She gestured to a cloth napkin that covered a small stack of mincemeat pies and two skins on a nearby table. "I thought it best we eat on our journey."

"I ate already," Lutian said. He patted his stomach. "It was very tasty and well served. I still would rather have had my first request, though. A prime maid to feast upon." His gaze went to Adara. "What man could ask for more?"

Christian frowned at that until she brushed a

hand against his brow, which immediately succeeded in calming him. "You shouldn't do that so much. You'll get wrinkles before your time."

Christian opened his mouth to speak, then paused as he heard something odd from outside.

If he didn't know better . . .

A dagger went whizzing past his face, narrowly missing it.

Adara screamed as she moved away from him to shield the children. Lutian quickly joined her in the corner.

Before he could unsheath his sword, the door slammed open and a body was flung through it.

Christian pulled his sword out and angled it to the man on the ground, only to realize he was already dead. He stepped back as another man came through the door with a drawn dagger in his hand.

Adara held the girls' faces to her gown to shield them from the sight of the dead man as she tried to understand what was happening. Even Lutian stood as motionless as a statue.

Christian still held his sword at the ready, but made no move to attack.

The newcomer was almost as tall as Christian. He had black hair that flowed long past his broad shoulders. In truth, she'd never seen hair so long on any man. His skin was a darker tan than most Europeans. If she didn't know better, she'd swear he was Saracen.

But his eyes were so pale that at first glance,

they looked white. They were as startling in their mercilessness as they were in their color.

"Phantom," Christian said in a low tone. "Are you friend or foe this night?"

"If I were foe, Abbot, you'd be dead now," the man said in an accent that was definitely Norman.

In one fluid motion, Phantom wiped his bloody dagger on his thigh before he tucked it into his black sleeve.

"Mercy, mercy!" the hostel owner said as she entered the room and saw the dead man on her floor. She rushed to the girls, then herded them out of the room.

Phantom turned his cold, eerie gaze to Adara, who stiffened instantly. There was something very chilly and frightening about this man. And at the same time, there was something eerily familiar about him, too, but she was most certain that had she ever met this man before, she would definitely recall it.

"What have we here?" he asked with a note of excitement in his voice.

Christian placed himself between them. "She's no concern of yours."

A slow, wicked smile spread across Phantom's face. "Is she your concern?"

"Aye."

The man inclined his head almost respectfully to them. "Then you're right. She's none of mine." He bent down and hoisted the dead man up onto his back.

Adara was awed by his strength as he stood up and headed for the door.

"What are you doing?" she asked him.

He shrugged even with the weight of the other man on his shoulders. "I figured the goodwife and her daughters wouldn't want me to leave her place in a mess."

He left the hostel, then returned a moment later without the dead man. "So why was he after you, Abbot?"

Christian glanced at her and Lutian. "It appears someone wants me dead."

Phantom passed a curious look from one to the other. "You should be more careful, then, shouldn't you?"

Christian didn't respond. "What brings you here?"

"I was on my way back to Paris and thought I'd rent a room for the night when I saw Titan in the stable. I was inspecting him as I caught sight of the shadow headed toward the hostel. Good thing I followed."

"Indeed."

The two men were extremely uncomfortable around each other and Adara wondered why.

"Thank you, kind sir," she said, interrupting their rather stilted conversation.

Phantom scowled at her. "I know that accent. Queen Adara?"

Her blood ran cold, that he had suddenly recognized her.

"You know me?" she asked at the same time Christian asked, "You know her?"

"Aye," Phantom said with a speculative gleam in his eyes. "I know her. I was even paid to kill her."

Adara stepped back and collided with Lutian as Christian went ramrod-stiff. "Paid by whom?" he asked.

"I didn't ask his name, but he looked official enough." He rubbed his chin thoughtfully. "You can both relax. I don't take money to kill women." There was an odd note in his voice that concerned her much.

"Do you do it for pleasure?" Lutian asked.

He laughed darkly. "There are some lines even a damned man won't cross. Rest assured, I turned the money down, then cut the throat of the man who offered it."

Christian gave him an arch look. "What did you do with the coin?"

He shrugged. "I left it for the beggars."

She shivered at his nonchalant frankness about death.

Phantom cocked his head as if listening for something. "The townspeople are stirring. I'd best go before I have to kill one of them as well." He started for the door.

"Wait," Christian said. "We're heading toward the Scot's."

"So?"

Before they could say another word, Phantom stepped out of the hostel and was gone.

Adara crossed herself at the unholy way he vanished into the evening. There was something about him that didn't seem quite human and he definitely wasn't sane. She crossed herself again, just for good measure. "What is that man?"

Christian sighed as he sheathed his sword. "He claims he's the son of the devil and a whore. Sometimes I don't doubt it."

Lutian stepped forward. "Why did he call you Abbot?"

She didn't expect him to answer, so when he did, it caught her off guard. "We used to live someplace where names weren't important to us. It was actually easier to pretend we didn't have names at all. My friends called me Abbot because they knew I was from a monastery and many thought I was a monk."

Lutian ahhed. "I take it Phantom was named for the fact that he looks like an ungodly ghost."

He nodded. "And he moves like one as well. The only problem was that we were never quite certain whose side he was on."

She could well understand that. "It seems to me he's on his own side."

"Aye, but just when you think that, he does something completely altruistic, such as killing the man who was after us, and places himself in great peril to help another." Christian motioned for them to join him. "Come, we best be on our way."

Adara gathered up their food and skins, then followed him and Lutian through the door.

Outside, there were a number of local men studying the body that Phantom had propped beside a building, while the hostel owner told them about Phantom.

"He was evil," she breathed. "Possessed by the devil himself. 'Tis the devil's witchcraft, I know it."

Adara started toward the crowd, only to have Christian pull her away. He motioned for her and Lutian to be silent before he set her up on her horse, then mounted his own. Lutian followed suit.

He took her reins and led her quickly and stealthily away from town.

"Why did you do that?" she asked once they were away from the area.

"The goodwife could see that I knew Phantom, and I didn't want them to start pointing at us and crying witchcraft. Best to get out before it's too late."

She agreed. "I must say, my lord, you do keep interesting company."

He snorted at that. "You have yet to meet the most intriguing ones."

Hmm, that might be true. But she doubted if any man could ever be more intriguing than the one she was looking at right now.

Christian was an enigma to her. What kind of

man dressed as a monk, while he concealed a sword and armor beneath his priestly robes? For that matter, what kind of man would give away his kingdom to keep company with an unholy killer?

And Phantom wasn't even the most intriguing member of his company, according to his own words.

Just what kind of man was she married to?

But then, what did it matter? Prince or demon, she needed this man's presence to secure her kingdom, and that was her first priority. Somehow, she must seduce him to her cause.

Adara watched Christian as he led her through the dark, foreign countryside. His face was barely discernible, but his commanding presence and power were undeniable. This was a man who had led a hard, harsh life.

"Christian?" she asked quietly.

"What, Adara?" There was a tired note of exasperation to his tone.

"Do you have any place that you call home?"

Christian fell silent at her question.

Home. Such a simple word, but in truth, he had no knowledge of its meaning. As a child, he and his parents had traveled constantly. They'd stayed in hostels, inns, or the homes of friends. Occasionally, they might happen upon his father's Norman family who held land in Outremer, but those times were extremely rare.

He couldn't even begin to count all the countries they had visited. Some were nothing more than blurred memories, while others were more clear. He'd fall asleep in a bed one night and by the time he awoke, he'd be cradled in his father's arms while they were off to a new location. Whenever he'd asked his parents why they constantly traveled, they'd only said that they liked to see different people and countries.

Now he wondered at the truth. Were they being pursued?

Damn you for not telling me.

But then, he couldn't truly damn the parents he'd loved so much. All these years, their love for him had been the only thing he'd held on to in order to keep him sane. The only thing that had kept him human.

The closest thing to a home he'd ever known had been the monastery. But if that was truly a home, then they could keep it.

"Nay, my lady," he said quietly. "I have no home."

"Then how do you live? Where do you get your coin?"

"I live by my sword. It shelters me and it feeds me. As for coin, I have enough. Should I need more, I tourney for it."

"He who lives by the sword shall die by it," Lutian said from his place behind her.

Ignoring Lutian, Adara was humbled by Christian's words, which tugged at her heart. "You always travel alone?"

"Aye."

"And this life suits you?"

"Aye."

Adara frowned at that. But how could it? How could a man be completely alone all his life and not want friend or family near him? It made no sense to her.

"You are a lonely man, Christian of Acre. Basilli and Selwyn have taken much from me, but you . . . you've lost it all, haven't you?"

"Nay, Adara. I haven't. I still have my life and I have my dignity and my morals. Take my word for it, I still have much to lose."

The tone of his voice said it all, and as she thought back to Phantom, she realized how right Christian was.

"I am glad for you, then. You must have fought hard to maintain all three of them."

He reined his horse to a stop and didn't speak until they were side by side. The look he gave her chilled her soul deeply. "You have no idea, my lady, and I hope that you never learn."

"You hope or you pray?"

He gave a short, bitter laugh. "I hope. I ceased to pray a long time ago."

He kicked his horse forward and left her behind to contemplate that revelation. She glanced at Lutian, who exchanged an uncomfortable look with her.

"He is a man of many demons, my queen," he said in a whispered tone.

Adara agreed, but now she was even more confused. She kicked her horse forward until she caught up to Christian. "I don't understand. If you have ceased to pray, why wear the garb of a monk?"

"It suits me to."

"Why?"

He slowed at that and cast a piercing look that not even the dark could conceal. "Why are you dressed as a peasant?"

"I didn't want anyone to know that I'm a queen."

"Why?"

"Because my life would be in danger if . . ." Adara frowned as she followed his line of thinking. "You are afraid for your safety?"

"Nay. Never. In all honesty, I couldn't care less for my safety. I dress as I do so that most will ask me no questions and leave me in peace."

"Tell me, my lord. Does that include meddlesome wives who should have stayed home?"

She saw the slightest lifting of the corners of his lips. "You keep that up, Christian, and you might actually manage a smile."

His face turned sober again. "There is little about this situation that I find amusing, Adara."

"Are you so certain, my lord prince? I think being tossed naked from a window is rather amusing, myself. Or at least I am rather sure I will once the embarrassment of it wears thin."

She had a distinct impression that he was forcing himself not to smile at that.

"How can you find humor in what has befallen you?"

She shrugged. "There is humor to be had most places. My father always said that it is a wise man indeed who can laugh at himself."

"Only a fool laughs at himself and 'tis a greater one who allows others to do so."

"Pardon?" Lutian chimed in.

Adara motioned him to silence. "Laughter is the music of the angels. It clears the soul of its melancholy and adds the beauty to our lives. 'Tis why I value Lutian so. Without laughter and humor, we are all barren inside."

"Then I am barren. Now will you leave me in peace?"

Adara sighed at the somberness of the man her parents had chosen as her husband. Poor Christian, to have no mirth.

She opened her mouth to speak, only to have him hold his hand up to shush her.

Reining his horse, he cocked his head as if listening to the woods around them.

"Is something amiss?" she whispered.

"Aye. We are being followed."

Four

Adara's heart returned to its frantic beating while she scanned the dark forest around them. "Where?"

He put his finger to his lips to silence her as he listened. After a minute, he moved his horse closer to hers so that he could speak in a low tone. Lutian rode to her side so that he could hear as well.

"Withernsea Abbey is only about a league from here. If we are attacked before we reach it, continue to ride due north and at full speed. Do not look back. Do not slow until you reach the abbey's gates. Ride to the backside of the abbey, where Brother Thomas should be manning the small alm's door. Tell him Christian of Acre sent you for sanctuary. Do you understand?"

She nodded.

"Good. Now gallop."

Adara squeezed the horse's ribs with her knees.

The horse sped up. She thought at first that all would be well until she heard an inhuman cry. It was the call of the Sesari, a special, elite group of the Elgederion army. Lightning fast, they were the bodyguards of the king.

She slowed her horse. "They're your men," she told Christian.

"What?"

"I know that sound. They are the king's bodyguards. They're here to protect—"

Before she could finish the word, the Sesari attacked.

"Go!" Christian snapped, slapping his reins against her horse's flanks.

She reined her horse while he unsheathed his sword. "They can't hurt you. It is forbidden."

An arrow went whizzing between them.

Christian gave her a fierce glare. "Apparently they don't share your belief, Adara. Now go, so that I can fight without fear of your being harmed." He looked to Lutian. "Get her to safety."

She didn't want to leave him to this, but he was right. She wasn't a warrior and neither was Lutian. They would only compromise Christian's ability to defeat their attackers.

"*Ecri denara,*" she said, wishing him luck in his native language. She caught a glimpse of blue in the woods an instant before she set her heels into her horse and sped north with Lutian following her.

Christian took a deep breath in relief that she'd listened to him. Now he just had to hope that he could hold off the attackers and give Adara and Lutian time to reach their destination.

His sword gripped tightly in his hand, Christian wheeled his horse about and watched as one by one six men dressed in dark blue robes broke through the forest into the small clearing.

A clear, masculine voice rang out speaking Elgederion as they spotted him. "The regent wants the imposter dead. Paradise and riches to the one who takes the imposter's life."

Christian laughed at that. Poor men. They had no idea who or what they were dealing with. "Paradise or hell will be determined by the Lord our God," he said to them in Elgederion. "Not your ruler. Anyone who wants his judgment this night, step forward and I'll be more than happy to speed you on your way."

His horse reared as it sensed the battle to come. Christian brought the beast back under control, then spurred it toward those who would kill him.

And as he neared them, he realized they were only the forefront of more of their kind.

Adara thought her heart might fair explode before she finally saw the walls of the old abbey before her. The light of the half moon above shone brightly against the stark stone. As per Christian's words, she rode to the back and found the small door he'd described.

She dismounted quickly and ran to it. She

struck the old bluish gray wood hard, hoping the monks weren't in prayer.

A small window opened on the door. "We've no more alms left for the poor," the old monk said. "Come back tomorrow, child." With two fingers held upright, he made the sign of the cross on the small opening. "*Pax vobiscum.*"

"Brother Thomas?" she asked before he could close the window all the way.

He opened it wider so that he could see her better. "Aye?"

She dropped her cowl and stood on her tiptoes so that he would know she posed no threat. "I was sent here by Christian of Acre. He told me to beg sanctuary from you."

The old man's face became a mask of horror. He slammed shut the window, then immediately opened the door. "Come in, child. Is Christian . . ."

She could see he didn't even want to ask lest the news be painful. "I know not. We were on our way here when we were attacked. He sent us"—she indicated herself and Lutian—"on ahead while he faced those who were after us."

"God be with him," he whispered as he crossed himself, then waited for them to enter the monastery's confines before he locked the door behind them.

Adara's breath caught as she saw a small mark on the monk's hand. Before she could think better of it, she captured his hand and held it under the rushlight to see the same mark there that Christian bore on his own hand.

"This sign . . . what is it?"

The pallor on his face increased.

"Please, Brother. Christian bears it as well and refuses to speak of it to me."

"And who are you?"

"His wife. Adara."

Tears came to the man's brown eyes as he looked at her as if she were a ghost. He embraced her like a sister and pounded her hard on the back.

"Adara," he whispered as he continued to hug her. "It does this old heart good to see that Christian has finally found some comfort in this world. God knows, he deserves it."

Lutian opened his mouth to speak, but was silenced when Adara flung her hand out to his stomach in warning. He quickly snapped his mouth closed, glared at her, and rubbed the area she'd struck.

Sniffing, the old monk stepped back and smiled at her. "You are beautiful, child."

"Thank you, Brother. But the sign?" she asked. "I need to understand why it pains my husband when I ask after it."

By his expression she could tell the brand bothered him as well. "It was the mark of our prison and has since become the mark of our Brotherhood."

"Mark of your prison?" Lutian asked.

"Aye. After we were individually captured and thrown into the bowels of the prisons, the heathens branded it into us as a way to remind us of our lowly, beaten status." He turned to face Adara. "Thanks to men such as your husband, it was turned into a mark to fortify and unite us."

That gave her hope that the monks would have at least a warrior or two in their ranks. "Is there anyone here we can send to help Christian now?"

His gaze saddened. "I wish it were so, my lady. But alas there are no knights here, only champions of God. But I know Christian well. He will prevail."

Adara prayed for that to be true, but she knew the Sesari well and they weren't easily defeated by anyone. She considered going back for him herself, but the last thing Christian needed was for her to do something stupid.

"He will be fine, my queen," Lutian said to her.

Thomas's eyes widened. "Queen?"

She could feel her face flush. That had been something she'd rather the monk not know about her. "Aye, Brother. I am a queen."

"Then it is true that Christian is a prince?"

"Aye."

He shook his head as he took the rushlight and led them toward a small group of buildings in the center of the yard. "Well, I'll be. It is nice to know he has finally found his place in the world. Many are the times that I never thought he'd find peace or home."

She didn't have the heart to correct the man and tell him that Christian had no desire at all to be her husband or to return to his home. He denied both with equal fervor.

"You were with Christian while he was in Outremer?" she asked.

Thomas nodded as he continued to lead them across the well-tended yard. "I was already a captive when they took him. In those days, I was a merchant who had gone to see Jerusalem on pilgrimage and I am sad to say that I had lost all faith in God after they captured me. It is hard to maintain your faith when your prayers go unanswered and you live among constant suffering and death for no reason.

"Then they brought in this man-child who stood strong against our Saracen tormentors. He was like a lion possessed of God's faith and love. Whenever we wanted to die, it was Christian's words of comfort and hope that kept us alive. His faith that saw us all through."

His old eyes were haunted. "Indeed, he was the only one we had to confess to and to perform Last Rites for those of us who didn't survive. Most of the boys his age ran from the constant death around us, but Christian didn't. He wouldn't allow any to burn for their faith. No matter the disease or injury, he spoke the final words to save their souls. God bless his kindness and mettle."

A lump settled in her throat as she thought about how horrible it must have been for him. She couldn't imagine a higher responsibility. Not even one as ruler.

"Is that why they called him the Abbot?"

"Aye, and I have since taken my vows so that I may serve God more truly, since it was He who sent Christian to us to give us the strength to survive our nightmare."

"And there is truly no one we can send to help him now in his hour of need?" she asked again.

"Nay, child. But fear not. Christian is like no other in battle."

Christian sank his sword into the body of his latest attacker. He'd held his own, but the tide was swiftly turning against him. Several of the enemy had already wounded him and his sword grew heavier by the heartbeat.

As he grew more tired, they grew in number.

Just how many of them could there be?

Suddenly a blinding light streaked through the darkness. It landed near him, then exploded into fragments that flew against the men attacking him. They screamed as the fire ran up their bodies and consumed them.

More fire rained down. Christian stumbled back, away from the men and the source of their anguish.

As if from an unholy source, the sound of hooves came near. Christian barely had time to move before the horse and rider were upon him.

"Take my hand, Abbot."

He looked up into the face of Phantom.

Christian took his arm an instant before Phantom pulled him up behind him. Phantom kicked his horse into a run while Christian held on to the saddle.

"Where's your horse?" Phantom asked him.

"I know not. It was a farmer's horse. The fighting scared it."

Phantom laughed darkly. "Threw you, did he?"

"Aye."

Phantom shook his head as he veered his horse into the thickest part of the forest in order to escape any who might be pursuing them.

Christian took slow, even breaths as the pain of his injuries seeped through him. It was always like this. During battle, the mind was occupied by survival. Pain had no place in a man's thoughts. But once safety was reached . . .

The body's agony made itself plainly known. And his was singing royally this night.

Christian glanced behind them to see if they were being followed, but if they were, the darkness concealed it. "We need to head toward With—"

"I know. I followed your queen there earlier to make sure she arrived safely before I doubled back to help you."

That news surprised him. "I thought you were headed back to Paris."

"I lied."

Christian frowned at Phantom's bland tone. "So you followed us, then?"

"Aye. I had a feeling the one I killed wasn't alone."

"You could have just told me and traveled with us."

Phantom scoffed at that. "Not my way."

Christian understood that. Phantom had always been a solitary creature. Even more so than Christian himself was. In prison, the young man had always been extremely reserved and sullen. He'd only grudgingly interacted with Christian and the other prisoners, and even then he'd been suspicious and cautious.

In many ways, he reminded Christian of a dog that had been beaten one time too many and was hesitant to let anyone else close enough to him for fear of being hurt again. Not to mention, the man carried a severe scar across his throat that he now kept concealed. In prison, there had been no way to hide the mark, which looked as if someone had once tried to cut Phantom's head off.

So Christian had always done his best to give Phantom the isolation the man seemed to crave.

The two of them remained silent the rest of the way to the abbey. Christian dismounted first, then stumbled as the pain spread through him.

"Jesus, Mary, and Joseph," Phantom snarled as he joined him on the ground. "How wounded are you?"

Christian stiffened in indignation. "I was significantly outnumbered."

Phantom made a rude noise before he seized his arm and draped it over his shoulders.

Christian shoved him away. "I can walk on my own."

"Not bloodly likely. By the looks of you, I'm amazed you can even stand."

It was difficult. Even so, Christian started for the small alm's door. After he stumbled again, Phantom grabbed him and offered him his shoulder.

"Damn your pride, Christian. You're about to pass out. No one, least of all me, will think less of you for accepting aid."

Christian reluctantly leaned against Phantom and allowed himself to be helped to the door. He couldn't tell who answered Phantom's knock. By the time they had the door opened, everything went black.

Phantom caught Christian against him as he passed out. Groaning, he hefted him up into his arms. "You would have to be wearing armor, you bastard, wouldn't you?" he growled.

The priest gave him a harsh stare.

Curling his lip, Phantom glared back. He couldn't care less what the monk thought of him. For that matter, he couldn't care less what anyone thought of him.

"Phantom?"

He turned his head at the familiar voice that approached them from the north. "Thomas?"

"Aye," the old man said as he came forward wearing the brown homespun and tonsure of a monk. "I was hoping when I heard the bell that it was Christian. Bring him this way. I already have quarter for him."

Grateful, Phantom followed him to the monk's dormitory. The building was clean but sparse, he noticed, as they walked down the hallway toward a small room.

Phantom grimaced at the plain furnishings that were designed for practicality and not comfort. But at least he could finally put down the overgrown knight who weighed as much as his horse.

Thomas pulled back the rough cover on the inhospitable-looking cot. Phantom laid Christian down carefully before he pulled the black robe off him to expose the suit of chain mail beneath. He quickly removed the sword and sheath.

"He's been badly injured," he told Thomas. "Is there a monk here who can tend him?"

"Aye. Brother Bernard. I'll get him and let the queen know that Christian has made it."

Phantom nodded while he started unlacing the mail pieces. He could see the bright red stains where the blood was seeping between the links, not to mention several gashes in the metal where weapons had cut through it. There were quite a few injuries, and in truth he was amazed Christian had gone so long before he passed out.

Then again, pain wasn't anything new to either of them.

He pulled the mail hauberk and quilted aketon off, then paused as he saw the old scars that marked Christian's right shoulder. Unbidden, his memories surged.

Instead of the monastery where they were currently, he saw the old mold-covered prison walls. Smelled the stench of decay and death. Heard the echoing screams of pain and whispered prayers of the hopeless and dying. He could even feel again the heat of the fever that had ravished his body.

"Here, Phantom," the boy Christian had said as he offered him a cup of rare bitter water to drink.

The sight of it had terrified him. To be caught with unrationed water meant a severe beating, which was what had given Phantom his current fever. "Where did . . . ?"

"Shhh, fear not. Just drink. You need it for your fever."

Phantom had barely consumed it before their guard found them.

Christian immediately took the cup and pretended that he was the one drinking from it.

"Thief!" It was one of the very few Arabic words that Phantom knew at the time. The guard grabbed the cup and then commenced to beating Christian for it.

Christian took the blows in silence until Phantom tried to tell the guard that the water was his.

The guard paused and asked Christian something that Phantom didn't understand. Christian answered in Arabic and then was beaten even more.

Phantom wanted to stop it, but knew from experience that the guard would only beat Christian longer for Phantom's interference.

When it was over, Christian crawled back to his side. His lip was split, his eye swelling. "Here," he said, his hand trembling as he gave Phantom a small skin that had been tucked into his breeches. "There's more water for you inside it."

To this day, Phantom cherished that sacrifice. It had been the first time since the death of his father that anyone had ever shown him such kindness. Christian had had nothing to gain and everything to lose by helping him.

It was why Christian of Acre was the only man alive he'd give his life for. He was the only man alive who held Phantom's cynical loyalty. The rest of humanity could burn in hell as far as he was concerned.

Forcing those thoughts away, he tore pieces of Christian's robe into strips for a tourniquet against the worst of the wounds . . . a sword slash down Christian's right shoulder and arm.

"What happened?"

He looked over his shoulder to see Adara entering the room. "He was attacked."

She knelt by the cot. "What can I do to help?"

"Keep this pressed against the cut and let me see if there are any others as deep."

Adara did as he said. She held the cloth with as much pressure as she could without hurting

Christian more and watched as Phantom removed the mail leggings and breeches. "Thank you, Phantom, for saving him."

He responded with a subtle nod. If she didn't know better, she'd think that her words embarrassed him.

Phantom had just covered him with the rough blanket when Brother Thomas returned with another monk, who looked as if he'd been asleep. Tufts of bright orange hair were standing on end as the rotund man squinted at them.

"Not good, not good," he muttered as he neared the bed where Christian lay. "Brother Thomas, fetch my kit."

"I already have it, Brother Bernard." He handed it to him.

Bernard looked at it as if it were a stranger. Scowling, he took it into his hands and shooed Adara away from the small chest beside the bed. "Best take them out while I work."

Phantom looked less than agreeable. "I think I should stay and—"

" 'Tis God's work I do. Now go."

"It'll be all right, Velizarii," Thomas said. "He won't allow anything to happen to Christian."

"Velizarii?" Adara asked as sudden recognition hit her. No wonder she had thought this man looked familiar. She had known him well when they were children.

How could she not have realized it the moment

she glimpsed those pale eyes? "You're not Velizarii yon Kranig?"

His face hardened. "I'm no one of consequence." He turned and left the room.

Adara rushed after him. By the time she caught him, he was halfway down the hallway, headed toward the refectory.

She pulled him to a stop. "Velizarii?"

"Velizarii is dead," he said from between his teeth as he wrenched his arm free of her loose grip. "He died a long time ago."

Tears gathered in her eyes as she heard the hatred in his deep, raspy voice. "'Tis indeed a shame, then, since I loved the boy I knew. Greatly."

A muscle worked in his jaw as he glared down at her. He looked as if he were fighting within over whether he should talk to her or run.

She searched his face for some semblance of the pretty little boy who had once come to her palace with his father. While their parents spoke of politics and treaties, they would play in her back garden. There was nothing of that innocent child left in the man before her. He was hard. Callous.

And that broke her heart.

When he spoke again, his words were as harsh as his cold stare. "How could a princess have ever loved a peasant?"

"You weren't a peasant."

He laughed bitterly at that. "My mother was."

"Your father was a prince."

"And all that got him was an early death at the hands of his own brother."

Her heart ached for him. She knew exactly how much his father had meant to him when he was a child. Never once had she seen his father Tristoph that Velizarii wasn't with him.

Many times over the years, she had wondered what had become of her playmate. But no word of him had ever reached her and so she had assumed that he, like the rest of his family, had been slain.

"Does Christian know you are his cousin?" she asked.

"Nay," he growled, "and he is *never* to know it."

"Why?"

"What good would it do him to know?"

"You are all the family he has left."

"Nay, Adara, *you* are all the family he has left. I am a felon and a ghost. Like Christian, I have no desire to return to Elgedera, where I live under a death sentence and where I will be reminded of how my father died, fighting for his life against his very kin. Our blood is tainted."

She refused to believe that. "Yet you saved Christian this night."

"I saved a man I owe my life to, that is all. Need I remind you who is out to kill both of you? Our family. Yet again they strike, and they will not rest until all of us are dead."

Perhaps. But that still didn't negate the fact that Velizarii had twice saved Christian this night.

"What happened to you, Velizarii?" she asked, desperate to understand how such a happy child could become the angry man before her. "When last we spoke, all you wanted was to make your father proud. You were going to join the *hauen gras* and be a captain someday."

Bitterness darkened his eyes as he pulled down the leather piece that obscured his throat. There below his Adam's apple was a deep, vicious scar, which explained his deep, gravelly voice. It was a gruesome mark that made her cringe in sympathetic pain for him.

"What happened? My father killed my grandfather, and in the middle of the night, under Selwyn's command, the wasps descended on my dormitory and slew every man and boy there to make sure we didn't retaliate against the bribed Sesari who had allowed the murders to take place."

Adara remembered the night the *hauen gras*, the royal Elgederion knights who protected the country, were slain. "How did you survive?"

"Foolish persistence is ever the hobgoblin of fate."

His flippant comment set her ire off even more. "How did you survive?" she repeated.

Releasing the leather piece on his neck, he shifted his haunted gaze to the floor. In the depths of his eyes, she could see his horror. His agony. "I crawled out from under the bodies of my friends while Selwyn's men burned down our quarters.

Half dead, I crawled out the back, fearful that at any moment they would see me and finish me off. I found a place in the woods and hid until they were gone. I lay in a stupor for days until a farmer found my hiding place and took me to his wife to nurse back to health."

"Then how is it you ended up in Outremer with Christian?"

"Dame Fortuna. She forever spits on even the most resourceful."

Adara sighed. "Velizarii—"

"Don't call me by that name. I've no wish to recount that part of my life, Majesty. The kindest thing that happened to me there was having my throat cut. Believe me, you've no desire to know what really happened to me after the death of my father."

She patted his arm gently, wanting to console him, but knowing that nothing could. "Did they train you and Christian to be so evasive or is this a talent the two of you picked up on your own?"

"It was a necessary skill we cultivated so as to survive." He turned and headed toward the refectory where she had left Lutian eating before she went to see to Christian.

"You'll have to forgive him, Your Highness," Thomas said from behind her. "Both of them, for that matter. Neither of them has ever known comfort or solace. They've seen enough tragedy to make any man mean."

She smiled at the old monk. "And yet both men have your loyalty."

He nodded. "They were mere boys when I met them and yet they fought like seasoned, fearless champions. I was lucky to be a man full grown before I was taken. They grew to manhood under the lashes and abuse of our tormentors." He motioned for her to join him. "Come, and I shall talk Brother Bernard into letting you stay with Christian. He needs the tender touch of a woman to comfort him."

Adara returned to Christian's bed, where Brother Bernard was finishing up the dressing of Christian's wounds. His skin held a grayish cast to it. The wound on his shoulder was already bleeding again.

"How does he?" she asked Brother Bernard.

He harrumphed at the question. "Somebody wanted him to die, that's for certain. God's will be done in these matters." The monk made the sign of the cross over Christian before he gathered his kit and headed for the door.

He paused beside her. "If you wish to aid him, my lady, you can bathe his brow this night and make sure his fever doesn't rage too wildly. If he begins to thrash, send for me immediately."

"Thank you, Brother Bernard."

He nodded and headed out of the room.

"I shall be with Velizarii if you need me," Thomas said.

Alone now with her husband, Adara approached the cot slowly. She pulled the small stool that Brother Bernard had left closer to the man who, even while unconscious, looked imposing.

He was a prince who refused his throne. It was inconceivable to her. All her life, her royal responsibility had been impressed upon her. She'd never once considered just shrugging it off and turning away.

Christian had and she wondered what it must feel like to live that way. To not have the constant, nagging weight of making the wrong decision hanging over her head. She was all that stood between her people and tyranny. Her people and slavery.

At times that burden was more than she could bear. She was still considered a young woman, and yet in the dark of night when she was alone she felt ancient.

But then, Christian didn't know his people. He'd never seen the beauty that had been Elgedera before the bloody coups that had left his family completely destroyed. There in the green hills and golden valleys was more beauty than the very Garden of Eden. Like her parents before her, she would ride through the villages that surrounded Garzi in disguise so that she could talk to her people, meet them as one of them, and know their troubles.

Christian had no idea of their customs or their skills. They were faceless strangers to him.

Just as she had always been.

Her heart heavy for him, she went to the small bowl where Brother Bernard had left water and a small cloth. She wrung out the cloth and took it to Christian. The instant she touched his forehead, he came awake with a curse as he grabbed her hand and held it in a powerful grip that bit into her flesh.

"Easy, Christian," she breathed.

Christian blinked as he recognized the face of a dark angel . . . His wife.

"Adara?" he asked, wondering when they'd arrived at the monastery.

She covered his hand with hers. "Aye, now please release me. Your grip hurts."

He let go immediately. "Forgive me, my lady. I don't wake well to touch."

"I noticed. How do you feel?"

He grimaced and forced the pain away as he lay back down. "Truthfully, I've felt better. How long have I been unconscious?"

"Not long."

She placed a cool cloth to his head. Christian savored the warmth of her touch. The gentleness of her actions. It'd been years since he last had a woman touch him like this. For comfort.

She still wore the gown of a pauper and yet only a fool would fail to recognize the inherent nobility of the woman before him. She was graceful and kind.

"Where is Phantom?" he asked.

"I believe he went to eat."

"Have you eaten?"

She nodded. "Would you like me to get you something?"

"Nay, I am fine."

"Really, you should eat. We didn't have time to even taste the pies I bought."

She was so close to him that all he could do was stare into her eyes. They weren't a simple brown color, but rather they had specks of gold in them. Her long black hair fell forward over her shoulder, down to his hand. The silken ends of it tickled his flesh. Before he could think better of it, he let the sable strand wrap itself around his finger.

There was something extremely surreal about this moment. Something peaceful. Calm. Friendly. It awakened a foreign part of himself, a part of him that desperately craved moments like this when someone cared for him.

Since escaping his prison, he'd never thought about home or family. His only thoughts had been to stay away from any binding ties.

Yet what she offered him this night . . .

He lifted his hand to his lips so that he could inhale the sweet, feminine scent of her hair. Feel the softness of it against his flesh.

Adara couldn't breathe as she watched him savor the feel of her hair. It was as if he'd never beheld anything so precious, and that tugged greatly at her heart.

He reached up with his other hand to cup her cheek gently in his roughened palm. His thumb brushed against her lips in a sensuous caress that caused chills to spread all over her.

"Have you ever been kissed, Adara?"

"Nay, Christian. I have kept our vows most sacred. No man has ever touched me in any fashion."

He stared at her in wonderment. And then she saw the guilt that came into his eyes as he dropped his hand. "I didn't know we were married."

She took his hand into hers. "I know and I don't hold you at fault."

"There is no absolution in ignorance. Adultery is punishable by death."

"I don't want you to die, Christian."

"Nay, you want me to return home with you."

She nodded.

"Would you have waited out your entire life for me to come home?"

She let out a long breath at that. "Honestly? I have to say that I have long grown impatient for a husband and child. Had we not been on such tremulous terms with your country, I would probably have sought an annulment years ago and then married another."

Christian wasn't sure if he was happy or not that she had maintained their marriage. But lying here, staring into her eyes, feeling a peace the likes of which he'd never known, he wondered how he could feel anything but pleased.

He lifted her hand to his lips and kissed the tender flesh over the delicate bones of her knuckles. She stared at him with a guarded look. His body sizzled with her nearness. Every part of him craved this brave and noble woman who had come for him. She lured him with a snare that was most irresistible.

And yet, like a caged beast, he couldn't survive in chains. He couldn't. Not again. His time in prison had taught him well the madness that came with captivity. The price. No matter how gilded the cage, it was still a cage.

Adara saw the light fade from his eyes a moment before he released her.

"I need to rest, my lady." He rolled away from her.

Adara clenched her teeth in frustration as she stared at his broad, well-muscled back. At least she did until she noted the scars that ravaged the once-smooth skin.

Her heart hammering, she reached out to touch the puckered flesh. "What caused all this?"

"Life, Adara," he said without looking at her. "It scars us all in some way."

Nay. Not like this. She'd never seen anything like this in her life and she remembered Thomas's words about their tormentors. Her hand paused at the bandage where he'd been wounded tonight. No wonder he didn't complain of it. Compared to the rest of the wounds he'd suffered, it must be paltry indeed.

And in that moment, she had a profound epiphany.

"I am truly sorry, Christian," she whispered softly.

"For what?"

"For all you have suffered. It was very selfish of me to come to you and expect any more of you. You have given enough for your people. I shall ask no more." She leaned over and placed a chaste kiss to his whiskered cheek. "Sleep well, my prince. God speed you on your recovery."

Christian listened as she paused to blow out the small candle on the table beside his cot. She left the room and drew his door shut, but as he lay there thinking, a part of him ached with the loss of her warmth.

He didn't even know her. But since the moment they'd met a few hours ago, his life had careened into chaos. And yet he'd never felt more alive than he did right now, with the scent of her still lingering in the room. With the memory of her touch still warming his skin.

"Focus," he whispered to himself. He mustn't think of her. He had other, much more important matters to think on. Men were out to kill them and he needed to rest so that they could continue on in the morning.

This night had taught him well that there was no escape for them. No escape for her.

He had to get the queen to safety and then get her home again.

Adara's heart was heavy as she returned to the refectory to find Brother Thomas sitting with Phantom and Lutian, who were passing snide comments back and forth.

Phantom sneered at Lutian. "So you came into her service by falling off a wall because you'd stolen a horse and were running from the guards?"

Lutian made a grand show of chewing his bread, then swallowing it before he answered. "Well, we can't all be the *king* of thieves, can we?"

Moving like lightning, Phantom shot out with his eating knife and buried it into the table between two of Lutian's fingers. "I don't suffer *fools* lightly."

His eyes wide, Lutian balled his hand into a fist and moved to sit at the other end of the table with his trencher and cup, far away from Phantom.

Adara paid them little heed as she walked into the room. She'd made a mistake by coming here. How simple everything had seemed all those weeks ago when she had set out on this journey.

Now she was a continent away from her homeland and didn't know what to do.

But one thing was clear to her now. She needed to release her husband from his role and find another way to save her country.

"Phantom?" She waited until he looked up from his porridge. "How much will you charge to take me home?"

Five

Phantom choked on the porridge. Brother Thomas pounded him on the back while Phantom reached for, then drank from a small wooden cup. He gave a menacing glare to Thomas, who immediately halted his hand in the mid-pounding stroke position.

"Pardon?" Phantom asked once he'd regained some composure.

"I wish to go home and I need a guide and guard."

He cleared his throat. "You'll get neither from me, Your Majesty. I will not return there. Ever."

"Why are we returning with Phantom, my queen?"

She glanced over to Lutian. "I'll explain later." Then she looked back at Phantom. "I can pay you a fortune."

Phantom scoffed at that. "Coin is ever useless to a corpse."

She arched a brow at him. "Are you afraid, then?"

He laughed bitterly. "Hardly, and you'll never get me to agree by calling me craven."

"Then what will it take?"

Phantom wiped his mouth, then gave Brother Thomas an almost amused smirk. "You haven't enough money, power, or influence to buy me, Your Majesty. There are some things—few, I grant you, but some—that are not for purchase. My loyalty, or in this case stupidity, will not be bartered for any price."

He picked his cup up and lifted it in a mock salute. "Work your wiles on your husband. He's the greater fool of the two of us."

Her throat tight, Adara struggled for composure. "And therein lies the problem. I've no wish to work my wiles on him, either. He's suffered enough in this." She approached Brother Thomas. "Know you who might have swords and lances for hire? I shall need an army to return and I'm willing to pay dearly for it."

"Aye, Majesty, I know several. *Der Tuefel* is—"

"Don't bring Lucifer into this madness," Phantom said, interrupting Thomas. "Leave him be where he is."

"He is ever after glory and coin. I should think this is just what he would covet. Either he or the *Lladdwr*."

"We shall go for *Lladdwr* in the morning. He

and his men are in York under the banner of the local earl. I would think Ioan is more than ready to go to war for such a cause."

All four of them turned to see Christian standing in the open doorway. He wore a pair of black breeches and a black tunic that he'd left untied about his neck, showing her that he hadn't donned his armor.

His handsome face was pale but determined.

"This is no longer your fight, Christian," Adara said. "I will raise my own army."

He scoffed at that. "Aye, but it is. They made it so the instant they traveled here like a pack of wild dogs to kill us."

Phantom laughed evilly. "No man kills me and lives."

Christian nodded. "Exactly."

Adara frowned at them, not understanding the phrase.

"It was a pact they took in prison," Thomas explained to her. "No one would take their lives without paying dearly for it."

Christian's pale blue eyes fairly glowed in the dim light of the refectory. "I never had any intention of going to Elgedera. But they didn't send a single man to kill me or Adara, they sent an entire garrison or more, and that was their mistake. They have dropped the gauntlet before me and I intend to return it fully met."

Christian looked at each of them in turn. "Basilli and Selwyn have no intention of letting this matter end until we are dead. Therefore I shall end it once and for all. The prince is going home to be crowned king and to exact his revenge. Swear your fealty to me, Phantom, and I'll see to it that you'll have the choicest land in the kingdom."

"Why would you choose me?"

"Because you have ever been in my shadow, lurking there and only emerging when I need you. I never understood why, but your loyalty has long been noted and appreciated. I would have no other man at my back for this."

Phantom seemed to consider his words. "Are you ready for the battle, Abbot?"

He nodded grimly.

Adara smiled in relief. Part of her was grateful, but the other part didn't like the thought of adding any more grief to a man who had suffered so much. "Are you certain you want to do this?"

Christian turned toward her. "They won't leave me in peace, therefore I intend to leave them in pieces."

Phantom lifted his cup. "God save the king."

"And the queen," Lutian chimed in sincerely.

Christian rolled his eyes at Phantom's sarcasm. "Thomas, I shall need one of the monastery's servants to return to the inn in Withernsea, where I was supposed to meet Pagan, and tell him that I won't be able to aid him in his quest for Lysander's killer."

"Consider it done."

Phantom's face was pensive. "What of Stryder

of Blackmoor? Should we send for him as well as Ioan?"

Christian shook his head. "He's newly married and has too many ties to the English throne. I would rather have unfettered mercenaries to fight this war."

"I don't trust mercenaries," Adara said. "Too often they can be bought by your enemies."

Thomas, Christian, and Phantom laughed at that.

"Trust me, my lady," Christian said, "no one could ever buy their loyalty."

"Many a dead man has made the same claim," Lutian said from his end of the table.

Thomas made a tsking noise. "He's right about that. I trust Ioan, but some of his men—"

"Will die if they betray us," Phantom said menacingly. He pulled his knife out of the table from where he had embedded it and tested the edge against his fingers. "I've sent many a man to his grave for lesser things." His eerie gaze became intense, almost mad-looking. "Death to any who betray our kinship."

"Aye," Christian agreed. Suddenly he grimaced, then gasped as if his shoulder were paining him again.

Adara went to him immediately. "You should return to bed."

He nodded. "I'll rest tonight, but we have much to do come morning."

She couldn't believe he would even suggest

such a thing. "Why not stay here a few days so that you can recover?"

Christian rubbed his shoulder. "The assassins sent after us won't wait and I've no wish to see the monks here endangered in my fight. Not to mention they wouldn't think kindly on an army being amassed on holy property."

Her husband did have a point. The Church did tend to frown on warfare.

"I still think you need to rest."

He smiled at that as if it amused him. "Good night," Christian said before he turned and left.

Adara followed him. She didn't speak until he was back in his room, getting into bed.

"I'm sorry that I caused your wounds, Christian."

"You didn't cause my wounds, Adara," he said as he lay down. "The men wielding swords did that."

She laughed at his unexpected humor. It was the first time he'd made a joke. She crossed the room and tucked him in.

Christian held his breath as she did something he was sure she gave no thought to, and yet for him . . .

It was a rare caring act. One no other woman, other than his mother, had ever done for him.

She brushed the hair back from his forehead and laid her soft hand against his brow. "You have a slight fever starting."

Aye, but it wasn't related to his injuries. His body was on fire from her nearness.

She reached to pull off his tunic.

"I prefer to sleep with it on," he said in a gruffer tone than he'd intended.

If she pulled his tunic off . . .

He didn't trust himself being almost naked with her. Not when his body was this aroused. Injuries or no, he might very well consummate this misbegotten marriage, and that would be disastrous to both of them.

"Very well." She left the bed to sit on a small wooden chair that looked terribly uncomfortable.

"What is it you do?"

"I'm watching over you. Brother Bernard said that someone should keep an eye on you this night."

"I will be fine, Adara. There's no need for you to inconvenience yourself."

"Inconvenience myself? Why, sir prince, you have twice saved my life. This is the least I can do for you."

He wanted to argue, but had learned enough about his stubborn queen to know it would be a useless effort. Being careful of his injuries, he rolled over.

Still he could feel her watching him. It made his entire body burn with needful heat. But it was a need he could never sate. It wouldn't be fair to either of them, since he had no intention of staying with her. He would return and overthrow Selwyn and Basilli, aye, but he wouldn't stay in Elgedera. Nor would he ever leave his child behind.

There could never be anything between Adara

and himself. Once he had her throne secured, he would petition the Church to grant them an annulment and see her free.

And yet, even as that thought went through him, some part of his heart protested it. What would it be like to have a home? To have a woman by his side to bear his children?

I want more than that . . .

It was true, even though he hated to admit it. He didn't want a cold, political marriage. He wanted what Stryder and Rowena shared. When they looked upon each other, the heat of their passion fairly scorched anyone who was near them. They loved each other.

What do you need with love?

But then, it wasn't a need so much as a craving. His parents had been taken from him so early and since that day he'd never felt that sensation of true acceptance, true happiness. That inner warmth that came to his breast because he knew someone cared for him. Aye, his Brotherhood cared for him, but that was friendship, which was a whole separate matter.

What would it be like to feel the desperate ache of Cupid's arrow? Just once. That compelling force that could make a man willingly die for the woman who held his heart. In songs and poetry, they likened it to the greatest force under heaven.

Methinks the attackers have addled your brains. Any more of this and you'll be as useful as Lutian.

Aye, it was true. He didn't want love. Never.

Sooner or later something would come and destroy it. He'd be alone again.

They could keep their love. Christian of Acre had no need of it.

Grinding his teeth, Christian closed his eyes. He was a man born of an iron will. He could ignore her. He could.

And he would.

Adara sat still for more than an hour before she saw Christian relax in his bed. She'd begun to fear he would never find sleep.

She got up and went to check his fever. It was slightly worse, but still nothing to cause her alarm.

Christian was truly a strong man. Perhaps too strong. And yet as she watched him sleeping, she didn't see a strong prince. She saw only a handsome man who looked peaceful and calm. A look that wasn't there when he was awake. Awake he was intimidating and fierce.

Glancing down, she studied the mark on his hand that betrayed his captivity. She traced the lines of it with her fingertip. It must have hurt badly when it was received. How much more did the indignity of it hurt now?

Her heart heavy, she lay behind him on the small cot and snuggled close to his warm body.

She shouldn't be doing this. Christian would no doubt protest if he knew what she was about. Yet she couldn't stop herself. She wanted to hold him. Needed to feel his strength with her body.

She felt lost. Alone. She didn't know what her future held anymore.

Truthfully, that terrified her. Uncertainties assailed her in the darkness and brought tears to her eyes. "What's to become of me?" she whispered as silent tears started falling. "I need guidance, Lord. Wisdom. My people need a queen who knows what she's doing, not one who is lost and unsure."

Suddenly she felt the strength of Christian's hand on hers. She swallowed in trepidation as he lifted her hand to his lips and kissed it.

She pulled back as Christian rolled over to face her.

"Don't cry, Adara," he whispered, wiping the tears from her cheeks. "I won't let them hurt you or take your kingdom from you. I know what it's like to be without a home and I will pledge my eternal soul that you will never know that feeling."

His words only succeeded in making her cry more.

Christian was at a loss as to how to cope with her tears. He'd never spent enough time with women to witness them often. The only woman he'd spent much time with was Mary, who had been a captive with them in the Holy Land. But Mary had never once wept.

His stomach tightened in hopelessness.

"Shhh," he breathed, wiping her tears with his hand.

"I'm sorry," she sobbed. "I don't normally cry. I don't. I'm j-just at a loss."

"I'm so often at a loss that it seems my most natural state." He couldn't believe he'd confessed that to her. Even when he was at his most perplexed, he refused to allow anyone to know it.

"You're just trying to make me feel better."

"Nay, my lady. Truly. I am often baffled by life. Struck dumb, point of fact."

One corner of her mouth lifted at that. "I don't believe you."

He watched her eyes glisten from her tears. Before he realized what he was doing, he was tracing the curve of her eyebrow with his thumb. This was the most intimate moment of his life and they were both lying fully clothed.

Yet he'd never felt more exposed or vulnerable.

She looked up at him as if he were some type of hero sent to help her. He'd never felt particularly heroic before.

More than that, he felt her nearness with every part of him. And he wanted nothing more than to taste her virgin mouth.

Adara licked her lips as she watched Christian watching her. It was intense, hot, and it stole her breath away.

He leaned his head closer. Closer.

Then he pressed his lips to hers.

Adara moaned as she tasted her first kiss. The warm, masculine scent of Christian filled her head as his tongue gently parted her lips to explore her mouth. Her entire body sizzled from the foreign sensation.

His arms tightened around her, pulling her closer to his hard, tawny body. She ran her hands over the rugged planes of his back, taking care not to touch his bandages. His lips and tongue teased her unmercifully.

So this was a lover's kiss . . .

She liked it greatly.

Christian struggled to breathe as he felt her returning his kiss with enthusiasm. She stroked his tongue with hers and uttered a soft, murmuring noise of pleasure that made his body harder than it had ever been before.

It was all he could do to keep from lifting the hem of her gown and exploring more of her soft, supple body.

How could a mere mortal man sate himself with just this little portion of heaven?

You must.

If he took her, there could never be an annulment. He would be bound to her and to a throne for all eternity.

No more freedom.

Let her go.

Growling fiercely, he forced himself to pull away. Her breathing was ragged as she stared up at him in wonderment. Two heartbeats later, she reached up, buried her hand in his hair, and pulled him back for another kiss.

Christian's head swam as she boldly renewed their kiss. Worse, she rubbed herself against him, exciting his body even more.

You're in a monastery!

That finally went over him like a dousing of cold water. Pulling back, he held himself away from her.

"Did I do something wrong?" she asked.

Nay, she'd done everything right. That was the problem with this matter.

He shook his head at her. "Nay, my lady. You've done nothing wrong, but I think it best for both of us if we forget this moment."

Adara was hurt by his words until she realized something. "You're not going back to stay, are you? You plan to leave as soon as you can."

She saw the truth in his blue eyes before he even spoke.

"Nay, I will not stay."

An unfounded anger and disappointment tore through her. Furious beyond her endurance, she bolted from the bed to confront him. "Then why bother to go home at all?"

"Because it is my duty and responsibility and I will not run from it."

"Why not? You've been running from it all these years."

His nostrils flared at that as he sat up. "What has possessed you?"

"Anger," she growled out. "Great doses of anger, my lord. And all of it is for you." She paced before his bed. "Please, spare me your pity and your charity. I most certainly don't need either one. I've come this far, I can make it back home on my own."

"And where are your guards?"

Her stomach knotted as she thought of what had befallen them because of her. "I can hire more."

"And the men after you?"

"What do you care? Up until a few hours ago, you knew me not at all. For all you knew, I was already dead."

"And now I know you for my wife. It is because of me that you are in danger. Believe me, I don't want to do this, but I can't walk away until I set this matter right and you are again safe."

Adara forced herself to calmness, even though inside she was weeping at his "noble" words. Noble, her left foot. She hated him for this.

Until this moment, she hadn't realized just how much she had opened herself up to him. And why wouldn't she? For years, she had dreamed of this man. Ever since she was a child, she had done nothing but prepare herself mentally for the day her "king" would return and claim her.

But her "king" wanted nothing to do with her. Nothing. It stung on a level she hadn't known existed.

"Very well, my lord," she said acrimoniously. "Set your matters right and be done with this, then the devil can take you for all I care." She went to the washstand and flung the cloth at him. "And you can tend your own bloody damned wounds."

Stunned as the cloth slapped him against his face, Christian watched while Adara stormed from his room. He pulled the cloth from his head and stared at the closed door.

The next thing he knew, he was actually laughing over her tirade. Why? He couldn't imagine. He should be every bit as angry himself.

He wasn't.

No woman had ever been angry at him before. None. They had cajoled and tried to seduce. But rage had never confronted him in such a promising package.

You are enchanted.

Aye. Much more than he should be. She would be quite a handful for any man.

He wiped his soggy brow with his arm before he tossed the cloth back to the washing bowl. Most likely he should go after her and apologize, though to be honest there was nothing to apologize for. He'd done nothing wrong. He'd only been truthful with her.

Honesty is for weak-minded fools, especially when it involves charming a maid.

That's what Ioan would say, but then his old friend was unique in his views of the world.

Sighing, Christian turned over and forced himself to think of other matters. Winning back his kingdom would take all his concentration. The last thing he needed was to allow Adara to distract him while he was leading so many men.

Adara had no real destination in mind as she stalked from the dormitory where Christian's cell was. She wanted his blood, but there was nothing to be done for it.

"My queen?"

She turned at Lutian's voice.

"You shouldn't be out here while the Sesari are after you. They could be here in the yard even now, observing us, waiting for a moment to strike."

He was right. She headed back toward him immediately. "I was so angry that I wasn't thinking."

"We all do that from time to time."

Adara paused by his side. Her precious Lutian. He'd been with her for so long. Always her friend, her confidant. Not once had he ever betrayed her.

If only he could have been noble-born . . .

"You are a good friend to me, Lutian. Thank you."

His eyes blank, he inclined his head to her. "Ever my pleasure and honor to serve you, my queen."

She patted him on the shoulder before she returned to the shelter of the dormitory and headed to her own cell without ever knowing that Lutian watched her longingly as she vanished from his sight.

"You're in love with her."

Lutian turned sharply at the deep, raspy voice that came out of the darkness surrounding him. He had no idea where Phantom was, any more than he'd known Phantom could see him with Adara. "Do you always make it your habit to sneak about?"

"They don't call me Phantom without cause." Phantom stepped out of the shadows to his left. Indeed, the man appeared to just move out of the wall itself.

Lutian glared at him. "I thought the Elgederions executed you for murder."

He gave a wry smile. "They tried. Obviously they failed."

Lutian started back inside.

"Have you ever told Adara how you feel about her? That you love her?"

A tic started in his jaw as pain swept through him. "She is unreachable to me, and well I know it. If I told her, I would lose her."

One corner of Phantom's lips quirked up. "I knew you weren't the fool you are playing. Tell me, how is it a thief ends up as companion to a queen?"

Lutian gave him a dry stare. "I suppose the same way the son of a prince ends up a legendary thief and assassin. The hand of fate ever schemes to keep us on our toes."

"Hmm," Phantom said thoughtfully.

Lutian was uncomfortable under that cold scrutiny. "What?"

"I'm only wondering what lengths you would go to, to possess your ladylove."

The underlying tone of his voice was dubious. Accusatory. "What is it you accuse me of?"

"How is it her guards were killed and you escaped? For that matter, who killed her guards?"

Angry over his presumption, Lutian started back for the dormitory.

Before Lutian could take more than two steps, Phantom grabbed him and ripped the sleeve from his tunic to bear his upper arm. Lutian cursed and tried to shove him away, but Phantom held tight.

There in the moonlight, Lutian wasn't sure whose face was palest as Phantom saw the mark on his biceps. He knew it wasn't the mark Phantom was expecting to see.

"I am not Sesari," he snarled as he covered the elaborate vine-shaped brand that marked him as a slave. "Nor did I kill her men. I was born property and I stole in order to live after I found the courage to run away from my abusive owner. I hid when the Sesari arrived at the inn because I know nothing of killing or fighting. It's not a skill anyone teaches a slave or a fool."

Phantom winced. "I'm sorry, Lutian. It's not in my nature to trust."

Lutian looked at the scar on the man's throat. "Nay, I guess it isn't. But know this: I would die before I ever betrayed Queen Adara."

"Does she know of your past?"

He shook his head. "And I would keep it that way."

Something almost kind darkened Phantom's eyes. "Have no fear. Keeping secrets is something I excel at." He released him. "Good night, Lutian."

Lutian inclined his head to him before he entered the dormitory and headed for his room.

Phantom watched the fool leave, then listened to the night winds that whispered around him. The Sesari were there. He could feel them. They would not stop until they had completed their mission.

But then, neither would he.

"It shall be interesting to see who wins this," he whispered, then laughed.

A wounded prince, a runaway slave, and a condemned thief were about to join forces with the devil and the damned to save a queen and her people.

The next few weeks would definitely prove interesting indeed.

Six

Christian woke up to the harsh morning light. For an instant there, he was a boy again in the monastery in Acre. His heart clenched as panic swelled and he waited for Brother Arthur to douse him with water, then box his ears for being late for prayer.

But he was no longer a child. The old monastery was gone . . . as was Brother Arthur. Christian grimaced at the reminder of how they'd all died the night of the attack that had come without warning.

"Cease," he whispered, banishing those bad memories. There was nothing in the past for him. Nothing.

He sat up slowly, his body loudly protesting every movement.

"Cease what?"

He turned his head to find Adara seated in the

uncomfortable chair where she'd been the night before, watching him. "I thought you were angry with me."

"I am, my lord. Make no mistake over that. However, I have done much thinking since I left you last night and I agree that you are right. What good would it do me to have a king who has no interest in my throne or his? For too long I have lived my life waiting for you. No more. Once we return to Elgedera and you depose your misbegotten relatives, I shall seek your annulment and find myself a consort who is worthy to be king."

Christian frowned at her words and her flat, emotionless tone. She spoke so matter-of-factly that they could have been discussing the weather as opposed to her future.

"What has brought about this change in you?" he asked.

She shrugged nonchalantly. "Common sense. Since you have no wish to be king, you will need to choose a successor. That successor will be my spouse."

Surely she was jesting. "And if I choose someone you revile?"

"You won't."

She was so cold as she resigned herself to such a heartless fate. Of course, that was the fate of most women in her position, and yet a part of him that he didn't want to acknowledge rebelled at the idea of her marrying another man. Surely a woman such as this deserved something better. Someone who could at the very least value her.

What do you care? She is after another poor sap to marry. Be grateful. You are free of her now.

Then why didn't he feel better about it? Why did something inside him feel like it had been battered by her decision?

'Tis your pride that she would accept another man. Nothing more, nothing less.

Perhaps . . .

Adara got up and headed for the door. "Thomas sent a servant out at first light to return to the inn so that he could wait for your friends and tell them what has happened to you."

"Then the rest of you must have been waiting for me."

She nodded.

"I shall be ready shortly."

She inclined her head to him and headed for the door. Christian watched her leave. She was again dressed in the plain watchet gown of a peasant with her hair braided sedately down her back, and yet there was something about her that was compelling. She looked calm this morning, but some inner part of him missed the hellion of the night before.

Do get dressed, Christian, and put the matter aside.

That would be the wisest course of action. Christian got up and wasted no time getting himself armed and dressed again. Once he was ready, he went in search of his party.

He found Adara in the refectory with Phantom, Thomas, and Lutian while they broke their fast.

"How do you feel?" Phantom asked him as he set his cup aside to pin him with a frown.

Christian leaned his head to the right to stretch one of the sore muscles in his neck. "Fit to ride."

Phantom scoffed. "Interesting, since you look as if you're only fit to fall over."

Christian gave him a gimlet stare.

Phantom disregarded it. "But if you're willing to die—"

Thomas cut him off by clearing his throat. "I was telling Velizarii earlier that this monastery was built during the height of the Viking invasions, so there is an old tunnel beneath it that runs for a league out into a shallow bit of woods on the outskirts of a small village."

"At first light," Phantom continued, "Thomas had several servants leave the monastery one by one with our horses, to await our arrival in the village."

Christian smiled at their plan. "So if the Sesari are watching, they will think we are still here."

Thomas nodded. "They may be soldiers, but according to Adara they are Christian and won't dare to attack the monastery."

Phantom laughed bitterly at that. "I wouldn't bet my life on that presumption, Thomas."

Christian concurred. The best thing they could do for the monks would be to leave as soon as they were able. "Where is this tunnel?"

Thomas took a torch from the wall, lit it in the

fire, then led them to the antechamber of the church. He lifted the corner of a bright red tapestry that depicted Christ rising from the cross, to show a door behind it. The old door hadn't been opened in quite some time and it took both Phantom and Christian to shoulder it back into working order.

Lutian was "kind" enough to hold the tapestry out for them and verbally encourage them.

"He could hurt himself," Adara said when Phantom commented on the fool's lack of use.

"Better him than me," Phantom muttered as they finally managed to get the door open.

Christian rubbed his sore shoulder as he stepped back from the opening. "Might I make a comment, Thomas? In the event of the monastery being attacked, this would prove a most useless escape route if it takes the monks an hour to open it."

"Aye," Phantom concurred. In a feigned ancient voice that sounded much like an old monk, he added, "Wait, good and decent attackers, don't burn us out yet. We've still got a little more pushing to do. We'll be through with it shortly. Here, pull up a seat and give us a few so that we might escape you. God will bless you for it."

Adara squelched her laughter, while Lutian and Christian gave full rein to theirs.

Thomas looked less than pleased. "You really are a heathen, aren't you?"

Phantom shrugged as if it concerned him not at

all. "To the farthest depths of my damned and rotted soul."

Mumbling a prayer for him. Thomas led them into the dark, damp passageway that reminded Christian far too much of the place where they had spent most of their youth.

"Oh, what fond memories this evokes," Phantom said sarcastically as he followed them. "All we need now is the stench of excrement, rats running over our feet, and the tortured screams of men."

"Better than riding straight into your enemy's clutches," Thomas reminded him.

Phantom snorted at that. "If I have to die, I'd rather do it with the sun on my face and fresh, untainted air in my nostrils."

"Well, with any luck none of us shall be dying today," Lutian said.

"How far is this York?" Adara asked as they continued on their way. "Will we have long to journey?"

"Nay," Phantom answered. "If we move quickly, York is but one day of hard riding south of here. We should make it shortly before nightfall."

Adara was aghast. "Christian can't ride that long with his injuries. He shall need rest."

Christian scoffed at that. "I shall be fine."

She exchanged a doubtful look with Lutian.

"Look to the bright side of the matter, my queen. If he dies, then you can get his necklace and have your proof of him as your husband."

Christian cast a murderous glare at him, but said nothing as they walked onward.

It didn't take too long to get to the village. There Thomas met his servant, who already had the horses saddled and waiting for them.

"Godspeed," Thomas said as soon as they were mounted.

"And may He be with you, Brother," Christian said with a respectful tilt of his head.

Thomas blessed them, then sent them on their way. Christian took the lead, while Adara and Lutian rode side by side, with Phantom at the rear in case the Sesari should find them.

Just as Phantom had predicted, it was a hard day of riding, with them only stopping long enough to rest the horses. Adara watched Christian closely, afraid that he would succumb to his injuries. He didn't, but as each hour came and went, he was definitely paler and a fine sheet of sweat would dapple his brow from time to time.

Still, he refused to stop or to slow, lest it put her in danger. She'd never known any man with his fortitude.

It was well into the evening before they finally reached the town of York. It was a bustling city, even at this hour. Adara looked about as they passed carts and people coming and going on the cobblestone streets.

"How will we find your friend Ioan?" Adara asked.

Before Christian could respond, a man was thrown through an open doorway and went sprawling before them into the street while raucous laughter, taunts, and insults rang out after him. Two more men quickly joined him in the street. They all lay on the ground, groaning.

"I think we found him," Christian said with a hint of amusement in his voice.

"Or if not, we found someone who can take us to him," Phantom added.

A large, burly man left the building, and a small crowd gathered in the doorway to watch him as he picked up the first man he'd tossed out. His clothes rumpled, the man's shoulder-length black hair was in sore need of a trim. He had large brown eyes and a vicious scar that ran from his temple down his cheekbone.

"And for that . . ." The man's voice trailed off as he looked up to see Christian on his horse.

The man blinked, then narrowed his eyes as if trying to get them to focus properly. "Abbot?" he asked gruffly. "Is that you, man?"

"Aye, Samson. 'Tis I."

The man laughed as he allowed the man he held to crumple back to the street. He came toward them with his arms outstretched in greeting. The crowd, realizing that there would be no more bloodshed, headed back inside, while the burly man stopped before the travelers.

"God's blood, Abbot, it's been too long."

Christian dismounted. "Indeed, old friend."

Samson embraced him until Christian hissed. "Are you wounded, brother?"

Christian nodded as he moved away from him. "Where is your lord?"

Samson scratched his scraggly beard. "We're camped on the outskirts of the town, just below the castle's hill. Last I saw, Ioan was headed for his tent." Samson's dark gaze went from Christian to Adara. "My goodness, what precious vision have we here?"

"You're death by Christian's hand if you touch her," Phantom said.

Samson laughed. "Phantom. Now, you are indeed a ghost from my past. Since when do you travel with anyone?"

"Hugh?" a woman called from the doorway before Phantom could answer. "Are you not coming back?"

Samson turned his head toward her. "Aye, love, give me a moment and I'll return." He moved away from Phantom back toward the tavern.

"Vaden?" he bellowed inside the doorway.

A boy around the age of ten-and-six who appeared less than fully sober came running outside. He was thin yet handsome, with dark blond hair and golden eyes. "Aye, m'lord?"

"Take Lord Christian and his companions to Lord Ioan and be quick about it, or I'll have your arse skinned and tanned."

As the boy ran for his horse, which was tied to a

post a short distance away, Samson turned back to Christian. "If Ioan isn't there, Vaden will find him for you."

"My thanks."

Samson inclined his head. "Now, if you'll forgive me, I have a previous engagement with the bosom of a goodly woman."

"And the only question to that is just what exactly is she good at," Phantom said in a low tone.

Samson clucked his tongue at him. "After you find Ioan, come back here, Phantom, and she'll educate you well on what she excels at."

Christian shook his head at them before he remounted.

"Follow me, m'lord," the boy said as he headed due north toward the castle on the hill.

Just as Samson had said, there was a massive encampment of multicolored tents between the town and the castle. Lutian gaped at Adara as they saw the large number.

"How many camp here?" Adara asked Vaden.

"My Lord Ioan leads one hundred and twenty-six knights, my lady. Then we have some three score archers and servants and squires for them all."

Adara was shocked by the size of the army. "And they are all mercenaries?"

"Aye, my lady."

"Ioan never does anything in a small way," Phantom said from behind her.

Apparently not. She'd never heard of a single man leading a free company of this size.

The boy led them to a large red-and-white-striped tent that was in the midst of the others. As they dismounted, Adara noted that Christian was slower to move than he'd been earlier.

"Are you all right, Christian?" she asked, concerned that he might have hurt himself.

"Aye."

But she didn't believe it. He moved too carefully and slowly. It was obvious to her that he was in pain.

Christian handed the boy a handful of coin and thanked him, then led their small group into the tent.

Inside, the tent was sectioned off by cloth walls. In the main area where they entered, there was a table with four chairs and an arming stand that held the knight's chain mail, helm, and sword.

"Ioan?" Christian called.

No one answered.

As they turned to leave, they were confronted by what appeared to be a young archer who was surely no older than the boy who had led them here. Several inches shorter than Adara, he was gangly and thin, with raven-black hair and brown eyes that watched them warily.

He held his bow at the ready with an arrow already nocked. "Who are you and what business have you with Lord Ioan?" he asked in a gruff, low tone.

"We are old friends," Christian said calmly.

Phantom moved toward him.

The archer turned quickly and let fly the arrow. Phantom caught it midflight, but before he could take another step, the archer swung the bow and caught him upside his head with it.

Phantom staggered back from the force of the blow.

The archer struck again and knocked him to the ground.

Christian moved toward them.

Before Adara could blink, the archer had another arrow nocked and ready to fly into Christian's chest.

"Corryn, cease!" The Welsh-accented voice rang through the room like thunder.

Adara looked at the entrance to see a tall, well-muscled man there who bore a striking resemblance to the archer. His wavy black hair fell to his shoulders and a full beard covered his cheeks. He looked wild and untamed as he put himself between the archer and Christian.

"What has gotten into your head, Spider?" he asked the archer in his thick, rolling accent.

"They came here looking for you," the archer said brashly, as if the larger man's anger didn't concern him at all. He finally unnocked the arrow. "After the message from Stryder saying there were assassins out to kill you, I thought I was protecting you, *brawd*."

The man she assumed must be Ioan made a disgusted noise at him. "God save me from your protection. Did it never occur to you that an assassin wouldn't bother to come into my tent and announce himself?"

He said something in a language Adara didn't understand, but by Corryn's reaction, it must have been a curse or reprimand of some kind. "Now apologize. You almost took the head off the Abbot, and it's the Phantom who you've knocked to the ground."

The archer's face went pale at that.

Ioan stepped away from the boy to offer his hand to Phantom, who took it. He helped him back up to his feet. "You'll have to forgive my brother, Phantom. He's a damned fool."

"Are you the Abbot?" Corryn asked Christian.

"Aye."

The boy's lips quivered before he threw himself into Christian's arms. "May the saints guard your blessed soul throughout all eternity!"

Christian looked awkward as he frowned at Ioan. "Brother?"

Ioan's gaze turned dark, dangerous as he pulled Corryn back.

Still Corryn stared at Christian with hero worship. "Thank you, Abbot, for bringing my brother back to me."

"Get out of here, scamp," Ioan said gruffly, "before I skin you."

Corryn curled his lip at Ioan. "I spoke too soon, Abbott. Curses to you, that you brought his surly hide home. Methinks you should have left him there to rot." He turned to Phantom. "My apologies to you, sir. I hope you'll forgive me."

Phantom shook the boy's arm. "I admire anyone who can get the better of me. It doesn't happen often."

"Corryn!"

"I'm leaving," he snapped. "To the devil with your hoary hide."

Scowling, Christian watched the boy leave.

As soon as they were alone, Ioan's face softened. "To what do I owe this pleasure, Christian?"

"We are in need of an army."

"Done," Ioan said without hesitation. "My men are yours."

"We'll have to go back through the Holy Land," Phantom said.

"That bothers me not."

It was Adara's turn to frown at the man's blasé acceptance of their mission. "Don't you want to know why we need your army?"

Ioan shrugged. "I assume it is to fight."

"Aye," she said slowly, "but don't you want to know why you're fighting?"

"I am fighting because Brother Christian needs me."

Lutian scratched his cheek. "Methinks our new ally is even more simple than I am, my queen."

"Queen?" Ioan asked with a frown as he looked at her with new interest.

"Aye," Christian said. "I have sworn to return her to her throne."

Ioan nodded. "Consider it done. I'll need a day to ready my men, then we can march to wherever it is that you need us."

"How much will your army cost me?" Adara asked.

Ioan appeared highly offended by her question. "I would not be here today if not for Christian, my lady. This army would not exist. A man needs no coin to help out his brother." He headed for the entrance. "Tobias!"

A few seconds later, a young man entered the tent. "My lord?"

"Have four tents set up for my friends for the night."

"Aye, my lord." The young man dashed out to do his bidding.

Adara waited for Christian to correct Ioan on the number of tents they would need, since as his wife she assumed they would share a tent.

When he didn't she felt a small pain in her chest. Especially as she realized that he had yet to tell the Welshman that they were married.

So be it. If he didn't want her, she would start her search for a new king here. After all, she was in a camp surrounded by strong men who would most likely jump at the chance to marry a queen and share a throne.

"You are a good man, Ioan," she said to him. "By all appearances, a fine and capable leader as well. A queen could do well with a man such as you by her side."

Christian's ears perked up at her words. Even though his body was throbbing from pain, he didn't miss the look of heat that came into Ioan's eyes, or the speculative gleam in Adara's.

It made his vision dim.

Ioan gave her a hot, seductive smile. "I appreciate your compliment, Majesty. While we await your quarters being prepared, would you like to have something to eat?"

His wife all but preened under the Welshman's look. "Aye, my lord. We are truly famished and your kindness would be most appreciated."

Christian's sight dimmed even more as he watched her coy smile. She even batted her eyelashes.

This was more than he could stand.

"Abbot?" Phantom asked. "Are you all right?"

"I am fine," he said from between clenched teeth.

Phantom scoffed. "Whatever you say."

"He looks ill to me," Lutian said. "Rather green and red. Can't tell if he's angry or vomitous."

Christian slanted a look at the fool that had him retreating.

Adara felt a modicum of satisfaction at her husband's ill humor until she saw the reddish stain that was barely discernible through the black cloth of his robe.

"You're bleeding," she said sternly, moving to stand beside him.

Christian tried to brush her off, but she would have none of it.

Her anger flared. "Cease with your stubbornness, Christian. Your wounds need to be tended."

He glared at her.

She glared back.

Ioan whistled low. "Phantom, who is the queen, that Christian would tolerate her thusly?"

Phantom folded his arms over his chest as he watched them. "His wife."

"Only until our marriage is annulled," Christian snapped.

Adara put her hands on her hips as she continued to glower at him. "Well, if you stand there until you bleed to death, we won't need an annulment, now, will we?"

Phantom sucked his breath between his teeth. "The queen has gotten a bit snippy, eh?"

Christian looked to Ioan. "Have you a healer in your company?"

Ioan snorted at that as he looked back and forth from Christian to Adara. "Heed my words well, Abbot, no man who possesses his full sense will ever come between a woman and her husband."

He pulled back a corner of the fabric that formed one wall, revealing the sleeping area of the tent, where a large, ornately carved bed was placed. "You may tend him here, my lady. I shall have fresh linens and herbs brought for you."

Adara was relieved that at least one of the men was cooperative. "Thank you, Ioan."

War was clearly etched on her husband's handsome face. But then, it also raged in her own heart.

If he wanted a battle, she was more than ready to give him one.

"Pull off your armor, Christian, or else."

"Or else what?"

"I'll pull it off for you," Ioan said for her.

Christian stiffened. "You wouldn't . . . then again, *you* would."

"Aye, and you'd best be remembering that." In spite of his dire tone, Ioan winked at him.

Christian was ready to beat them all, but knew better than to try and take on Adara, Phantom, and Ioan at once. His fury snapping, he stalked toward the bed and removed his monk's robe.

The next thing he knew, Adara was there, unlacing his mail hauberk while the others dispersed from the tent and left them alone.

"You know, Christian," she said after she was assured the others couldn't hear her, "I don't understand you. You don't want me and yet you get angry anytime another man looks at me."

He could feel the muscle working in his jaw as she loosened his armor, then helped him pull it up over his head. For once he welcomed the absence of its weight. In truth, it had chafed his injuries all day.

The armor slinked to the ground.

Still, his wife gave him no reprieve. "I think you need to decide what it is you want of me, my lord. If you do not want me, then you need to come to terms with that and stop glowering at me whenever I speak to other men about being king in your stead."

He whipped at the laces of his quilted aketon. "Is that really what you want, Adara? A cold marriage that serves no purpose other than to provide you with a strong sword to protect your people and to give you a child for your crown? Do you not crave someone who cares for more than your money and titles?"

She was aghast. "Is this argument not backwards? Is the woman not supposed to be the one who decries the loss of love? I am a queen, Christian. My first marriage is to my people and they are my priority."

"Marriage? It sounds more to me as if you're willing to whore yourself for them."

She hissed at him. "Caution, Christian. I am a woman of infinite patience, but you are sorely testing the limits of infinity."

He was being unreasonable, he knew it. He just didn't understand why.

And then it dawned on him. His anger at her wasn't for the fact that she wanted another man. It was that she wanted *any* man, and not him alone. He was nothing more to her than any other.

"That is all I am to you, isn't it? I could be any man and you would tend my wounds and strip your clothes off for me. I am a duty to you. A burden you have to tolerate."

"Nay, I—"

"Don't deny it," he snarled. "You already told me it was so. When I asked you if I chose a man to be king whom you would revile, you told me you wouldn't. Because in the end, it doesn't matter to you what a man is or what he looks like. So long as he does his duty, you will do yours."

"What is so wrong with doing your duty?"

Everything, when it involved intimacies. He had no use for a bride who wanted nothing more than a warm body in her bed and on her throne. He wasn't a dog to be ordered about or a fool to do her bidding, or anyone else's.

"Leave me," he snarled.

Adara tried to understand his anger, but for her life she couldn't. "You need someone to tend—"

"Then send me a leech. 'Tis his *duty* to tend me."

"Fine," she snapped at him, losing her own patience. She turned and left, then drew up short as soon as she saw Ioan, Phantom, and Lutian on the other side of the fabric wall. They must have returned.

Lifting her chin high, she refused to show them her dismay. "Christian wishes a physician."

"So we heard," Ioan said.

She felt the heat creep over her face.

"Archer!" Ioan bellowed out the entrance of the tent.

Almost instantly, Corryn appeared. "What?" he snapped angrily.

"Fetch a leech for the Abbot and take the queen and her man to your tent to wait for food to be brought to them."

His brother bristled under his stern command.

"I am not your servant, nor am I a child to be ordered about."

"Go."

Corryn made a face at him. With a look of resignation, he turned toward Adara. "Come, Majesty."

Her pride bruised, Adara gratefully left the tent, with Lutian following closely behind her.

Christian gingerly pulled his aketon over his head as his body protested the movement. He sensed someone behind him. Turning, he saw Phantom and Ioan watching him.

Ioan looked disgusted. "Tell me, Phantom, what kind of man turns aside a bride like that one?"

"A raging imbecile, surely."

Christian dropped the aketon to the floor. "Be warned, I'm in no mood at present to deal with either one of you."

Still, Ioan gave him no reprieve. "So your bride wishes nothing more than your arm and your prick, Abbot. Most men I know would be throwing themselves down for such a blessing."

"Yourself included, no doubt."

"No doubt. A throne and a beauty in your bed. Are you completely mad, to turn that aside?"

Christian clenched his teeth at Ioan's condescending tone. "I've had beauty in my bed before, as have you. And like me, you have coin and land aplenty to provide for said beauty. Why, then, have you never married, Ioan?"

Ioan shrugged. "Women need a home to live in to feel safe. A traveling band of soldiers is no place for one."

Phantom frowned. "Then why do you travel with your sister?"

"What say you?" Ioan asked in sudden anger.

Phantom indicated the entrance of the tent with his thumb. "Corryn. 'Tis obvious she is no man or boy as you claim."

Christian concurred. "I noticed the same myself."

Ioan's gaze turned deadly. "You tell anyone that she is a woman and I shall kill you both, Brotherhood or not."

"Why are you passing her off as a man?" Christian asked.

Deep sadness darkened his eyes. It was obviously a sore subject for him. "I wasn't here when our father died. We were still captives then. Corryn was cast out and forced to find her own way. She disguised herself as a boy so that she could find legitimate work and live until I came home."

"And after?" Christian asked.

"As I said, a woman has no place in this life I have chosen. I tried to leave her behind in Wales with servants and coin, but she refused. She donned her boy's garb and followed me. I am all she has in this world and I will kill any man who touches her."

Phantom frowned. "So your men know she's a woman?"

"Nay. I won't chance that temptation. I travel with a rough troop of men."

"Then they must be blind as well as stupid," Phantom said with a laugh. "No boy has hips shaped as hers. Nor a mouth so tempting."

Ioan turned on him with a growl.

Phantom smirked at him. "Calm yourself, *Lladdwr*, I would never trespass on your family."

"You'd best not."

"Excuse me, I need a few moments alone with Christian." They looked up to find Lutian back in the tent.

"Now," the fool said in a forceful voice that surprised Christian. He hadn't heard the fool be forceful before.

To his further shock, Phantom pulled Ioan away and left the tent.

Lutian waited until they were alone before he turned on him with his full anger. "You should be glad I'm not a warrior."

"Why?"

"Because if I were, I would kill you."

Christian rubbed his aching head. He was in no mood for the man right now. "I've no time for this, fool. I hurt and—"

"You hurt?" he asked in disbelief. "Good. It pleases me no end to know that. I just wish you hurt more."

Christian scowled at him. "What has gotten into you?"

He curled his lip at Christian as he clenched and unclenched his fists. "You bastard. I wish I could give you the beating you deserve."

Christian was baffled by the change in the normally good-natured man. "Have you gone mad?"

Lutian moved to stand before him. He had to tilt his head up so that he could meet his gaze. Even so, the fool didn't back down or relent.

Christian admired his courage. Few men who knew he wasn't the monk he appeared had ever stood toe to toe with him.

Lutian shook his head. "For years now, I have envied you. God's blood, I even wanted to be you. But you know what? For the first time since the day I met Adara, I am glad that I am only pretending to be a fool. You, on the other hand, are truly an idiot."

Never one to tolerate an insult, Christian grabbed him. "Caution your tongue, Lutian. Addled or not, I will beat you for your insults."

His anger had little effect on the man. "Then beat me if you will. I assure you any physical blows will be far less painful than the ones you have dealt your wife this night."

Stunned by the revelation, he released him. "What do you know of her?"

"Everything. There is no thought in her heart or head that I haven't been privy to. I have been her only friend all these years. I was there when her father beat her for her refusal to divorce you and marry another when she was ten-and-eight. I was there when they executed her brother and then locked her away to rot because her father was afraid she would turn on him as well. And I was there moments ago when you broke her heart and killed the only dream she has ever allowed herself to have. I have had it with you, my lord, and I wish you to suffer."

Christian ignored the fool as the words soaked in. Adara had been beaten? Locked away?

Was that possible?

"What say you?"

"You heard me. I have spent wasted hours of my life listening to her sing your praises as if you were some noble and kind prince who would come and be the man she deserves. You wore blue trimmed with gold the day you came to her palace for your marriage and you rode a dappled gray stallion named Hercules.

"Your father was taller than a giant, and possessed a thundering voice and wore a black and gold surcoat. He had well-trimmed golden hair and laughing blue eyes that brightened every time he looked at your mother. She was as beautiful as an angel. Her black hair was coiled around her head with no veil and she wore a gown of scarlet with a golden mantle that was trimmed in topaz and diamonds."

Christian was stunned. Lutian described it as if he'd been there. Indeed, he knew details about Christian's parents that even Christian had forgotten.

"Whenever your parents would sit, your father oft kept his hand resting on your mother's shoulder so that he could toy with her earring and lobe.

He was prone to lean close and whisper in her ear things that would make her blush and laugh. You thought nothing of running up to your parents, who would pull you into their arms and hold you close. Your mother always tickled you before she released you to go play."

"How do you know that?"

"Adara." Her name was said like a prayer on Lutian's tongue. "She has every nuance of you and your parents memorized. Do you know she has a gilded box that she keeps in her room at home and in it is everything you touched while you were there? She has the knife you used at dinner. The goblet you drank from. You and her brother were playing a game of chase in the gardens and a piece of trim was torn from your tunic when you ran too close to her mother's roses. She has that as well, and every night before she retires, she opens the box and touches her only link to a man she has dreamed of. She even sleeps on the pillow that you used while you were there."

"Why?"

Lutian's gaze bored into him. "Because she saw the love your parents held for each other, the love they held for you, and she has burned to taste that kind of love ever since. Her father was not a kind man. He was a king and he trusted no one, not even his own children. Her parents never coddled her. There were no playful tickles, no kind hugs or kisses in her world. Only a mother who cast her off to a myriad of nurses and a father who had no use for her until after he executed her brother and then needed to have her trained to be a queen.

"But before your mother left with you, she told Adara that you would come back in six years to consummate your marriage. She promised Adara that if she was a good, chaste, and dutiful wife, you would love her just as your father loved your mother."

Tears came into Lutian's eyes as he looked at Christian as if he were the lowliest of life. "She has nurtured that dream in her heart ever since. Why do you think she came here for you? She could have forged your necklace and found any blond man to pass off to your people as their king. They would never have known the difference. But she didn't. Even when her father told her it would be in their best interest to divorce you and find another husband, she refused. 'Tis not a king she wants, Christian. She wants her husband. She wants *you*."

Christian didn't believe him. "She cares not who her husband is."

"You couldn't be more wrong," he said from between clenched teeth. "Listen to her when she speaks to you. You are not her king or a prince. You are her *husband*. That is the only word she has ever used for you. And you have spat on her and tossed her away. She thought that when you saw her, you would greet her with kindness and respect, that you would be like your father and treat her as he treated your mother. Instead, you threw her from a window and denied her.

"Adara is proud, and yet she offered herself to you, not as a queen but as a woman, naked and willing, because in her mind you were her husband and her champion.

"You've no idea how many times I have caught her with a faraway look in her eyes while she rested her hand on her neck, stroking her earring as if she were dreaming of you touching her the way your father touched your mother. How many times she has told me that her husband, not her king, would return for her."

"Then why does she flirt with you and with Ioan?"

He made a sound of disgust. "She's a woman. She wanted to make you jealous, since you have done nothing but promise to have your marriage dissolved. But when she talks of replacing you she never says she is taking a new husband, only a new king. Those two are not the same in her heart or her mind.

"The only reason she speaks of seeking another king is to save her people. But at the end of the day, she doesn't want another king. For some ungodly reason, she wants you, Christian of Acre. Think you she would tend the wounds of anyone else? She's a queen, not a maidservant, and yet for you she is willing to put aside her status and be a woman."

Christian stepped back as he thought over what she'd said to him since they had met. Lutian was right. She did always refer to him as her husband . . .

"I have only seen her cry twice in her life. The day her father had her brother executed for treason and this day, when her beloved husband called her whore because she was trying to be practical after he destroyed her dreams of a loving marriage."

Lutian shook his head. "You think you're alone, Prince. You're not. You have your precious Brotherhood behind you. You have friends aplenty who would die for you. What does Adara have? Only a pathetic thief who pretends to be addled because if I had ever shown myself to be intelligent her father would have banished me from her and left her bereft."

Christian couldn't understand a parent being like that with his child. "Why?"

"Distrust," Lutian said simply. "Ten years after you played chase with that little boy in her courtyard, he was a man who made the mistake of trusting his best friend Basilli. Basilli turned Gamal's mind and convinced him that he could rule over two powerful kingdoms if he killed his father and imprisoned his sister, the Queen of Elgedera."

"How did her father find out?"

Lutian sighed as if it pained him. "Another friend of Gamal's betrayed his trust by telling his father what he had planned. Gamal was with me and Adara when he was arrested. I don't think I shall ever forget the look of horror on her face. She loved her brother more than anything, and when she heard what he had planned for her, it broke her heart.

"She vowed she would never trust another soul as long as she lived. Her father made it easy for her to keep that vow, since he made sure that no one, save me, the mindless fool, ever stayed with her long. She was taken and locked away in a small manor to our northernmost border, where her maids and servants were changed every few months to ensure that no one befriended her."

Christian stood in silence as he thought over everything Lutian had told him.

He had sorely misjudged his wife and it pained him that he had been so harsh with her.

Wanting to rectify it, he pushed past the fool and started for the entrance. He met the physician who was coming in, but said nothing as he left the tent, then realized he had no idea where Adara had gone.

Corryn was approaching him from the path between the tents. Her eyes widened as she caught sight of him without his tunic on.

"Where is Adara?" he asked.

She pointed to a green tent that was next to Ioan's.

Christian headed for it and didn't stop until he threw back the flap and caught sight of Adara sitting at a table with her back to him. Her head was bent low and she looked weary as she held a slice of apple in her hand.

She lifted one hand up and wiped at her face. "Adara?"

She jumped as if startled, but didn't turn around. "What, Christian?"

He moved around her until he could see her face, and there he saw the truth of what Lutian had said. Her lashes were wet. Her eyes and the tip of her nose were red. He felt like a complete louse that he had caused this.

"I'm so sorry if I hurt you, my lady."

She didn't speak.

Christian sank down to his knees next to her chair. He looked up at her and hoped that his sincerity showed on his face. "It took a lot of courage for you to come all this way to seek me."

He noticed her grip tightened on the apple, but still she said nothing.

She was so beautiful sitting there. Like a peaceful angel. He covered her hand with his and without thinking he placed one hand to her neck and stroked her earlobe.

She bolted from her seat. "Don't do that," she snapped, putting more distance between them.

"Why does that bother you?"

She looked terribly uncomfortable. "It is an intimate touch that one lover gives to another."

"It is a touch that a husband gives to his wife."

Sadness marked her face. "But I'm not your wife, Christian. You have no wish to be saddled with me. You've made that plain enough."

Aye, he'd been cruel and unkind to the one person who deserved his utmost respect. For that he truly was sorry. But he didn't know what to do. There was no place in his life for a bride.

He didn't even know who he was. All he knew was that from the moment he had first met her, he'd been assailed by unfamiliar emotions and feelings. Half of which he could neither name nor identify. Part of him wanted to hold her, to kiss her, and the other wanted to run as far and as fast away from her as he could.

"Tell me what you want, Adara."

Her answer was automatic and emotionless. "I want my people to be—"

"Not your people," he said earnestly. "What do *you*, the lady, not the queen, want?"

Adara couldn't say the words. They were too painful because she knew she could never have what she wanted most. Christian had made it readily apparent that he wouldn't give her her wish. "I want peace for my people."

"Is that all?"

She stared at him, at the golden highlights in his hair and the curiosity in those crystal-blue eyes. She wanted him, her husband. She wanted him to be the man she had dreamed of.

But he wasn't.

That Christian would love her in her dreams. He danced with her and he laughed with her. He cuddled their children and held her close to his heart.

Saints and martyrs, how she ached for that man to be real. How she needed him to be real.

It was useless. Her dream Christian didn't exist.

The man before her was contemptuous of her. He wanted to leave and be done with her forever. And that made her want to cry again. How could she have been so stupid as to think for one minute that the real Christian could be anything like the man she had made him in her mind?

She wasn't a foolish woman, and yet she had sold herself on this ideal. She felt stupid and ashamed.

He moved to stand before her. "Answer me, Adara. What do you want?"

She lifted her head to give him a haughty glare, but before she could, he captured her lips with his.

Adara moaned at the taste of her warrior husband, at the feel of his hard body pressing against hers. She brushed her hands over the naked skin of his back that burned her palms.

His kiss was wonderful. Hot and maddening. Possessive. Christian filled her senses completely. His skin was like a velvet glove stretched tight over an iron hand. His hair, silky and smooth and cool to her touch. He tasted like wine and smelled divinely masculine.

This was better than any fantasy kiss she had ever shared with him in her daydreams.

Christian's emotions warred inside him as he tasted her sweet innocence, felt her touch. It had been far too long since he last took a woman. Far too long since he'd been this unsettled by anything.

For some reason he couldn't understand, he

wanted to taste this woman fully. The sight of her greeting him naked went through his mind as his body hardened even more.

Let her go!

But it wasn't that easy. He craved her on a level that he neither understood nor knew. She filled him with more than just simple desire or lust. She did something to him that he didn't comprehend.

It was as if she awakened a feral beast inside him that wanted nothing more than to possess her.

All he knew was that he was hopeless against this woman who had remained faithful to him all these years when he had barely remembered her. How had she remained so loyal?

It defied his imagination. Surely he wasn't worth her sacrifice. She should have divorced him and found another.

But she hadn't. He wanted to touch the belief in her that had allowed her to stand strong. Wanted to feel it. Most of all, he wanted to feel her.

Adara's breath caught as she felt Christian lifting the hem of her gown. His hand skimmed over the bare flesh of her hip. His palm was rough but gentle as he stroked her virgin skin. He deepened his kiss while his warm hand cupped her bottom and pressed her hips closer to his. She felt the swell of his manhood as he rubbed himself against her. A foreign ache started deep inside her body.

She couldn't think for the bittersweet pain. "Christian?" she breathed.

He answered her with another scorching kiss as he slid his hand down between their bodies until he touched the source of her need. She moaned deep in her throat as his long, lean fingers separated the tender folds of her body so that he could stroke her intimately.

Her head swam at the sensation of his touch. His fingers swirled and probed until he slid one deep inside her that made her entire being shiver. Adara moaned at the foreign feeling, wanting more of her husband.

Christian couldn't think straight as her wetness coated his fingers. The sweet, tender smell of her filled his head as she sank her hands deep into his hair and held him close.

She was his wife. His.

And he wanted to possess her. That thought consumed him as his body strained to take her. No reason could permeate him at this moment.

Nothing could stop him.

Adara saw the wild look in his eyes as he leaned her back against the table so that it supported some of her weight. His hand left her as he moved it toward the laces of his breeches.

Was he going to . . .

Her thoughts scattered as he freed himself from his breeches. He left her mouth to bury his lips against her neck an instant before he drove himself deep inside her body.

Adara hissed as pain overrode her pleasure. Christian was a large man who filled her to capacity and her body didn't seem to like that in the least. He held one of her legs against his hip as he pulled himself back, then thrust himself even deeper into her.

She was stunned by the burning sensation of his body stroking hers. This wasn't the blissful sharing that she had heard about in poems and songs. This hurt!

Biting her bottom lip to keep from crying out, she buried her head against his neck and held tight, hoping he would finish soon and be done with her.

Christian reveled in the tightness of her grip on him until he looked down to see her eyes tightly closed. He paused as he realized she wasn't enjoying this. She was actually cringing.

"Adara?"

"Is it over?" she asked in a brittle voice.

His desire faltered. He was far from sated, but the hopeful look on her face as she asked her question squelched his need as his body softened against his will.

The fear and pain in her eyes softened him even more.

Embarrassed and shamed, Christian pulled out of her. He let her dress fall back into place. "Aye. I am finished."

In more ways than one.

Completely humiliated, he pulled his breeches up and tied them closed as he silently berated himself.

What were you thinking?

In one moment of stupidity, he had consummated their marriage. And he hadn't even enjoyed it.

What had this woman done to him? Nothing had gone right in his life since the moment he had first laid eyes upon her. Nothing.

Well, if she didn't hate him before, she certainly hated him now.

Look to the bright side, she'll never want to take another man to her bed.

Feeling even worse now, he moved away from her. There was an awkward silence between them. In truth, Christian had no idea what to say to her. He'd never taken a virgin before. His lovers had always been experienced and well sated by his touch.

He'd never had such an encounter. Never. Not even his first time had been this horrifying.

"I'm sorry I hurt you, Adara," he said softly. "It was not my intent."

Afraid to look at her and see the pain he'd caused, he turned and left her alone and returned to Ioan's tent, where the physician was waiting.

Christian grabbed a flagon of ale before he sat in a chair to await the man's examination.

"Whatever you do," Christian growled, "make it hurt."

Disregarding the man's shocked look, he tipped back the flagon to drink from it.

He needed the pain to drive away his shame and guilt. Most of all, he wanted it to drive away the unsated lust that still tempted him to take his wife.

And if he was lucky, the physician might actually kill him.

Seven

The marriage was now consummated. Adara should feel elated and relieved. She didn't.

She felt horrible. Awful! For the first time since their marriage, she actually dreaded the idea of Christian remaining her husband. Saints preserve her, but how many more times would he want to do that with her? From all she had heard, men liked conjugal relations. A lot.

Not to mention she would have to have more sex with him to become pregnant. Oh, this was horrible! If only she'd known just how painful sex was, she wouldn't have pressed him for a consummation.

Why had no one told her? But then, why would they? If other women knew, no one would ever have sex again.

The entire world would die out, and truthfully

she would rather that happen than her husband take her again.

"Is something amiss, my queen?"

She turned at the sound of Lutian's voice. He was standing in the opening of the tent's entrance as he watched her.

Adara sat down again in her chair and sighed. "Did I make a mistake by coming here, Lutian? Honestly?"

He came forward to kneel beside her much like Christian had done. Taking her hand into his, he stared up at her with an inquisitive gaze. "What has that bastard done now?"

His angry tone on her behalf warmed her, but she couldn't allow him to go unchastised. It wasn't his place to insult Christian. More like she would do it herself.

"He's a prince and would-be king, Lutian. You shouldn't be so impertinent."

"And he's a bastard who hurts you."

She smiled at him while she squeezed his hand, grateful for his friendship. "I know not what to think of him. I truly don't." She shook her head. "I should have stayed home and fought Selwyn myself."

"We couldn't have, my queen. Our army is no match for the Elgederions. You know that. They would have destroyed us and you would have been imprisoned again or killed."

That was true enough.

"But that isn't what is truly bothering you, is it?"

She glanced away from him. There were times when Lutian was far too intuitive for his own good and he knew her far too well. There was never any hiding from him.

He lifted her hand to his lips and kissed her knuckles. His beard tickled her skin, but there was no heat from his touch. Not like Christian caused her.

"Tell me what has you so despondent, my queen."

She wished she could, but it was too horrible to contemplate. "It is too personal."

"Nay, there is no such thing where I am concerned, and well you know it."

It was true. She confided everything to him.

"I'm confused, Lutian. I always thought that when a husband . . ." She hesitated. She'd never spoken of such things before with anyone. Her nurse had merely explained the basics, then left the rest to her imaginings.

How could she broach such a topic with her friend? For that matter, she wasn't even sure if Lutian had experience in these matters. If he had been with a woman, he'd never mentioned it to her.

"When he what?" Lutian asked.

"When he . . . when people . . ."

He cocked a brow as he waited while she searched for the right words.

All she could remember was her old nurse and what she'd told her. "You know there are birds and bees and they have to pollinate . . . well, not really pollinate per se . . ."

He cocked his head as if he were starting to understand. "Has your prince consummated your marriage?"

She felt heat flood her face. She couldn't look him in the eye.

Lutian cursed. "Did he hurt you?"

Reluctantly, she nodded. "He apologized for it afterward, but aye, he did." She looked at him beseechingly. "Why did no one ever tell me it would be so painful? And I don't believe he even finished. It was marvelous in the beginning and then it turned awful. Horrible. I don't think I should ever want to do it again."

A tic worked in his jaw. "Methinks your noble prince is an incompetent man, my queen. I assure you, the experience can be most pleasurable for both the man and the woman when it is done properly."

Adara's chest was tight. "Think you he didn't care enough to make it pleasurable, then?"

"Nay. I think your husband is a great fool and wholly unworthy of you."

"What should I do, Lutian?"

"What should I do?"

Christian lay in the bed, staring up blankly at the tent's ceiling over him. He had a wife now. One who had carried a memory of him from her childhood. A woman who had guarded a throne for him that he didn't even want.

In all his life, he'd only had two things that belonged solely to him. His sword and his horse.

He'd never wanted anything more than that. But Adara was right, they provided a cold comfort to him at night.

Now he had a wife and a throne. People who looked to him for leadership. Whether he liked it or not, it was time he grew up and took his rightful place in the world. Time he stopped running from his past and his parents' memory.

"Slave to a throne . . ."

His worst fear. He would have no one to trust.

He would be like Adara.

Pain lacerated his heart at the thought. Lutian had been right. He knew his wife's isolation and yet she had borne it with grace and dignity. Unlike him, she wore the chains of her slavery without complaint.

God's blood, she must think him a childish cur, and in truth, at this moment, he thought it of himself.

Now it was time to be the man Adara had expected. He only hoped he didn't disappoint her again.

Adara spent the night in Corryn's tent, far away from her husband, who might wish to exercise his marital rights. Truly, it was the last thing she wanted.

So she and Corryn had spent an interesting

night getting to know each other. She'd been more than a little dismayed when the young woman had confided her gender to her.

She couldn't believe she'd been fooled so easily. But then, Corryn wasn't the most feminine of women. Still, she was kind and amusing, and Adara liked her a great deal.

They had arisen early and broken their fast, then set about packing up Corryn's tent while the men in the camp did the same.

"Don't lift that," Corryn said as she rushed to Adara's side to stop her from moving one of the arcs by her cot. "We'll make Ioan do it." She winked at her.

Adara laughed. "You enjoy abusing your brother, don't you?"

Corryn shrugged. "All women need a man to lovingly abuse, and I'm lucky to have a whole camp full of them. It keeps them on their toes."

She handed Adara a large leather-bound book. "If you would like something to do, Majesty, please carry this to Ioan in his tent. 'Tis a list of the men and their pay and he gets rather upset if I keep it too long."

Adara studied the thick ledger. "Why do you have it?"

"I was adding new names to it. We picked up three new archers while we were here. Ioan is in charge of his knights, while I oversee the rest."

That made sense to her. A bit apprehensive, Adara left Corryn's tent to cross the way to Ioan's.

She expected to see Christian or Ioan in the tent, but neither was there. Frowning, she went to the bed, where she found Christian's robe discarded.

Was he walking about naked?

Surely not. But what else did he have to wear? She'd never seen her husband in anything else. Could something have happened to him? Surely the Sesari hadn't found them.

Placing the ledger on Ioan's desk, she left the tent in search of him.

She found Phantom and Ioan, who were helping to load a wagon of weaponry. "Have you seen Christian?" she asked them.

"Last I saw he was in the tent with the physician," Phantom said.

"Is anything amiss?" Ioan asked after he loaded one large trunk.

"Nay. He wasn't in the bed. I was but curious." She looked around the men and noticed that Lutian had vanished as well. "Have you seen my fool?"

"I already said I know not where Christian is," Phantom said.

Adara gave him a droll stare.

"Oh," Phantom teased, "you meant Lutian. The *other* fool who does your bidding."

"Aye."

Ioan laughed at them. "I sent him off to aid in packing the spare tack, my lady."

"Thank you, Ioan."

Adara left them to find Lutian, but he wasn't

with the others who were packing the tack and none could tell her where he'd gone.

A bad feeling went through her. Surely Lutian hadn't challenged Christian. Had he? Her mind ran away with ideas of her friend doing something profoundly dangerous where Christian was concerned.

"Oh, please, Lutian, please don't get yourself killed."

"I'm going to kill you for this, Lutian," Christian snarled as he looked at himself in the polished steel mirror. His face was clean-shaven, his hair trimmed and styled by a hired razor. Good God, he'd even allowed the man to curl his hair, and for what?

He looked like a stranger.

"You asked me what she wanted, my lord, and that is what she dreams of."

Christian grimaced at his reflection as he stroked his smooth and oiled cheeks. He looked like a bloody woman. How could any female find this attractive?

Sighing, he got up and paid the man who had shaved him.

He felt like a complete and utter ass and he still wasn't sure why he was doing this to please a woman he'd only just met. A woman he had inadvertently made cry.

He'd bathed in scented water, had bought a new mail hauberk, gloves, and a horse. He'd even dragged out his court clothes, which he hadn't worn since Stryder's wedding.

"Have you memorized the poetry yet?" Lutian asked as they left the small shop.

"Of course I have." Sentimental slop that it was. The entire piece was an ode to a woman's beauty. "You are certain that this is what a prince does?"

"Aye. All women dream of a golden knight who plies them with gifts and words of beauty."

Christian reached up to brush his hand through his hair, only to have Lutian slap his hand away. He glowered at the fool.

"It has taken us hours to make you presentable, my prince. Don't undo it on a whim."

Christian tightened his grip on his sword as he fought an urge to pull it out and skewer the man. This had best please Adara or he would indeed skewer him.

A group of women watched him as they passed by, then burst into giggles as they stared at him with lust in their eyes.

Christian smiled devilishly.

Mayhap he didn't look so imbecilic after all. But he wouldn't bet his life or his soul upon it. He only hoped his wife appreciated his efforts. If not, her fool would be hanged by nightfall.

"Oh, saints preserve me. Who is that fine specimen of manhood? I know he's not one of ours. But with any luck, that might change."

Adara turned at the sound of Corryn's lust-filled words to see a knight riding down the pathway between the tents. She couldn't see his face, but the setting sun glinted off his form, making him appear to be golden fair, like an angel with a halo.

His stallion was white, with a black and gold drape that matched the surcoat of the knight. A golden rampant phoenix was embroidered on his chest and painted on the black shield that hung from his saddle. He carried a rippling black banner embroidered with the same symbol in his hand. He posed a fearsome sight.

Adara furrowed her brow as she continued to watch him. She knew those arms, but couldn't remember where she had seen them before.

"I'll be buggered," an older knight said from her right as he paused his own packing. "I haven't seen the arms of Michel de Chelrienne in years."

"Michel de Chelrienne?" Adara asked.

"Christian's father," Corryn answered as she cast a new look at the knight. "His father was the son of the duc there."

Adara felt her jaw go slack as she turned back to look more closely at the approaching knight. *That* was her husband?

Mercy, the man needed to discard his monk's robes more often.

She didn't fully believe it until he reined his horse before her and his blue eyes seared her with heat. She'd known her husband was a handsome man, but this . . .

This was unbelievable.

He buried his banner into the ground beside his

horse. His gaze never wavering from hers, he slung one long, well-muscled leg over his steed before he slid to the ground. She didn't move as he approached her. She couldn't. The sight of him had her completely riveted to this spot on the ground.

Adara wasn't sure what he had planned, but when he dropped to his knee before her, she was dumbfounded.

He struck himself on his left shoulder with his fist as a salute to her, then bowed his head. "My sword is ever at your disposal, my lady."

Laughter rang out from the men around her.

"As is mine," someone called out.

Christian ignored them as he looked up at her like something out of her dreams. The moment seemed surreal. Truly, it was a fantasy come to life.

"What has possessed you, Christian?" she asked.

"Your beauty. It has . . ." He paused as if searching for the words. "Your great beauty has possessed my soul and . . ."

More laughter and taunts rang out.

Her husband's eyes flashed angrily, but still he stayed there. "I would be your champion, Adara, and—"

"Simpering milksop," one of the knights finished for him.

Christian dropped his head and shook it. "This is not who or what I am," he muttered before he looked up at her again. "I'm sorry, Adara."

"For what?"

His answer came as he rose to his feet. With a determined stride, he went to the men who had been tormenting him. He struck the first man he reached so hard that he was knocked to the ground.

"Milksop with an iron fist," he snarled. "And you'd best remember that."

The knights attacked. Even wounded, Christian fought them off, then drew his sword to keep them back.

"Cease!" Ioan's Welsh accent cut through them all. He pushed his way through his men to see Christian in his finery. Ioan looked at him, blinked, then burst out laughing. "Abbot? Since when do you dress like a woman?"

His expression hard, Christian tossed his sword into the air, where it twirled around. He caught the hilt upside down in his fist and in one smooth motion sheathed it.

Christian paused beside Ioan and glared at him. "Be glad I carried you out of the Holy Land on my back. That fact, and that alone, is all that precludes me from hurting you. For both our sakes, don't try my patience and make me kill you after such a sacrifice."

Ioan's eyes twinkled in merriment. He leaned forward and sniffed. "My God, you even smell like one. What happened to you?"

Christian let out a tired breath and headed for the tent they had pitched for him.

Phantom tsked in her ear as soon as Christian

was out of his hearing range. "Only a woman can make a man sacrifice his dignity on the altar of humility. Tell me, Adara, did Christian just sacrifice his for naught?"

Nay, he didn't.

Adara did something she hadn't done since she was a child. She ran toward his tent, then drew up short as she saw Christian angrily unbuckling his sword and tossing it to the cot. The anger from him was tangible.

"Bloody damn fool," he growled under his breath. "I should have known better."

"Was that for my benefit?"

He turned sharply to face her and grimaced. "Well, I most certainly wasn't trying to turn Ioan's head in my direction, now, was I?"

She squelched her smile at his dour words. "I surely hope not. If you were, I would say it didn't turn out well."

Her words didn't seem to have the lightening effect on his mood that she had hoped. If anything he appeared even angrier. "I've been mocked enough this day, Adara. If you wish to laugh at me, then join the others outside of my hearing."

She approached him slowly. "I'm not mocking you, Christian. I think you look noble. Kingly." She reached up to cup his smooth cheek. "You even shaved."

Christian held his breath as she stood up on her tiptoes and placed a chaste kiss to his cheek. Her warm lips were softer than silk and they made his skin burn, especially as he recalled even softer areas of her body. Her breath caressed his flesh as she nuzzled her cheek to his. The tenderest of chills went through him.

"I think you smell wonderfully manly. I could inhale you all day."

He hardened at her words and fought the urge to crush her in his arms and make love to her again. "I'm not the man you dreamed of, Adara. I am coarse and used to doing for myself. I know nothing of royal manners or decorum or even how to dance. I have spent my entire life either confined in cells in the company of men or on the battlefield. I'm not the cultured knight my father was. In truth, I feel like some sort of pretender in his clothes. How can a man such as I ever be king, prince, or husband?"

Those words set her heart to pounding as she pulled away. "I can teach you anything you need to know about royal etiquette. 'Tis far simpler than swordplay or battle strategy."

Christian was captivated by her dark gaze, by the flecks of gold in her eyes as she stared up at him with an adoring gaze that somehow erased all the embarrassment he'd suffered outside. He laid his hand against her cheek so that he could feel more of her softness. "I thought you would hate me after I hurt you."

"I was confused by it, but then Lutian told me that when a man knows what he's doing—"

He cringed and cursed at her words. "You spoke to Lutian about it?"

"Was that wrong?"

"My humiliation knows no boundaries."

"You are overreacting, Christian. Lutian explained that it is oft times painful for a woman her first time, but that afterwards it is better."

Christian wanted to kill both her and Lutian over this. "You shouldn't be speaking to another man about such matters! 'Tis indecent."

That set off her temper. "Don't you dare call me indecent. I have done nothing wrong."

Aye, but she had. "You have unmanned me before your fool and I have unmanned myself before the rest. I should have known better." Cursing, he snatched his surcoat off and would have burned it if it hadn't belonged to his father. "I shall never dress like this again," he snarled under his breath.

"Why did you dress yourself like this?"

"Because, I . . ." Christian stopped himself before he told her the answer. It would serve no other purpose than to give her and Lutian more room to mock him.

"Because why?"

"Just leave me."

"Nay, not until you answer."

He turned to leave, only to find her blocking his way. "I will not allow you to flee until you answer me."

"I will give you no more reason to mock me."

"I don't want a reason to mock you, Christian. I want a reason to love you."

Christian went ramrod-stiff at that. His heart

leapt at her words, which both terrified and elated him. "You don't want love. You want a king. You said it yourself."

"Everyone wants love, Christian, especially those of us who have never had it. Have you ever loved anyone?"

He glanced away from her as he shook his head nay.

"I have," she whispered tenderly as she reached out to run her hand along his arm. "He was a little boy with a generous smile who laughed with my brother as they ran in play. Since that day I have dreamed of having a house full of golden-haired children who aren't afraid of me while I've been tormented with dreams of them one day trying to kill me in my sleep. I, too, am scared of marriage. I'm scared of being used. But I am willing to accept you, my lord. To trust that you won't kill me or imprison me."

Her words tore through him. She was laying herself bare to him and it made him ache. "It seems to me, Adara, that you and I are both haunted by the same image."

"And that is?"

"My parents' love."

"Aye," she whispered. "They were beautiful together. I never knew anyone could be so happy as they were together and with you. I always yearned for my father to look at me just once the way your father looked at you, with pride and love shining in his eyes. For my mother to brush her hand through my hair and kiss my cheek as your mother did you."

No one had ever loved him since. There had never been another tender touch or word of praise.

In truth he missed it more than he ever allowed himself to admit.

"Let me love you, Christian. Let me give you the comfort of home and wife."

"Why do you wish to give me that?"

"Because I know that you are capable of the same love that your parents shared. The little boy in my palace glowed from the fire of it and I know that it still exists somewhere inside you."

He met her gaze levelly and hoped he could make her understand the truth of him. "That boy died a long time ago, Adara. They locked him inside a cold, dismal hell that extinguished that light. He is barren now. The embers are long dead. There is nothing left to spark that flame. Nothing."

She gestured toward the cot where his surcoat lay. "Then why has that man forsaken his robes for his father's finery to please the bride he denies?"

"Because he is trying to atone for what he did to you." He locked gazes with her. "I don't want love, Adara. I don't. Ever. What I had with my parents was paradise and I loved the life we had together. It has haunted me every day of my life. I still remember when they left me at the monastery. They promised that they would only be gone until morning and they never returned. In the blink of an eye, everything I knew, everything

I had was stolen from me and I was cast out into a cold hell where there was nothing for me but pain."

He looked away as he let the agony of that moment wash through him anew. "I don't ever want to hurt that badly again. All I suffered at the hands of the monks, at the hands of my enemy was nothing compared to the way my heart shriveled and died with them. I will not allow anything to hurt me like that again. You yearn to have what you have never known, but take my word for it, you are far better off not knowing the beauty and then the horror. I refuse to lose something like that again. Do you understand?"

Adara's throat tightened in sympathetic agony for him. "You would deny yourself love because you're afraid of being hurt?"

"Nay. I deny myself nothing but more pain to be had. I am tired of hurting and of grieving. I only want peace from my past."

Adara placed her hand to his lips. "Let me inside you, Christian, and I will give you the peace you crave."

He shook his head before he stepped back, away from her touch, and donned his monk's robe. "I took your virginity and your choice. For that I am sorry. I will try and be a good king for you, but I will never allow you to love me, Adara. Nor will I ever love you."

And with that, he turned and left the tent.

Adara wanted to scream out in frustration. She

went to the opening and watched as he made his way through the men who had returned to work.

A few cast an amused look at him, which his grimace and growl effectively quelled.

Without looking back, he seized his banner and jerked it from the ground. And as he did so, a realization came to her. He had agreed to stay and be her husband, but not to love her.

Adara's mind raced with that. He had budged a little in their war.

Smiling, she watched as he headed for Ioan's tent. "I'm going to make you love me, Christian of Acre. Mark my words and heed them well."

She wasn't sure how. Not yet. But some day she was going to find the path to his heart and make it beat solely for her.

Eight

It was late when Adara went to find Phantom in his gray tent. As she entered, he had his back to her. He'd stripped to his waist and was washing his face.

She paused as she saw that his body was riddled with as many scars as Christian's, if not more. "Velizarii?"

For once he didn't castigate her for using his name. Grabbing the towel that was folded near the washbasin, he turned and wiped his face. "Aye, Adara?"

She was struck by his remarkable good looks. Like Christian, he was well muscled and lean. Where Christian's chest was bare, Velizarii's was lightly dusted with short black hairs. He was as dark as Christian was fair and no less handsome. But it was her husband she wanted.

"Tell me what happened to my husband in the Holy Land."

"I told you, Adara, you don't want to hear those stories."

"Please. I have to understand him if I'm to have a marriage with him and to help him heal those wounds that seem to be ever raw. Why is he so closed to me?"

Phantom sighed wearily as he headed toward a table where a flagon and goblets rested on a tray. He poured two goblets.

"Not so much," Adara said as he filled the bowls.

"Trust me, Adara, you will have need of it before I finish . . . as will I."

Handing her the full goblet, he indicated for her to take the chair across from his. Adara sat down immediately before he changed his mind.

Phantom sighed even more heavily as he sat down, then leaned back in his chair to look at her with a hooded expression. His long legs stretched out before him as he rested the goblet on his stomach. "Christian had already spent six months in the prison when I was taken there by the Saracens."

"How did you end up there?"

His eyes turned dull, haunted. "The same way any man ends up in hell. I was damned by my own deeds."

He took a deep draught of mead before he continued. "I wasn't expecting kindness of any sort from anyone. Having already spent a year in an

Elgederion prison, I was feral, waiting to have to fight my fellow inmates for peace and for survival. I was shoved into a dark hole and as I lay there bleeding, beaten, and in absolute agony, these two boys came to me."

By the look on his face, she could tell he was recalling that instant with crystal clarity. "One was dark, the other fair, and both looked as if they'd been ground up on a butcher's block." He twisted the goblet around in his hand. " 'Welcome to our Brotherhood,' the fair-haired boy said as he started to bandage my wounds. 'I am the Abbot and this is the Widowmaker. We will take care of you.' "

"The Widowmaker?"

"Stryder of Blackmoor. He was our leader in prison. It was he and Christian who came up with the idea of the Brotherhood of the Sword."

"How so?"

"Christian said his father used to tell him stories of men who were born in the time of barbarian invasions and conquests. They came from all over the world to fight together against injustice and barbarism. Their leader was a king named Arthur for the bear banner that he carried, and Arthur's motto was that might should never make right. Right should make right. The duty of knights and men is to fight for those who can't fight for themselves. And that is what our Brotherhood is built upon. Whenever one of us is weak, the others protect him."

Adara smiled at their oath and their courage. "It sounds wonderful."

He laughed bitterly. "There was nothing wonderful about being tortured and starved. We were prisoners of war and our guards made us pay for every Crusader who had come to Outremer to fight them."

Clenching his teeth, he let out a long, deep breath. "Christian's role was doubly hard. He was the closest thing to a priest that we had and the boys and men rallied to him for help and for salvation. He was only a child and yet he became their confessor. The dying called for him constantly and it was he alone who held their hands as they left this world and said Last Rites over them."

Adara's throat tightened as she imagined all he must have heard and seen.

"I never understood his strength. No matter the illness or injury, he would pray with them and comfort them with priestly words, even though I knew he'd long since lost the faith himself. Not that I blame him. How can you believe in God and His mercy when mere children are being killed for nothing more than sheer meanness? Our worlds had been destroyed, our lives no more than that of a petty insect. And when we were finally free of our hell, Christian spent the first three years traveling to the homes of the dead to pass on their final words and wishes to their families."

That was something she wouldn't have expected of him, and yet it seemed oddly fitting. "How kind of him."

"Not really. He was an idiot, in my opinion. You can't imagine the grave responsibility it is to tell someone that their loved one is gone and that they died horribly, aching for the comfort of home and family.

"I was with him one night when he told a Burgundian lady how her son had perished of illness. She cursed and slapped him for surviving while her precious son lay dead. She said many hurtful things to him and her venomous words echo in my ears even now. I can only imagine how they must echo in Christian's. For every person who thanked him for telling them, three more cursed him for it."

"Then why did he do it?"

Phantom drained his cup and poured more. "Because he never got to say good-bye to his parents. There was no one there to comfort him when they died. No one to tell him that their final thoughts were of him and his welfare, and he had promised the dying that if he survived, he would carry their words to their families no matter what."

Adara sat quietly as she thought about that. Few men would honor their words to the dead when it gained them nothing and cost them so much.

"Your husband is a lost man, Adara. It's easy to recognize the species when you're one yourself. After our escape from prison, with only a handful of exceptions everyone headed for home. Christian had no home or family to head to."

"He had you. Why didn't you tell him you were cousins?"

Bitterness glowed in his pale eyes. "Truthfully?"

"Aye."

When he answered she wasn't sure what chilled her more, his cold stare or his harsh words. "Because I was sent into that prison to kill him. I didn't think that knowledge would endear me to his good graces."

She was stunned by his confession. "What?"

Phantom leaned forward and spoke in a low, sinister tone. "You want my guilty secret, Adara? I traded my life for Christian's. After you and your father demanded a body and they couldn't find one, Selwyn learned that the Saracens he'd hired to destroy the monastery had taken a lone survivor into their prison. I was scheduled to be executed, so Selwyn offered me a bargain. He would send me into Christian's prison and if I killed Christian and survived, I could return home and my many crimes would be expunged."

"What crimes?"

He snorted at that. "Theft. Murder. General mayhem. They are too many to recount."

"Then why didn't you kill Christian and go home?"

He laughed. "I'm not stupid. Selwyn would never have suffered me to live. He would have killed me the instant I returned. As for Christian, I realized that he was what our people needed. A king who was compassionate. One who wouldn't turn his back on those who suffered, no matter how much it hurt him. I knew one day he would return and I pray only that I live long enough to see the look on Selwyn's face when his retribution comes calling."

Adara felt for the man. Who would have ever guessed that the little boy who used to play war with her and her brother would have come to this pass?

If she could, she would ease both him and Christian. They didn't deserve what life had given to them. She couldn't change what they'd been through, but she would make sure that both their futures were far kinder than their pasts.

"How do I reach my husband, Velizarii? Can I make him love me?"

He scoffed at that. "Love. Now, there's a word I despise with every part of me. Love is a disease that gets inside you and poisons the heart and mind. Do yourself a favor, Adara, stay away from Christian. Have his children, rule his lands, but never, ever allow yourself to care for him."

"I'm sorry that you feel that way, Velizarii, but I don't want to be alone anymore. I thought I could be queen without emotion. But I can't. I want Christian's heart and I won't rest until I have it."

"Then you are even more damned than I am, Adara, and for that I am truly sorry."

* * *

Christian sat alone on his cot as he listened to the men outside who were still packing their wares to leave in the morning. He grimaced while he held a cloth to the wound on his rib, which was bleeding again.

Leaning his head back against the post that was behind him, he closed his eyes. As his thoughts drifted, they focused on the face of his tormentor. Only this wasn't the tormentor from the past. It was the one from his present.

Adara. Queen, lady, temptress, dungeon mistress. Indeed, she might as well learn to use torture devices—they would hurt no less than the wiles she used on him.

"You're bleeding again?"

He opened his eyes to find said temptress in his tent, nearing his cot. He shrugged. "It'll stop or it'll kill me—either way is a winning proposition from my way of thinking."

"You're not amusing me, my lord." She brushed his hand aside to examine his wound. "It looks to be gaining an infection. You need a poultice to draw it out."

"How is it a queen knows so much about healing?"

She wiped the blood away with his cloth. Her touch was so gentle that it didn't even scrape the wound. "I have many interests and we have some of the finest Arab physicians at my court. I love to listen to them talk about their science. It fascinates me."

"And what is it they talk about?"

She left his bed to travel to the table where the leech had left his bandages and herbs. "Well, Omar says that the idea of the body's humors isn't right. He doesn't believe in bloodletting as a way of preserving the balance between them. He thinks the whole concept of the humors is incorrect and that the blood circulates through the body and touches all the major organs of it."

Christian welcomed the intellectual diversion that took his thoughts away from the pleasurable curve of her backside and on to something less disturbing. "Galen said nothing of blood circulation, nor did Plato."

She looked at him with a smile. "You've read Galen and Plato?"

"Aye, and Constantinus Africanus, Aelfric, Aristotle, and many others."

By her face, he could tell that thrilled her. She poured some of the herbs into the bowl on the table, then brought it forward. "You are amazingly well studied."

He scoffed at that. "I grew up in a monastery. There wasn't much else to do except transcribe and illustrate manuscripts. Brother Ambrose always said that the great works should be preserved for future generations."

She took the wine from his hand and poured some into her bowl so that she could make a thick paste. "So you can draw, then?"

He nodded as he took the cup back. "I was forever getting into trouble in those days. I would become so fascinated by what I was transcribing that I would forget to copy it and I would start reading instead. Monseigneur Foley would turn bright red in his face, which would make his fluffy white brows stand out like the devil's horns before he gestured at me to get back to work. Afterward, I would have to stand in the refectory while the other monks ate and I contemplated my lazy ways and prayed for forgiveness." He watched as she spread the cold, lumpy paste over his wound. It burned a bit, but he could feel it drawing the poison out of his body already.

"Did you learn your lesson?" she asked.

"Nay. I fear I was a poor pupil and I missed many a meal."

She arched a brow at him as she paused her hand. "Well, for a man who missed many a meal, I have to say that you have certainly filled out."

Christian stared at the tawny skin of her cheek. She held such an exotic look to her. Not pale like the European women he'd known in the past, she possessed a glow to her face. Before he could stop himself, he held his fingertip to her lips so that he could trace the contour of them.

"What else do you study?" he asked her.

"Laws," she said nonchalantly. "I'm particularly fond of the *Codex Theodosianus* and *Corpus Iuris Civilis*."

Christian snorted at the irony of that. Many of the Civil Laws had to do with marriage. "It is the duty of a curator to manage the affairs of his ward, but the ward can marry, or not, as she pleases."

Adara looked impressed. "You have committed the Code of Civil Law to memory?"

"Only certain parts of it, such as a son under paternal control cannot be forced to marry."

She applied more paste to his wound. "Where a son, having been compelled by his father, marries a woman whom he would not have married if he had been left to his own free will, the marriage will, nevertheless, legally be contracted; because it was not solemnized against the consent of the parties, and the son is held to have preferred to take this course."

Now it was his turn to be impressed, even though her argument basically said he had no choice by law except to accept their marriage. "You are remarkable."

"Not so remarkable. I merely like to argue a lot with my advisors, much to their chagrin."

"And with your husband."

Her eyes glowed like fire and enchanted him. "Aye. You are a worthy opponent."

"Am I?"

She nodded. " 'Tis not often I meet my match."

"Nor I." Christian rubbed the backs of his fingers over her cheek. No wonder his father was always caressing his mother's face. Truly, there was nothing softer than a woman's skin.

He dipped his head toward hers and saw the hesitation in her eyes. Not since his first encounter with a woman had he blundered so badly as he had with her. "I won't hurt you again, Adara. I promise."

Adara sank her hand into his silken hair as he took possession of her lips. She could feel the muscles of his jaw flexing as he ravished her mouth. It was all she could do to breathe as she inhaled the spicy, clean scent of him.

Surely no man could give a better kiss than Christian. He pulled away from her mouth to bury his lips against her throat, where his tongue toyed with the tender flesh. "Your wound, my lord. You will reopen it."

"Damn the wound," he growled.

He rolled over on the cot with her, pinning her beneath him. She trembled as he gently stroked her breast through her gown and fire spread through her veins.

Christian knew he shouldn't be doing this, but his pride wanted to show her that he did know how to please her. Not to mention his body craved hers with a passion that he had a hard time fighting.

Adara held her breath as Christian lifted the hem of her gown. She tried not to cringe in fear of the pain that was to come.

"Relax, Adara," he murmured against her throat.

She tried, but couldn't, especially not when he spread her thighs so that he would have access to her. She forced herself not to lock them together.

He is your husband. You have to do this!

It was a wife's duty. If she ever wanted a child, they would have to do this again.

She felt him pause. Opening one eye, she looked to see him watching her.

"You look like a condemned felon on the gibbet." He gently stroked her inner thigh.

"I am fine, my lord. Please, continue."

He didn't look as if he believed her. "I'll make you a promise. Trust me in this, and if I do anything that displeases you in any way, all you have to do is call my name and I will stop immediately and let you leave."

Would he really? "Promise?"

"Aye. I promise."

Adara took a deep breath and forced her body to relax. Christian shook his head at her. He bent her legs up and draped her gown so that she couldn't see what he was about.

"What are you doing?" she asked as he positioned himself at her feet.

His answer came as a tender nibble against her inner thigh. Hissing in pleasure, Adara jerked and started to put her legs down.

"Keep your legs where they are," he said gently, his hot breath scorching her skin.

Adara did, but it was difficult while his tongue traced circles over her thigh and hip. Every nerve ending in her body jumped and twitched.

Christian took his time with her so as not to scare her again. But it was hard. Just as he was.

He worked his way from her knee, up her thigh,

toward the part of her that he yearned for. He couldn't wait to taste her. When he left her after this, she would never again fear his touch.

Adara arched her back as she felt his fingers gently stroking the hair at the juncture of her thighs. Her body was on fire. And when he lowered his thumb to gently massage her, she cried out in pleasure.

"Why does this feel so good while the other hurts?" She hadn't realized she'd spoken aloud until Christian answered her.

"I'm a large man, Adara, and you weren't adequately prepared for me last time."

Adara licked her lips as he stroked her with both hands. It was all she could do to stay reasonably still as he worked magic on her. And then he did the unthinkable.

Her body jerked in ecstasy as his tongue took the place of his fingers against her.

"Christian," she moaned, pulling her gown down so that she could see him.

He pulled back from her, his eyes dark. "Did I hurt you?"

Unable to speak, she shook her head.

His gaze held hers as he returned to what he'd been doing. Adara's eyes widened as she watched him please her. Surely this wasn't proper, was it?

But he was her husband and she was supposed to surrender herself to his will.

Christian growled at the sweetest taste that was his wife. He could see the uncertainty in her gaze, and the passion and pleasure. He pulled back from her long enough to reassure her. "There is nothing shameful in what we do, Adara." He gave her another long, luscious lick.

He pushed her gown up farther until the whole of her lower body was bared to him. She was beautiful.

And he wanted to see more of her. He placed his body between her legs as he leaned over her and kissed her rounded stomach.

Adara cupped his head to her as he gently lapped at her navel. He flicked his tongue over her flesh, making her quiver as she felt herself growing moist.

Then he rolled her to her side so that he could unlace the back of her gown. The heat of his hands was searing, but it was no match for his lips as he kissed her bared skin and set her up on her knees.

Suddenly he pulled her gown free. Embarrassed, she tried to cover herself with her hands as he moved to kneel before her on the cot.

"What is this?" he asked incredulously. "Is this the same brazen queen who bared herself to me the first time we met?"

"I wasn't fully sober then," she confided.

He pulled her hand away, then took her breast into his mouth. Her head spun at the sensation of his tongue and lips teasing her.

This was the most incredible moment of her life and it was her husband who gave it to her. Her stomach jerked with every lick he gave. He dipped his hand down to stroke her again until he buried his finger deep inside her. His body moved gently against hers while his fingers toyed with her body.

His touch consumed her as her body began to move of its own accord to seek out more of his touch.

And just when she was sure she would die from it, her body tore itself asunder. Her cry caught in her throat as Christian straightened up to watch her. Still his hand pleasured her while her body spasmed in absolute bliss.

Christian waited until he had wrung the last tremor from her before he pulled his hand away. "That is the pleasure to be had in a man's touch, Adara."

It was truly glorious. Even now her body felt sensitive, as if the slightest touch could send her over the edge again. "What of your pleasure?"

He moved away from her to remove his hose. Adara swallowed at the sight of him. He was a large man. No wonder he had hurt her so much before.

"Don't be afraid of me, Adara," he said as he lay down beside her.

Christian watched her as she looked at the size of him. He took her hand into his and kissed her palm before he led her hand to his swollen shaft.

Adara frowned at the foreign feel of him in her palm. "It's soft."

He laughed at that. "Not really. It gets much softer and smaller when you're not around."

"Really?"

He nodded. "However, when you are around, it tends to stay like this to the point that it causes me pain. Constantly."

"This hurts you?"

"If it goes too long unsated, aye."

Cocking her head, she studied him. His body was so different from hers. The hair between his legs was a dark brownish blond that nestled his rigid shaft. She traced the length of him until she reached the soft sac. She hesitated until he covered her hand with his and showed her how to cup and stroke him.

He gave a pleasurable hiss as he lifted his hips. Wanting to please him more, she carefully stroked him. "You're getting harder," she said in wonderment.

"I know."

"I can see why this hurt me. You are far too large for my body."

"Nay, love, I'm not." He rose up from the bed and took her into his arms.

Adara frowned as he moved behind her. "What are you doing?"

"I'm going to take you like a stallion takes his mare," he whispered raggedly in her ear.

Adara started to protest until he bent his head and buried his hot lips against her neck. She sank her hand in his hair as he nipped and teased the sensitive flesh below her ear. He cupped her breasts in both of his hands as he gently stroked and coaxed their tips into hard nubs.

The familiar fire started inside her. It roared to life as he dipped one hand down and returned to stroking her again.

He nudged her knees farther apart. She started to protest until he plunged himself deep inside her. Shocked by the pleasant fullness of him, she shuddered.

He nipped her shoulder, then pressed his cheek to the spot he'd kissed so that he could watch her. "Am I hurting you?"

"Nay."

His smile warmed her before he straightened and began to thrust himself against her while his hand stroked her in time to his movements.

Christian wanted to howl in pleasure. She felt wonderful. Her sleek heat welcomed him as he slammed himself even deeper inside her.

Even though she was a novice, she was the best lover he'd ever taken to his bed. He couldn't remember a time in his life when it had been this important that he please his lover. But with her, he wanted to give her satisfaction over and over again.

Christian ground his teeth as ecstasy assailed him. He thrust faster as she ground herself against him, heightening his pleasure.

Adara moved in time to him, wanting to feel

him even deeper inside her. This was an incredible moment of sharing. She felt connected to him in a way she'd never felt connected to anyone. No wonder they called this intimate relations.

She arched her back and cried out as she came again. Christian quickened his strokes and listened to her cry as it crescendoed. He took pride in her pleasure until his own body found its release.

He buried himself deep and let his release sweep him away from this tent into heaven.

Adara collapsed against him. She wrapped an arm around his neck, then tilted her head back until she captured his lips. In that instant, he swore something inside him shattered and released some forbidden tenderness that he hadn't even known he possessed.

It was something he'd never felt before.

"That was incredible." She practically purred the words at him.

It was indeed. He smiled at her before he pulled himself out of her body. She looked down at him and frowned. "It is smaller."

"Aye."

She reached down to touch him. Christian shuddered again as she gently squeezed him in the palm of her hand.

"Did I hurt you?" she asked.

"Nay, but if you keep doing that, I'll grow hard again and want another taste of you."

"Is that wrong?"

Nay, that would be paradise.

And that thought terrified him.

She gasped in alarm as she saw his side. "You're bleeding again."

Christian looked down to see his wound re-opened. "But it was well worth it."

Adara rolled her eyes at his teasing tone. "Lie down," she said, pushing him toward the cot before she got up to get a new bandage and her poultice.

Christian remained quiet while she tended him. In truth, he enjoyed the sight of her concern for him. Especially given the fact that she was naked as she cleaned and bandaged his injury.

"You have bewitched me," he said after she had finished.

"Is that so bad?"

Christian didn't answer. Truthfully, he didn't know.

As she reached for her gown, he stopped her. "We've come this far, Adara, you might as well stay with me. Come to my bed, wife, and lie with me this night."

Adara held the gown to her in indecision, but the contented look on his face succeeded in winning her to his cause. She dropped it and returned to his cot.

Christian scooted over to make room. As soon as she lay down, he wrapped his body around hers.

Adara inhaled the musky scent of him as he lay her head on his biceps and held her close.

Christian closed his eyes and breathed the

sweet scent of her hair as he rubbed his cheek against the softness of it. For the first time in his life, he felt peaceful. Whole.

He draped his arm over her and took her hand into his. Kissing her cheek, he savored her skin. "Good night, my lady."

"Good night, Christian."

He settled himself down behind her and let her softness lull him to sleep.

Adara lay there letting the strength of Christian seep into her. It was strange to have carnal knowledge of him after all this time wondering what it would be like, trying to imagine the feel of him.

Now she knew.

And he hadn't sent her away afterward. For a man determined to keep himself cold toward her, this boded well. Mayhap there was some hope for them. It was certainly worth a try.

Smiling at the thought, she stroked his strong hand that bore the mark of his Brotherhood and hoped that in the end everything would work out. She wanted the life she had glimpsed all those years ago. One of love and kindness. Mutual respect.

But they both had enemies who would see them dead and a war to be fought that could easily take her husband away from her.

For the first time, she understood why Christian's parents had run away from Elgedera, and she couldn't blame them at all. It was tempting to think of having a life where she lived for no one but her husband. Where nothing existed except the two of them.

But unlike his mother, she wasn't the younger daughter. She was queen.

He would be king.

And both of their first priorities would always be their people. Yet as she lay here, feeling his body pressed to hers, it was hard to think of royal responsibility.

Love me, Christian, she begged silently. Just once she wanted to hear someone say those words to her.

She only hoped her husband was wrong and that he was as capable of such emotion as she thought him to be.

Nine

Christian sat in his wooden chair, staring at Adara, who still slept in his bed with his blanket entwined around her lush, full curves. He was already hard and aching for her. Just the mere thought of her soft limbs around him was enough to fan his desire to a dangerous level.

"My lord?"

He held his hand up to silence Samson and motioned him out of the tent. Getting up, he moved so that the knight couldn't see his wife in her peaceful slumber.

Christian closed the flap behind him. "Aye?"

Samson handed him the large parcel in his arms. "This came from a merchant who said you wanted it at first light."

Christian nodded as he took it from him. He looked around at the small handful of tents that were left standing. Most of the camp had already been dismantled.

"Also, Lord Ioan wanted you to know that we will be ready to ride within the hour."

"My thanks, Samson."

He inclined his head, then walked off.

Christian's stomach clenched as he turned with the package to go back inside. Yesterday his path had seemed clear. Today, not so much. But he had started down this way and there was no way to undo it.

Strange, how he could face a full-grown man in armor in a fight to the death and not flinch, but one buxom, unarmed woman terrified him beyond all reason.

Uncertain, he returned to his wife and knelt beside her. "Adara?"

She stretched like a kitten and made a low murmur that set fire to his blood. But it was the smile on her face when she woke up and saw him that was his complete undoing.

No one had ever given him such a pleased, adoring look. "Good morning," she said as she reached to brush his hair from his face. "Did you sleep well?"

Aye, better than he'd ever slept before. He'd awakened to the scent of his wife on his body, to the feel of her wrapped in his arms, and had been unable to find a single fault with the world.

"Did you know you talk in your sleep?"

She pulled back. "What do I say?"

He smiled as he remembered her whispered words. "I know not, it is truly unintelligible."

"Did it disturb you?"

"Nay," he answered honestly. It had actually charmed him. "I hate that I have to wake you, but we've a long journey ahead and need to break the tent."

"I shall be but a moment."

Adara watched as Christian got up to leave. He hesitated in the center of the tent with a package in his hands.

"Is something amiss, my lord?"

"I . . ." He looked as if some matter had him torn. After a pause, he returned to her cot and set the package beside her. "I shall see you outside."

Adara frowned as he all but ran away from her. Why?

"I don't bite," she said, then smiled as she remembered biting him a time or two the night before.

Her entire body grew warm again as she remembered the way he'd held her. The way he'd felt inside her. Thrilled with the memory, she untied the parcel, then froze as she saw what it contained.

It was a gown of the softest red silk that was trimmed in sable. Elaborate gold trim decorated the hem and sleeves. There was also a silk bliaut to wear beneath it and a golden mantle.

Truly, 'twas a gown fit for royalty.

Adara got up and washed, then dressed. She wished herself home, where she had a full-length looking glass, so that she could see the beauty of the gown that shimmered in the dim light of the tent. She quickly combed and braided her hair, then wove it around her head.

As she finished, she heard someone ask for admittance from outside the tent. Adara pulled back the flap to find a short bald man who carried a square leather box in his hands.

"May I help you?"

"I am looking for a lady named Adara. Are you she?"

"Aye."

He looked relieved as he handed her the box. "This is for you, my lady. I hope you like it."

Adara opened the box and felt her jaw fall open at what it contained. 'Twas a golden crown encrusted with diamonds and rubies, as well as a necklace and two brooches to match.

"Where did this come from?"

"My lord, the master jeweler of York. He is truly the finest in all of England."

"But who commissioned it?"

"It was a collection my master prepared for the faire this coming fortnight that he'd hoped to sell. A monk came in yester afternoon, saw it, and purchased it immediately. He bade my master to have it delivered to you this morn."

She couldn't believe Christian had gone to such expense for her. "Thank you. Tell your master that I adore his work. 'Tis truly the finest I have ever beheld on any continent."

He beamed delightedly. "I shall tell him, my lady."

Adara blinked back her tears as the man left her and she returned inside the tent. Her hand shook as she removed the crown, then placed it on her head. The good jeweler had even included pearl-tipped pins to hold it in place.

She'd never expected her husband to do something so thoughtful.

She used the brooches to fasten her golden yellow mantle into place, then put her necklace on. Even though she had finer gowns at home, none of them had ever been more beautiful to her than this one.

As she turned to leave, a thought struck her. Christian's mother had been dressed in scarlet and gold when she and Christian had married. Had he done this apurpose?

But then, she knew he didn't remember their wedding. Not the way she did.

Wanting to thank him for his gifts, she left the tent to find her husband. He was in the middle of the camp, with knights all around him.

She paused as she saw him there. He was again garbed as a black-robed monk, but he had taken time to shave this morning. There was no sign of the sword she knew he had strapped to his hips and she could barely catch a glimpse of his mail-covered leggings beneath it.

He was handsome, her prince. More so than

any man in the group. He, Phantom, Ioan, Lutian, and three men she knew not at all were standing in a circle as they discussed some matter.

Her heart light, she approached her husband from behind.

Ioan was speaking. "You know, Abbot, I hear wormwood helps with that problem." He held his hand up and crooked his finger down as if it were suddenly limp.

All the men save Christian laughed, while Christian glared murderously at Lutian.

"Look to the good of it," Phantom said as he sobered. He appeared to be imparting grave advice to her husband. "I hear all men have trouble from time to time with their sexual performance. Mind you, *I* have no personal experience with that, but . . ." His voice trailed off as he looked past Christian to see Adara glowering at him.

Struggling not to strangle the men who mocked him, Christian turned to see what had disturbed Phantom to find Adara standing behind him.

His groin jerked awake at the vision she made in her finery.

She was beautiful. The gown fit even better than he had hoped. Unlike her peasant garb, this one laced in the front and at the sides, pulling the cloth into a perfect fit that showed every lush curve of her body.

The only thing that sparkled more than her jewels were her brown eyes.

"Thank you," she said softly before she kissed his cheek. "I had a most wondrous night."

Christian was too dumbstruck by his lust to even respond.

Lutian bristled at her actions and if she didn't know better, she'd swear he was jealous. "Nay. Tell me this isn't so. Why are you kissing him, my queen? It was me. *Me.* I'm the one who told him what to do. He had no idea how to please you. None. He was lost and confused when he sought me out. He didn't even know how to do the most basic thing. It was me, all me."

Every man there gaped at Lutian's words.

"Christ's toes, Christian," Ioan said in disbelief. "Are you a monk in truth? Don't tell me you had to take advice from the fool on how to please a woman? You should have come to me. At least I know what I'm doing."

"You can't be a virgin," Phantom said. "What about that Norman tart in Hexham? Surely you did more than talk to her when the two of you vanished to her room?"

"Nay," another knight said. "I saw him drunk in Calais with two women."

"Aye," another knight began. "I was with him in London when he vanished for three days with a widowed countess."

Christian ground his teeth as this conversation quickly degenerated, while Lutian continued to take credit for instructing him on how to please Adara.

Lutian still held Adara's attention. "I'm the one who got him—"

Enraged, Christian lunged for the source of his current humiliation.

"Christian!" Adara snapped as he seized her fool. "Don't hurt Lutian."

He wanted to do much more than hurt the fool. He wanted to tear the man's head from his shoulders. Growling in frustration, he let the fool go.

"Thank you, my queen."

"'Tis my place to hurt him." She glared at her fool and smacked him on his arm. "I fully intend to take this up with you later."

She walked over to Ioan. "And for your information, my lord . . ." She lifted his hand and put his index and middle finger upright. "I assure you that there is nothing wrong with Christian's technique or prowess."

Corryn, who had paused beside the group after Christian had lunged at Lutian, broke into laughter.

Ioan hissed at her. "What are you laughing at?"

"I was just thinking of why we can't go to Scotland anymore. Someone should tell Christian about your *little* problem." She held up her pinkie and wiggled it, then burst into laugher.

"You're not supposed to know anything about these matters!"

Corryn rushed off before her brother could grab her.

He yelled out something in Welsh, then glowered at all of them. "We needs be going. Break your fast, my lady, while we pack your tent."

"And I wasn't a virgin when I took her," Christian called after him. "I've had more than my fair share of women."

Adara propped her hands on her hips and gave him a miffed look.

Christian started sputtering. "I mean, I was—"

"Surrender before you sink in even deeper," Phantom said, clapping him on the back. "You should have held your silence." He inclined his head to her. "Later, my lady."

The group broke apart to leave her alone with her husband, who was still squirming a bit.

"I am sorry they teased you," she said quietly.

"Don't be. I'm rather used to it, though not quite on that subject matter, I have to say. Up until you—"

"You had best stop referring to these other women, husband, else I might seek retribution on you after all."

"I'm sorry, Adara."

"It's all right, I am teasing as well. For the most part." She took his hand into hers and squeezed it tight. "But I do thank you for the gifts. They were most welcomed and unexpected."

He looked at her sheepishly. "But there is one missing."

"There is?"

Adara frowned as he pulled up the hem of his robe to reach his purse.

"There's one last thing that you should have."

He took her left hand into his and slid a large ruby ring onto her third finger. Adara's throat tightened at the sight of it there.

A wedding ring. A real one.

Without thinking, she walked into his arms and kissed his lips. He seized her fiercely and crushed her to his chest as he gave her a hot, exhilarating kiss.

"Should we leave your tent intact for a bit longer, since you seem to have found your missing manhood?" Ioan asked as he passed by them.

Christian pulled back to glare at his friend. "My patience runs thin, *Lladdwr*."

"As long as the steel to your sword is as thin, I have nothing to fear, eh?"

Christian gave her a disgusted look that made her laugh.

"You certainly know how to pick your friends, my lord."

As Christian led her toward the wagon where they'd packed up their foodstuffs, she saw a great commotion as an earl rode into camp with three knights behind him.

"Ioan ap-Rhys?" he called angrily.

Ioan sauntered out from his men to address the nobleman. Corryn came up behind her brother to see the man, too.

"What have you with me, my lord?"

"My steward told me that you were packing your camp to leave. What do you think you're doing?"

Ioan looked around his men. "Leaving."

The earl glowered at him. "You cannot leave. I forbid it."

Ioan gave him a devilish grin. "Well, see, therein is your problem. We are all freemen here. Not a serf amongst us. We come and we go as we please."

"I have paid you good money!"

"Corryn!"

His sister moved to his side. "Aye, *brawd?*"

"Have you the earl's purse?"

She handed it to Ioan, who in turn handed it to the earl. "I prorated our services, but the refund is all there for the rest of this month."

The earl's face turned bright red. "I need this army. You cannot do this!"

Ioan shrugged. "I can do anything I please, my lord. I lead more men than you."

Cursing them all, the earl snatched the money from him, then led his knights away.

"Why did he need your army?" Adara asked Ioan after they left. "We are not putting his people into danger by taking you from him, are we?"

Ioan shook his head. "Rest assured, Majesty, the earl didn't need my army. He had a minor skirmish with a serf rebellion that was quelled before we even arrived. My men were here for no other purpose than to intimidate his peasants and townsfolk."

"We've long grown weary of being here," Corryn said. "The knights are fat and lazy."

"Careful, little Spider," Ioan warned. "They think you're a man and might attack at such an insult."

Corryn gave Adara a droll stare. As soon as Ioan left them, she came forward. "No man here believes for an instant that I am male. But none dare to contradict him for fear of his sword, nor will they come near me. You would think I carry the plague."

Adara laughed. "Be grateful you have such a brother, Corryn. He loves you."

"I know. It is what keeps me from poisoning his mead at night."

Christian listened to them talk for a few moments as he dwelled on what Adara had said. According to Lutian, her brother had betrayed her. Though how he could have, Christian would never understand.

He went to get her some bread, cheese, and wine to break her fast, while they spoke about Ioan's death at his sister's irate hands.

Christian handed the bread to her after Corryn left them. "Do you miss your brother?" he asked quietly.

She paused for an instant as if his question startled her. He held her wine while she tore a piece of bread. "In truth, I do my best not to think of him at all."

Christian watched the way she daintily ate her food. Like a queen. She was flawless in her manners and bearing.

"I'm sorry."

She swallowed her bread and offered him a sad smile. "There is much in life that I wish were different."

"Am I included in that?"

She looked up at him as if she were studying him. "At times, aye. But this isn't one of them. I find you oddly endearing."

He frowned at her words. "Oddly endearing? I think I have been insulted."

She tore a small bite of bread and offered it to him.

His eyes never leaving hers, he leaned forward to feed from her hand. He took her fingers into his mouth and gently nibbled them before he pulled away.

He swallowed the bread. "Are you seeking to tame me, Adara?"

"Nay, my prince. I seek only to claim you. I don't mind your wildness in the least."

He was struck dumb by her playfulness as she stepped past him to join Corryn, who was ordering a group of men about.

Christian took a deep draught of the wine she'd neglected.

"You'd be better off to pour that down your breeches," Phantom said as he joined him.

"What say you?"

"The look of you says it all. You're aching to taste her again."

Outwardly, Christian scoffed even though he knew that attitude for the lie it was. "You are mistaken."

Phantom paused beside him. "Nay, Christian. Lie to yourself if you must, but never to me."

Christian frowned at him. "Why are you still here? It's not like you to travel with a group."

"You offered me land."

"Which I know means nothing to you. Not really. Why have you always been at my back all these years?"

"I respect you, Christian. You should be king, and if you are determined to seek your throne, then I am determined to help you."

Christian couldn't have been more stunned by his words. "What has gotten into you?"

"I wish I knew. Promise me that should I discover what it is, you'll exorcize it."

Christian laughed. "I wish the same promise from you."

Phantom looked back at Adara, who was busy castigating her fool. "I know what plagues you, my brother, but from that I hear there is no cure."

Christian sobered as he feared Phantom might be right. His wife was slowly seeping into his very soul.

He heard Ioan giving the call to mount. It'd been a long time since he'd traveled with an army. God be with all of them. They would have a long, hard journey ahead of them and then a battle.

He only hoped they all made it.

* * *

Adara spoke little as they traveled. Her gaze kept drifting over the knights and archers of this army.

"Is something wrong, Majesty?" Ioan asked.

"I was just thinking that even with the addition of my army at home, our numbers are too few to go up against Elgedera and win. Perhaps we sought you out too soon."

Christian laughed at that. "There will be more soldiers to come."

"Aye," she said, remembering the man he had mentioned, "but this Lucifer will have how many men? A few dozen?"

"About that," Ioan said. "He had just under three score when last I saw him."

Her stomach drew tight in apprehension. " 'Tis not enough."

Phantom gave her a wicked grin. "I cannot believe I'm about to say this. But have faith, my lady. The Lord will provide for us."

Adara had no idea what he meant by that until they reached Calais, where they stopped to rest and restock. The men had decided that the easiest way to move the army would be overland, which would be more grueling than traveling by sea, but would allow them to stay together in force for morale and safety.

It would take them approximately five months from Calais to reach Taagaria, which was two months longer than it had taken her by sea to find Christian. It was something that concerned her greatly. 'Twas a long time for Thera to be on the throne without her.

Ioan had claimed his men could cover the distance in half that time, which set off an argument between him and Christian over the greatness of Ioan's army versus their being too tired to fight once they got there.

"If we crawl down there like snails, the Elgederions will have too much time to prepare for our force," Ioan had growled as they supped the first night after they left York. "I'm sure by now the little garrison that they sent to kill you has headed back home to tell them that we're coming."

"They won't be prepared for us," Phantom had said with a sinister laugh. "Trust me."

Christian had shaken his head. "I've no wish to stress the men or the horses. A strenuous pace would cost us much in illness and injuries. What good does it to reach Elgedera with only a portion of our force?"

Ultimately, Corryn had come up with a compromise that left them traveling faster than Christian wanted, slower than Ioan could tolerate, while both men cursed the pace completely, every step of the way. However, Ioan had sworn that if any of the men or horses became injured or unduly stressed, he would slow his army to Christian's pace.

Of course, Ioan had cheated a bit and pushed the army hard to reach Calais in just over a fortnight.

Now they were trying to find a place to stay

without pitching tents, but it looked as if Calais were under siege. Everywhere they went, there were soldiers already there.

"What is going on?" Adara asked as the third inn they tried turned them away.

"Abbot!"

A handsome man near the age of thirty and with long dark brown hair came toward them. He was dressed in a blue and yellow surcoat that covered his black mail armor.

"Dragon," Christian said, offering his arm to the man. "What are you doing here?"

"Thomas sent word that you were in trouble. Some bastard has taken your throne, eh? So here I am with my men at your disposal." He turned toward Adara and took her hands into his. He kissed the back of each one as if it were a holy relic. "And you, lovely lady, must be Christian's bride. Thomas said you were as beautiful as Helen and I can see he did not lie in the least."

"Thank you, Dragon." Adara was both flattered and aghast at the man's presence. "This is your army here?"

"Along with a few friends."

"Who?" Christian asked.

"Falcon, Goose, Wyvern, and Sphinx have come. Together we have seven hundred and thirty-two knights for you."

Adara was stunned at the number. "How could you gather so many so quickly?"

Dragon looked less than impressed by their

numbers. "Not so many now. Had we had more time . . . But more will join us en route as they're able."

Christian offered Dragon his arm. "My gratitude is eternal to you, Michel. Thank you."

Dragon took his arm, then hugged him quickly. "We are brothers, Christian. No one threatens a single member without incurring the wrath of us all. You know that."

"There's no room here, either," Phantom said as he left a nearby inn. He paused as he caught sight of Dragon standing before them.

Dragon's eyes narrowed on him in instant hatred. "Phantom. Stab anyone in the back lately?"

The look on Phantom's face was one of pure evil. "Never, Dragon. I only stab from the front so that I can see the expression on my victim's face while he dies. Care for me to demonstrate?"

The hostility between them was tangible. "Come, Christian," Dragon said. "I have saved room in my inn for you."

"I appreciate it, Dragon. But I owe Phantom much and would rather he have the room than I."

Dragon curled his lip. "Fine, I'll allow him to join us as well."

Phantom smirked at the knight who hated him. "Hurts so well to do the right thing, doesn't it, Dragon?"

Adara had to suppress a smile at Phantom's teasing, when it was obvious Dragon truly wanted to trounce the man.

Without further comment, Dragon led them to an inn on the outskirts of the city.

He left them alone to freshen up while he went to find Ioan and tell him that there was space for him as well.

"Why does the Dragon hate Phantom so?" she asked as she washed her face while Christian placed a small trunk of personal items beside their bed.

"Basically everyone hates Phantom, Adara. He was never one to go out of his way to make a friend."

"Yet you befriended him. Why?"

He shrugged. "No one deserves to be alone. He needed a friend, he just didn't know it."

Adara smiled at him. "You're a good man, Christian, and I think that one day you will be extremely grateful that you treated him well."

"What do you mean? Do you know something about him that I should?"

"Aye, I do, but I promised him I wouldn't tell you. It's something that needs to come from him whenever he's ready."

He nodded. "Then I will respect you both and not ask after it."

Adara went to him and placed her cheek against his just so that she could inhale the precious scent that was her Christian. She kissed him lightly, then withdrew even though she didn't want to. Something inside her wanted to hold on to him and keep him near. But he often grew rigid if she stood too close to him for too long.

"Now sit, my lord, and let me look at your wounds."

Christian hesitated. If he possessed a brain, he would tell her nay and send for a leech.

But he didn't. Instead, he stripped to his waist, then sat down so that Adara could examine his injuries.

He closed his eyes as she trailed her hand down his back, touching his skin as she carefully inspected, then cleaned his few remaining stitches.

Adara felt that familiar heat start in her blood as she took in the whole of his muscled back. There was one little area at the base of his spine that she felt a peculiar urge to taste.

"You are healing very well. I think I should be able to remove the last of your stitches tomorrow night."

She moved around him to look at his shoulder and side, but it was the swelling between his legs that captured her attention. He hadn't touched her since they'd left York.

And it wasn't from lack of trying on her part. But the man had an iron will that should be legendary. Even Lutian was stunned by his wherewithal.

Adara leaned toward him.

He shot to his feet and whipped his robe back on. "I should check on the others."

He was out of the room so fast that she barely saw him leave.

"Fine, my Lord Difficult. You can run, but not fast enough." Nay, she had plans for him yet, and little did he know it, but he was doomed.

Ten

Adara sat alone at a table eating her supper of lamb and cabbage while Christian and the others were off planning battle strategies . . . and still arguing over their pace of travel.

One would think that at the very least they would become bored with the topic and find something new to argue over.

"Has the Second Coming come and I missed it? If so, I need to find a priest quickly."

Adara looked up from her food to find Corryn watching her from a short distance away. As always, Corryn was dressed as a bony man in a white tunic and brown leather breeches. "Nay. Why do you ask?"

Corryn shrugged as she drew near to take a seat across the table from her. "You look as if it came and passed you by." She pulled a piece of bread from the loaf on a wooden trencher near Adara's elbow. "So what has happened to cause you to look so miserable?"

Sighing, Adara set down her knife. "I was merely trying to understand why it is that my husband runs from me as if I'm a leper."

Corryn swallowed the bread she was chewing and gave her an arch stare. "Are you?"

"Nothing's fallen from me yet."

Corryn laughed as she reached to share Adara's wine cup. "Men are ever woman's bane. 'Tis a pity they look so delectable in armor, otherwise I would say good riddance and be gladly done with them."

Her outspokenness was startling to Adara, who would never speak of such things . . . Of course, she might think it, but she would *never* say such. Then again, Corryn spent a great deal of time in male company.

"Does Ioan know you think in this manner?"

"Ioan?" Corryn asked with a laugh. "He still thinks I'm ten-and-three in age. Would you believe he told the men that the reason they can't ever let me see them naked is that I was once a prisoner in the Holy Land and that the Saracens . . ." She paused as if trying to think of a way to phrase her thoughts. "Well, please don't be offended, but that my male member was cut off for spite and that if I saw any of theirs, it would either devastate me or cause me to go insane and kill them while they sleep. More like, Ioan would kill them while they slept, but he would blame me for it nonetheless."

"Are you serious?"

"Aye. The man is most mad. He claims 'tis also the reason my voice is so high and unchanged." She rolled her eyes as if even the merest thought of Ioan were too much to bear. "But let us return to your problem with Christian. I think you should tie him down until he learns not to flee from you anymore. From what I hear of our men, a lot of them like that."

Adara burst out laughing. "I sincerely doubt it."

"Nay," Corryn said sincerely. "I'm telling you, they have many fantasies about it. You'd be amazed at what I overhear."

Then again, she would not. Adara knew from her own guards, who sometimes became talkative outside her chamber doors, how bawdy most men became when they didn't realize a woman could hear them.

But the thought of a man wanting a woman to tie him down . . .

Ludicrous.

"Well, I can't imagine Christian being such a man. I think he fears ties of any kind."

"Well, then, I know of something else that will have him eating from your hand."

"And that is?"

Corryn's eyes glowed as she took a drink of wine before she answered. "Find your fool and meet me in my room. Trust me, after this Christian will be begging you not to leave him."

Christian had postponed returning to his room for as long as he could. It had been easy to avoid Adara in the past few weeks. They rode hard all day, then at night they had to pitch tents. By the time their cot was ready and he'd met with Ioan and the others, Adara had been asleep.

So he'd spent hours watching her sleep in his bed while damning himself for not sating the ache in his groin.

But to what purpose? Aye, he intended to stay with her now that their marriage was consummated, but he'd meant what he said about not loving her. There was no way under heaven he would allow himself that fallacy.

Completely exhausted by all the day's events and from arguing with Ioan for the last three hours, he opened the door to their room, then paused.

Adara wasn't asleep. She was sitting before the fire wearing nothing but her silk bliaut, mending a tear he'd gotten in his robe yesterday when one of the trunks he'd been trying to put onto a wagon had slipped and ripped his sleeve. God's blood, she was beautiful sitting there like a peaceful angel, oblivious to everything around her.

Her raven hair fell free around her shoulders to her lap, and had waves in it from her earlier braid that she had worn all day. Cocking his head, he watched as she knotted the thread, then bit through it. He swallowed at the sight of her white, perfect teeth and the image he had of her sinking them into his flesh . . .

Aye, she was a tempting siren as she worked.

The worst part . . . it was a homey scene she presented. One that made his entire body sizzle with need and ache with want.

She turned her head to see him standing in the doorway.

Christian straightened up immediately and pretended that he hadn't been staring transfixed by her. He tried to act as if everything were right in the world and that his groin wasn't swollen and aching for her touch.

"Good evening," she said with a tender smile. "I wasn't expecting you back so early."

Early? 'Twas almost midnight. But then, given how late he had stayed out in the past to avoid the temptation that was her body, he supposed it was rather early for him to seek his bed.

"We shall have an early start. No doubt you will want to retire very shortly."

Preferably in another room. Or better still, shire. But alas, he wasn't to have such a reprieve.

"Ah," she said as she folded his robe and placed it in the small coffer that they shared. It was sad, really, that all they had with them fit into something so small.

As she set about readying herself for bed, Christian couldn't help but notice that her silk garment was so thin her nipples were plainly evident beneath the gauzy material . . . as was the dark triangle at the juncture of her thighs.

When she crossed before the fire, the whole of her body was clearly visible to him.

His mouth watered.

"I have warm mulled wine for you," she said as she indicated a small flagon that was resting on an iron piece above a candle. "I thought it might help you rest."

'Twould take sheer drunkenness to allow him rest after this torment.

Adara went and poured him a cup before she brought it to him.

Christian thanked her, then took a sip of the warm, rich brew. Still, it was no substitute for what he wanted to feel on his tongue.

"Here, Christian. Let me remove those stitches."

She came forward to help him disrobe. Christian remained unmoving while she pulled his clothes from him. Her soft hands felt like heaven against his skin and he yearned to feel them against more of his body.

One part in particular.

When she had him stripped to the waist, she sat him down on a stool.

"Lean your head forward."

His mind dulled by his rampant lust, he obliged her without question. She brushed her hands through his hair and gently massaged his scalp. It felt so good that he had to bite his tongue to keep from moaning aloud. Her fingers slid around the contours of his skull, tugging ever so gently on his hair, stroking and teasing until the pleasure was almost blinding in its intensity.

Then she moved her hands lower to his neck and shoulders.

His body became liquid. "What is this you do?" he asked, his voice thick.

Adara kneaded her fingers into his rigid muscles, easing them. " 'Tis something Corryn taught me. She said she learned it from an Asian woman she met in Venice four years past. Do you like it?"

"Aye," he breathed as her hands worked magic on his body. Her touch was forceful yet so tender that it caused no pain, only joy.

"If you lie down on the bed," she said, "I can get to more of your back."

Adara pressed her lips together to keep from smiling as he quickly complied. Corryn had been right. Her husband wasn't complaining or seeking to leave her now.

He lay down dutifully as if he craved her touch.

"Put your hands under your head," she instructed before she gently kneaded the muscles of his back like Corryn had shown her. Adara couldn't believe this was actually working. Mayhap she should have listened even more carefully about Corryn's advice on how to handle men.

She bit her lip excitedly.

Christian exhaled as complete ecstasy went through him. He'd never felt the like. Her hands worked magic on his sore, strained muscles, soothing him in a way nothing ever had before. There was truly no one else like his wife.

The fact that she tended him . . .

It would be so easy to let himself love her. Something about her completely erased the pain of his past. Just looking into her eyes was enough to make him feel better.

But then people died. He more than anyone knew that. He'd lived the whole of his youth surrounded by the grim reaper and he never wanted to bury another person who meant anything to him.

It hurt too much.

Adara felt him tensing. "Shhh, Christian," she whispered in his ear, moving her hands back to his head, to stroke his scalp and temple. "Put your ill-founded thoughts aside and think of nothing but happiness."

She began humming in an effort to help him.

Christian closed his eyes as her gentle voice soothed him as much as her hands did. He felt so incredibly calm. Peaceful. At no time in his life had he ever experienced anything close to this.

It was perfection.

And he owed it all to Adara.

Adara smiled as all the tension left him. She gently dug her thumbs under his shoulder blades, then moved her hands down his spine until she reached the small of his back.

She traced one of the scars there. It was deep and angry as it ran from his hip down across his left buttocks. She wasn't sure if it had been caused by a sword or some other weapon or fall. Either way, he would have had to suffer much whenever he received it.

So much pain . . .

Before she could stop herself, she leaned forward and placed her lips to that spot. She heard Christian hiss in pleasure, but he didn't pull away from her.

Smiling with hope, she slowly trailed her lips up his spine to his muscled shoulders. Even with all the scars, his back was perfect to her. Beautiful.

And she wanted to taste every inch of him. To know him as a wife should know her husband.

Christian felt himself growing hard as she gently laved the scars on his back. It was strange to feel so much pleasure over something that had given him so much pain. But then, that was Adara. It was what she excelled at.

Rolling over, he caught her before she pulled away. He cupped her face in his hand, then brought her near to kiss her. He could taste the wine on her lips, the desire, feel the heat of her body.

And he wanted more.

Every day they had been together had been pure torture. Being so close to her and yet unable to touch her . . .

Now his resistance melted under the onslaught of her presence. He was too tired to fight, too weary to deny himself her comfort. Whether he liked it or not, he needed her touch to soothe him.

Adara closed her eyes and let the masculine scent and feel of Christian wash over her. He tasted of decadence and power. She couldn't believe that Corryn had been so right, but she was grateful to the woman for her advice.

His kiss was fierce and passionate, filled with promise.

Love me, Christian.

The words were a prayer deep in her soul. He was all she'd ever wanted in her life. How strange to have every comfort and luxury her wealth and position could provide and to still want the dream of her golden champion.

He'd been the symbol of all things good to her. He was love. Nobility. Passion. She couldn't imagine lying with any man other than him.

She trembled as he left her lips to trail his kisses down her throat to her neck. His hot hand cupped her breast, spreading chills over her. His grip tightening, he pulled her beneath him so that his weight was pleasant yet crushing.

His caresses weren't slow and playful as they'd been before. Tonight they were bold and fast, as if he couldn't get enough of her. As if he wanted to touch every part of her body at once.

And she was every bit as hungry for him. Her body thrummed with fervent need that was stoked by his own urgency.

He pulled the hem of her bliaut up so that the lower half of her body lay bare to him.

"What have you done to me, Adara?" Christian whispered in her ear before he licked her lobe and sent white-hot chills exploding through her. "I crave you more than I have ever craved anything."

Is that not how it should be between husband and wife? But she didn't say those words aloud. They would drive him away from her, she was sure of it.

"Show me how much you crave me, Christian," she said instead. "I want to feel you inside me again."

Christian's groin jerked at her brazen words. He felt her hands unlacing his breeches before she slid them down to cup him in her hands. He rubbed himself against her touch, delighting in the coolness of her skin on his fevered flesh.

"How do I feel inside you, Adara?" he asked, wanting to hear her describe it.

"Full and warm. It's as if I can feel the tip of you all the way to my navel."

He growled as she cupped him and gave a light squeeze. Hissing, he rolled over until she was on top of him. "Show me what you like, my lady. Our passion is in your hands."

She bit her lower lip as she pulled back and removed her bliaut. Christian held his breath as she sat up on her haunches and surveyed his body. She trailed a blinding circle around his nipple before she spread her thighs and straddled his body.

His heart thundering, he reached to touch the part of her that was now opened for his delight. He watched the ecstasy on her face as he gently stroked her with his thumb until she was thoroughly wet for him.

Needing more, he slid her back until he was completely sheathed by her body.

Adara gave a small cry at the perfect feel of her husband inside her. He lifted his hips, driving himself even deeper into her.

He held her hips and showed her how to ride him. It was glorious.

His lips curled into a perfect smile as he watched her. "That's it, love. Have your way with me."

She returned his smile as she quickened her strokes. Christian arched his back as complete pleasure glowed in his light eyes.

He sat up beneath her to ravish her mouth so thoroughly that it actually made her dizzy. She loved the sensation of his breath mingled with hers, of his tongue spiking through her mouth in time to her strokes.

Christian laid his head against her shoulder as he watched her body giving pleasure to his. Her sleek wetness was a haven to him. Tenderness exploded through his whole being.

And he wanted to possess her with a ferocity that wouldn't be denied.

Their bodies still entwined, he lifted her up until he could lay her back against the mattress so that he could take control of their union. He was no longer in the mood to be easy and playful.

There was a bestial part of him that only wanted

to possess her. To bury himself in her over and over again until he was at last sated and content.

Adara bit her lip as Christian rode her fast and hard. His strokes echoed through her, sending pleasurable tremors through the length and breadth of her body.

Her head spun as she came in his arms.

Christian nibbled her mouth as he felt her climax. She dug her nails into his shoulder as his name was torn from her lips.

Two heartbeats later, he joined her there in that moment of perfect bliss. When his body was finally drained and sated, he collapsed on top of her. He laid his head against her breast so that he could hear her heartbeat pounding beneath his cheek.

She played lightly with his hair while she cradled his body with hers.

Neither of them spoke in the quietness of the night. He merely let her touch soothe him until he fell asleep, skin to skin, his body still resting inside hers.

Adara kissed his brow as she felt him fall to sleep in her arms. This was the most blissful moment of her life and she hoped to have many more times like this shared with her husband.

Closing her eyes, she held tight to that dream and hoped that he, too, felt it.

Christian came awake to the scent of his wife on his skin. Even before he opened his eyes to see her face, he felt her hand in his hair, her thigh resting between his, her breasts against his back.

Her loins pressed against his buttocks.

It fired his lust immediately. Still groggy from his sleep, his only thought was to feel even more of her warm, supple body.

Smiling, he lifted himself up and over her while she slept. Adara awoke to the sensation of Christian deep and hard inside her. Moaning, she realized that he had one of her legs bent up as he entered her from behind and thrust against her.

"Good morning," he whispered against her ear before he tenderly kissed her cheek.

She drew her breath in sharply as he went particularly deep. "Indeed. It appears to be a most spectacular one."

His laughter warmed her as he cupped her breast in his callused hand. He dipped his head so that he could run his tongue around her ear. Adara shook from the force of the chills that went through her. There were times when her husband could be a most greedy man. And she liked that about him.

Christian inhaled the scent of his wife as he reached up to smooth her midnight hair. In that moment, he never wanted to leave her body or her side.

He wrapped his arms around her and let her feminine scent wash over him as he thrust himself in and out of her body until he felt her spasm. She cried out and dug her nails into his arms.

Christian quickened his strokes until he joined her. He ground his teeth as his orgasm swept through him. The force of it left him weak and sated.

Closing his eyes, he lay entwined with his wife, never wanting to leave her.

"Christian!" someone knocked forcefully on his door. "Come quick, we need you."

His heart cried out in refusal. But he had no choice. It sounded too urgent to wait.

"Sorry, my love," he whispered to her as he pulled away and left the bed to wash. He quickly poured water over his body to cleanse himself.

To his amazement, Adara readied his clothes and helped him to dress in his monk's robe. For the sake of urgency, he forwent his armor, but grabbed his sword and went to see what had happened.

Adara quickly washed and dressed, then followed Christian. The inn was mostly empty below. It appeared as if the soldiers had all but vacated it.

"What has happened?" she asked the old man who owned the establishment as he cleaned dirty dishes from a large trestle table.

He straightened up to speak to her. "I know not. Apparently, something is amiss down at the docks. One minute the inn was full of men eating . . . the next we were empty."

Her heart stilled. Had the Sesari come for them?

Her chest tight in apprehension, she quickly made her way out of the inn and through the streets alone to where they had docked just the day before.

As she drew closer, it wasn't hard to find where her husband had gone. A large crowd of their army was already there. Most of them were silent, solemn. It was very eerie to see so many men that quiet.

"They are not heathens!" the captain was shouting at Dragon as she approached. "My crew are good and decent men."

"We understand that," Dragon said from between clenched teeth. "But you need to have mercy on the man below. All he sees are Moors and Muslims."

The captain's eyes flared. "And he's about to tear a hole in the side of my ship. If he does any damage—"

"We will pay for it," Dragon snapped. "Just give us time to get him out of there before you have him arrested."

Adara frowned at his words. She saw Corryn, who was making her way away from the ship, back toward their inn.

"What has happened?" she asked, stopping her.

Corryn sighed heavily as she glanced back at the captain, who was still arguing with Dragon. "Dagger was bringing home three men from the Holy Land. After they docked, one of the men saw two of the crewmen who are from Egypt and has lost all reason. He's in the bottom of the ship now, threatening to kill anyone who comes near him, including Dagger."

"Dagger?"

"Another member of the Brotherhood. Like Christian, he is one of a few who escorts and guards the Crusaders and pilgrims they free. They bring them all the way home again and make sure no one harms them."

So that was Christian's role in his Brotherhood. It made a lot of sense to her now.

"Why are you leaving?" she asked Corryn.

Corryn clenched her teeth as she stared out with an unfocused gaze. "You've no idea what they look like when they're released. I saw my brother when he returned home, and I lived with him before he was completely adjusted to his freedom. He was a frightened shadow, a shattered shell. Though he doesn't say it, I know that is why he has amassed this army. Our number is so great that no one will ever again be able to take him captive. I don't think they ever get over what happened to them down there. They are too strong to say it, but I can see it in their actions."

Corryn swallowed audibly. "Quite honestly, I can't face seeing another man like that." Then she left her.

Afraid Corryn's words were all too correct, Adara wanted to see if there was something she could do to help Christian and the others. Skimming past the crowd of men, she boarded the ship.

She'd only taken a few steps on deck when a loud shout made her pause.

"You have to leave," one of the sailors snapped as he left the rigging to approach her.

She gave him an arch look she hoped would let him know that she had no intention of letting him sway her. "I am here to help with the man below."

She could see him silently debate with himself for several heartbeats before he agreed to allow her on board. He finally led her down to where Ioan, Phantom, and several other men were gathered.

The sailor went back topside.

Adara paused as she took in the dreadfully small size of the ship's hold. All the men had to bend their heads to stand upright. The space was cramped and saturated with the stench of ocean salt and decaying waste.

The men were completely silent and crowded around a small area. In front of them was Christian, who stood before a man who held a sword angled for her husband's stomach.

It was obvious that at one time the man holding the sword had been huge. Well over six feet in height, he now appeared frail and skeletal. His face was gaunt, his eyes haunted and deep-set.

"You're not the Abbot," the man snarled at Christian. "I heard he was dead by Saracen hands."

"I'm not dead," Christian said in a calm tone as he held his hands up to show the man that he was unarmed. "And I swear no one will hurt you.

You're not going to be sold. No one is going to beat you anymore."

The man's face was anguished. "I saw them. I saw the devils! This is a trick they're using. I know it. You're lying to me!" He swung the sword at Christian, who stepped out of his reach, but made no move to disarm or fight him.

Terrified for her husband, Adara stepped forward.

Phantom turned at her action and quickly rushed to her side. She opened her mouth to speak, only to have him clap his hand over her mouth.

"Not a word," he said sharply in her ear as he blocked her way to the men. He quickly moved her back topside.

"What are you doing?" she asked angrily after he released her on the deck.

"You are dark-skinned, dark-haired, and dark-eyed, Adara. No offense, but you don't look European. If that man had seen you, there's no telling what he might have done to you or what Christian would have been forced to do to him to protect you."

She swallowed as that reality seeped in. "I only wanted to help."

"I know. But you have to understand that when you have suffered as we did, the mind plays tricks on you. You do things that even you don't understand. The simplest sound or gesture can terrify you. One wrong word and you go mad and lash out."

She couldn't imagine Phantom being like that. Nor Christian. They were too controlled and in charge of their emotions.

"Corryn said there were others with him?"

He nodded. "Sphinx took them to the inn where he is staying so that they could eat while we sent for Christian."

"Why Christian?"

"This is what he does, Adara. This is why he's so important to the Brotherhood."

Adara wanted to know more about her husband and his role in all this. "I want to see . . . Please, Phantom. I won't make a sound. I promise."

Phantom looked skeptical at first. But after a brief debate, he pulled his cloak off and wrapped her in it so that no one could see her. Then he led her below.

By the time they returned, the man had laid down his swordpoint and was weeping while Christian held him.

"I am free," the man mumbled over and over again.

"You are free," Christian repeated. "There is no one here who will ever drag you back. We will fight the devil himself if they try."

Ioan moved forward to take the sword from the man's hand. His grip tightened before he released it.

"We are brothers, Agbert," Ioan said to him. "There's not a man here who doesn't understand and know how you feel."

Agbert let go of Christian to wipe his eyes. "I

haven't stepped foot on French soil in over six years."

"It was nine for me," Ioan said.

"Seven for me," another knight added.

"Twelve here, and I kissed the sand of the beach where I landed like a hot whore in my bed."

That actually succeeded in almost wringing a smile from Agbert.

"Come, Agbert. We'll lead you to freedom and to home." Christian held his hand out to Agbert, who took it gratefully.

Ioan kept one hand on Agbert's shoulder as they headed for the ladder.

She and Phantom stepped back as they passed, then followed the procession up.

On deck, Agbert stumbled as he saw the French town. " 'Tis beautiful," he said, his voice catching.

"Just wait," Christian said. "Wait until you taste your first bit of real Norman cooking."

"I ate myself sick on peppermint tarts," one of the knights said.

Another knight laughed. "And drank enough French wine to flood the Thames."

The small group of men made their way down the gangplank until they were on the docks. Adara watched from the deck as the men who had once been prisoners themselves came forward to show Agbert the mark on their hands. Then they embraced him.

"It's amazing, isn't it?" Phantom said from beside her. "So long as Agbert lives, he will never want for anything. If he needs coin, one of them will gladly give it. If he needs shelter or clothes—"

"What of you, Velizarii?" she asked, remembering the way Dragon had greeted him the day before. "Do they all make such offers to you?"

His gaze blank, he started away from her.

"Velizarii?"

He didn't answer her question. "You can go to your husband now, Adara. I'm sure he needs the warmth of your touch to ease the painful memories that Agbert has awakened inside him."

"And who eases yours?"

He gave her a bitter, self-deprecating smile. " 'Tis why God gave us beer and wine."

With that, he headed off the ship to vanish into the crowd.

Her heart heavy for her childhood friend, she left the ship to go after Christian.

Adara caught up to him on the docks, where he frowned at her for wearing Phantom's cloak.

"I saw you on board the ship," she said quietly.

"I know. I saw you as well."

She glanced over to where Agbert was being led into town by the others. "Will he be all right?"

"In time he should heal enough to where he can be normal again. Dagger will take him to the castle of one of our members, where they will help him get used to being free and safe."

She frowned at that. "Would he not be better off with his family?"

He shook his head. "They wouldn't understand."

"Understand what?"

Christian's throat tightened as old memories assailed him. "When I first came to Europe, I couldn't sleep for days on end. I would walk the halls of Stryder's home, clutching my sword and searching every shadow for someone who might pounce on me. Stryder was the same. The only way we learned to sleep again was to have two beds set into his chambers. I would stand watch and guard over him while he slept and then he would watch over me. If I heard the simplest footstep or voice outside my room, I would awaken in a sweat, clutching my sword in expectation of an attack."

Her heart ached for the horror he described.

"To this day, I can't sleep well unless I can identify every sound around me and know that it isn't masking the sound of an enemy coming after me. It is only in the last year that I have finally learned to lay my sword aside at night."

"But you still keep it within arm's reach."

He nodded. "It is a hard way to live. Many of those demons are gone now, like shadows of a distant nightmare. But others . . . they are more resilient and they stalk me even now."

Christian paused to frown at her. She could feel him searching her gaze as if seeking something he needed. "At least they did until you."

He picked up a lock of her hair and stroked it

with his fingers. "I don't hear them whispering to me whenever you're near. I only hear your heartbeat."

Those words lightened her heart and gave her hope. "Then I am glad for you."

His eyes tormented, he pulled her into his arms and gave her a thunderous hug. Adara held him close, reveling in this moment. He had reached out to her. For the first time, he had spoken of his past and shared it with her.

It was a breakthrough.

As in all battles, his heart wouldn't be won by a single victory. It would take many small ones such as this to bring him to her.

She would be patient and she would trust that in the end, Christian would finally see all that she offered him.

And yet even as that thought went through her, she saw an image in her mind of Agbert holding Christian. Of his gaunt, terrified face that had only been eased by Christian's kind and patient reassurances. It was true that Christian's people needed him.

But now she was no longer sure if his people were the Elgederions or the ones who were still being freed and returned to their families.

Eleven

While Christian and Dagger settled Agbert, Adara returned to the inn to pack their things so that the army could march as soon as they were all ready.

She left out Christian's armor, assuming he would want to wear it beneath his monk's robe as he always did.

After Phantom and Lutian came to get her coffer and take it to the wagons to be loaded, she went below to buy bread, milk, and cheese to break her fast. She smiled at the inn's owner as soon as she saw him and asked for enough that she could share with Christian when he returned.

The short older man walked off, leaving her alone. While she waited, a strange sensation came over her. The hair on the back of her neck rose as if she were being watched and her senses were trying to warn her.

Still fearing that they were being followed by their enemies, she cast her gaze around the room until she found two unknown men in one corner who were glaring in her direction. Nay, on second thought, they were glaring straight at her and no one else.

The unfounded hatred in their eyes was extremely disconcerting. She looked about the inn at the other men who belonged to their group. Some were laughing. Some making ready to leave. Some were lounging on their benches, while others ate. None of them seemed to notice the suspicious-looking two men at all.

She hadn't seen either one before. Perhaps they were townsmen or travelers who were new to Calais. But that still didn't explain why they hated her.

Did she perchance remind them of someone?

She was relieved a few minutes later when the owner brought her the foodstuffs and she paid him for them. Wanting to get away from the men, who were still staring at her, she made her way back to her room, where she set the items down.

She had just poured herself a goblet of milk when someone knocked on her door. Assuming it was one of their party, she opened it to find the two men from below.

Her blood went cold, but she refused to let them see her panic. "Can I help you?"

They shoved her back into the room, then slammed the door shut.

* * *

Christian felt awful as he climbed the stairs to his room. Poor Agbert. He'd had a horrendous time in prison, but then, they all had. The worst part about being in the Brotherhood was facing others who were just coming out of their nightmare. There were times such as this when he wondered what it would be like to put the whole of it behind him and carry on free of the responsibility.

Unfortunately, he couldn't. This was his lot in life.

But at least he now had Adara. The thought of her waiting in his room had somehow made the past hour more bearable.

"The men are ready to ride," Ioan said as he came up the stairs behind him.

Christian nodded. "Knowing Adara, I'm sure we're already packed as well. I just need to don my armor and I, too, will be ready."

Ioan was about to leave him when they heard something shatter inside Christian's room. A heartbeat later, Adara screamed.

Terror, panic, and anger descended on Christian as he swung open the door to find her in the room with two other men who were trying to hold her down.

"I'll make you pay for that, bitch," the one holding her said as he tore open her gown.

Christian flew across the room, ready to kill them both. He grabbed the one holding his wife and knocked him against the wall, then turned to knock the other one back.

But when the one who had touched her came back to swing at him, he lost all control. All he could see was the man ripping Adara's gown, the terror on her face.

He slugged her assailant repeatedly, then grabbed his head and banged it against the floor until he felt Ioan pulling him back.

"Christian, stop! You're going to kill him."

Enraged beyond reason, he slammed the man's head against the floor one last time, then turned on the other, who was pushing himself up from the floor. His lip was busted as he stared at Christian in disbelief.

"Go see to Adara," Ioan snapped, pulling him away from the other attacker.

Needing to make sure she was all right, Christian went to her. She was huddled on the floor, weeping.

"Shhh," he said soothingly as he pulled her into his arms. She looked up at him, her lips quivering, to show him her battered face.

It was more than he could stand. Rising, he went after her attackers again, only to find Ioan blocking his way.

"Get out of my way, Ioan, or I'll thrash you, too. I mean it."

Ioan refused to budge. "Let the sheriff handle this."

"Why are you so angry?" the taller attacker asked. "You are one of us. 'Tis only fair we take a Saracen whore—"

Christian shoved Ioan away from him as he

lunged for the man and cut his words off with a vicious backhand. "That is my wife you speak of, you bastard. My *wife* you attacked."

The color faded from the man's face.

Suddenly Phantom was there, pulling him back as Ioan came forward.

"Let go of me!" Christian shouted. "I want justice."

"I can't let you hurt them, Christian," Ioan said apologetically. "They are the ones who have just come back with Agbert and Dagger. They spent the past seven years in a Saracen prison."

Still, he fought against Phantom's hold. "It doesn't give them the right to attack an innocent woman, and most especially not mine."

"Nay, it doesn't," Ioan agreed. "I will see them into the sheriff's custody."

Far from appeased, Christian finally succeeded in shoving Phantom away from him to return to Adara's side. Her tears were quiet and dignified and they tore through him like shards of glass, shredding his heart.

"I am so sorry, Adara," he said, his eyes tearing up for the pain she'd suffered as he took her into his arms again. "I should have been here to protect you."

"I'm just glad you came when you did," she said, sniffling as she wrapped her arms around his neck and laid her head against his shoulder. Christian rose with her in his arms and carried her to the bed.

Phantom came forward with a wet cloth. "I should have been watching her, too. I knew Dagger had sent them ahead, I just thought they were at another inn. I had no idea they were here. Forgive me, Christian. I never meant to endanger her."

"There's nothing to forgive, Phantom. I am far more guilty of neglect than you are."

Christian handed his purse to Phantom. "Go find her a new gown."

Nodding, Phantom took the purse and handed him the cloth. "I'll return as quickly as possible."

"My thanks."

Once he was alone with Adara, Christian laid her back on the bed so that he could examine her. Her cheek was swelling and her lip was split. There was also a clear outline of a man's handprint against her throat where they had held her down.

He fought against the rage that demanded he go kill the men. "Did they rape you?"

"Nay," she whispered. "You came in time."

Relief poured through him as he wiped the blood from her lips, then pressed the cloth against her right eye, which was starting to swell. "I should have killed them."

She covered his hand with hers. Her eyes were dark and filled with a forgiveness neither he nor her attackers deserved. "Nay, I wouldn't see you arrested for such a crime. No real harm was done."

Adara reached up to touch Christian's face

while he tended her. Tenderness swept through her. She was so grateful that he'd found her in time. She'd been terrified when they started insulting and hitting her.

Even though she had done her best to fend them off, she'd been powerless to stop them. It made her wonder how many times her husband had experienced that awful feeling of helplessness as a boy. How many times had he suffered wounds much worse than hers and had no one there to ease them?

"I brought you bread to break your fast," she said quietly.

"I will eat it shortly."

She nodded. "How is Agbert doing?"

He gave her a stern glower. "You would ask after him while you are injured?"

"Aye, as would you in my place. I hope you gave him some serenity."

He let out a tired breath as he turned the cloth over to let the cool side soothe her throbbing cheek. "He will be fine eventually."

"Are there any who don't heal?"

Christian's throat tightened at her question—that she would be so compassionate, when any other lady of her stature would be demanding the lives of the men who had assaulted her.

It was something his mother would have done.

"Unfortunately, aye. There are always some who can't adjust. Some kill themselves once they arrive home. A few have gone mad, and some, such as the Scot, live in perpetual torment and seclusion from the world."

She reached up to place her fingertips to his lips as she stared up at him with a warm, tender expression. "I wish you had come home to me so that I could have helped you."

He pulled the cloth away from her face and stared at her for a hard second. "Had I known what was waiting for me, my lady, I would have."

Adara's heart soared at his words. It wasn't an avowal of love, but it was enough to fill her with warmth.

Christian leaned forward and brushed a tender kiss across her brow. "If you like, I can tell Ioan to ride on ahead with the men."

"Nay. I'm fit to ride."

"Are you certain?"

She nodded.

Christian got up first, then helped her to her feet. As she set about straightening her mussed hair, he paced the floor, still struggling with his raw emotions.

He had actually attacked two men who had been through hell. Would have killed them had Ioan not been there.

Christian should be horrified over his actions. He wasn't. In truth, all he felt was the rage inside that still wanted to cleave the men's hearts from their bodies for touching Adara.

He was growing too attached to her. In spite of his efforts to keep himself immune to her wiles, it wasn't working. Slowly, bit by bit, she was weaving her way into his heart.

What was he going to do?

Someone knocked on the door.

"Enter," he called.

Corryn rushed in. "I just heard what happened. Is Adara all right?"

He nodded as Corryn saw her and went to inspect her. "Did Christian arrive in time?"

"Aye," Adara said quietly. "I suffered nothing more than a few blows. I shall be fine."

Corryn shook her head. "Ioan should have let Christian have their heads. I would have."

"Where did Ioan take them?" Christian asked.

"They were arrested for the deed."

In truth, that was probably a worse punishment than any he could have meted out. After being locked up for so long, a stint in the sheriff's cell would be debilitating to them.

A few minutes later, Phantom returned with a gown. " 'Tis not fancy, but it will suffice."

They left Adara alone to dress. Corryn ran off to wait with the men downstairs while Phantom and Christian waited in the hallway.

"If you want, I will go to the jail and kill them before we leave," Phantom offered.

It was tempting, but not realistic. Not even Phantom was that talented. "You can't do that."

Phantom laughed evilly. "Trust me, I could get into their cell and have their throats slit and be out again before even they knew it."

There were times when Phantom almost scared him. He didn't know what disturbed him more, the fact that Phantom offered or the fact that he seemed so willing to spill their blood.

"Adara says to leave them be."

Phantom shook his head as if he couldn't believe what Christian had said. "She's an incredible lady, isn't she?"

Christian nodded. "Her strength amazes me."

"Aye. She was always something to behold."

There was a note in his tone that gave Christian pause. "You speak as if you knew her before."

Phantom's eyes turned dull. "I shall wait outside with the others."

"Phantom?" Christian said as the man ran off.

Phantom didn't pause.

Christian frowned after him. He would go and pursue this conversation, but didn't want to leave Adara unguarded again.

There would be more time later to interrogate Phantom about this.

Irritated, he returned to the room where Adara was trying to tie the laces at her back. She was twisting and turning, like a squirrel trying to scratch an itch.

He smiled gently at the sight of her.

"You ever have trouble with this, don't you?" he asked.

She straightened and shrugged nonchalantly. " 'Tis why I have maidservants."

After closing the distance between them, Christian laced the gown shut, then placed his chin on the top of her head. He inhaled her sweet scent as he pulled her back into his arms. Warmth and serenity crept through him, making him hard and aching to possess her.

She awakened something inside him. Something fierce and wild. Something that, in truth, scared him.

"You need to dress in your armor, my lord," she said as she ran her hand down his forearm.

"I will."

Adara pulled away reluctantly. "I'll wait—"

"You will go nowhere alone."

The anger in his tone was almost enough to irritate her, but she understood his alarm. Inclining her head to him, she helped him dress.

The mail was heavy, but as always, she helped him suit up, then tied the laces for him.

Christian paused as he saw her tiny hand on his chain mantle while she smoothed it down. How precious that hand had become to him.

Turning around, he cupped her face and offered her a gentle smile.

The smile she returned to him made his stomach flutter, his groin tight. He growled at the sight of her and wished that they had more time.

Taking her hand into his, he led it to his swollen shaft and pressed her open palm to him. "How I wish they weren't waiting on us."

Adara shivered at his needful tone and the feel of him in her hand. Her own body heated up, wanting to feel him skin to skin with her. "Aye, my lord. Would that we had more time." She squeezed him playfully, causing him to let out an anguished moan.

He ground himself against her palm, letting her feel exactly how much he wanted to be with her.

"We'd best go," he said, his voice ragged. "Otherwise they will be waiting an hour or more and, knowing Ioan, I am sure he would come to investigate, thereby causing his own murder when I kill him for interrupting."

She laughed at that. "Aye. He hates to be kept waiting."

But before she pulled her hand away, she ran it up to caress the patch of hair below his navel to his groin.

Whimpering from his need, Christian finally forced himself to pull away.

He led her below to join the others. As they walked, Christian wasn't sure what would be waiting for him in the future. In truth, he could very well die on this journey or during the battle that awaited him.

For the first time in his life, he realized that he had someone who would grieve for him. Someone who would make sure his body was dutifully prepared and that a marker was there to say that he had lived in this world.

It was a strange realization, and he couldn't decide if it made him happy or not.

Lutian met them by the horses. His expression was hell-born as he saw her face.

"I am well, Lutian," she said charitably.

"And I am angry, my queen."

Christian met his enraged glare without flinching. "No more so than I am, Lutian, I assure you."

Christian picked her up and set her on her horse before he mounted his own.

Adara didn't speak as she rode between Christian and Lutian. Both men seemed reluctant to let her out of their sight, and truthfully, she was grateful for their care.

All of their company was somber and grave as they rode in virtual silence. It was as if something had placed a pall over the entire morning.

About an hour outside of Calais, their spirits seemed to improve. Adara could hear some of the men laughing and boasting as they marched their way through the beautiful French countryside.

A tall, well-muscled blond man drew alongside Christian. He inclined his head to them. "Abbot," he said to Christian in greeting.

Christian seemed pleased to see him. "Falcon. It's been a long time."

"Aye. I'm sorry I didn't get a chance to greet you yester eve when you arrived."

Christian offered him a lopsided grin. " 'Tis well understood. I heard about your escapade with the butcher's daughter and your near miss with her father's cleaver."

Falcon laughed. "Lies all. 'Twas the tanner's daughter and her father's ax."

Christian joined his laughter. "One day, my friend, you will meet the one father who can run faster than you."

" 'Tis why God gave us horses." He winked at Christian, then tilted his head so that he could see Adara. " 'Tis a pleasure to meet you, Queen Adara. I am Lord Quentin of Adelsbury and my sword is ever at your disposal."

Christian gave him a meaningful stare. "And your sword had best stay sheathed, Falcon, until you're on the battlefield."

"Your warning is well taken into consideration, Abbot, along with your sword skill and horsemanship. Have no fear of me. Your wife is ever safe from my designs. But no woman is safe from my charm."

Adara couldn't help teasing the man who seemed of remarkable good spirit and cheer. "However some women might find themselves immune from it, my Lord Falcon."

"What, ho?" he said with a laugh. "Congratulations, Christian. You have found a woman as intelligent as she is beautiful. Tell me, Your Majesty, have you a sister who is fashioned in your image?"

"Nay, my lord. I fear I am one of a kind."

He looked sincerely despondent at the news.

" 'Tis a pity, then. I shall just have to pray for Christian to lay aside his duties and become a monk in earnest."

Christian snorted at that prospect. "You would have a better chance courting my horse."

"Then I shall take my charm and work it on a woman who isn't immune to it. Good day to you both."

Adara glanced over her shoulder as he fell back into the ranks with the other knights.

"Don't look at him," Christian said in a teasing tone. "You'll only play into his overbloated self-esteem."

She gave him a meaningful look. "In that regard, he reminds me of someone else I know."

"Ouch, my lady, you wound me."

"Never, Christian. I would never wound you."

Christian smiled at that as he watched her from the corner of his eye. His lady was truly beautiful, but it bothered him greatly that her feathers were currently clipped. His anger had yet to dissipate. Had anyone ever told him that he could become this angry at another Brotherhood member, he would have denied it.

But for her, he had forsaken his solemn vows to protect them.

One life can never mean more than the whole. Stryder's words echoed in his head. They had made some hard decisions in prison and that one had been the hardest.

There were times when one had to be sacrificed.

And yet he had a sneaking suspicion that he wouldn't be able to see Adara harmed no matter the consequences, and that was enough to give him nightmares all over again.

Twelve

By the time they reached Venice, the weather was freezing, but they had picked up some thousand knights and nearly as many archers.

Adara still couldn't believe the sight that had become their army, and with every town they rode to, the natives became terrified. Some had even refused their admittance for fear that they were marching against them.

Their camp stretched on for leagues. She'd never seen the like. There weren't that many Brotherhood members, but many of them commanded armies that put Ioan's to shame.

She could barely name all the Brotherhood members who knew her husband and she wondered how Christian kept them all straight.

All of them had settled into an easy camaraderie.

True, fights would occasionally break out, but for the most part they were a harmonious crowd.

During their long trip south as they stopped at fairs and cities, Christian would buy her gowns or material that he would commission the women who followed their army to sew. She now had quite a collection of finery.

Anytime she tried to thank him for his kindness, he would quickly brush it aside. Meanwhile, he continued to wear the black homespun robe of a monk. Even his cloak was sparse when compared to the fur-lined ones she and the rest of the knights wore.

Now they were camped outside the city and had been here for three days—their longest stay anywhere to date. The men were growing weary and though Ioan wanted to press on, Christian had won their argument only after Corryn took ill.

Adara herself wasn't feeling much better. She'd been nauseated all day. It was all she could do to keep her stomach settled.

She was lying on the bed, trying to ease her sickness, when she heard Christian enter.

"Adara?" he asked, his tone concerned as he rushed to her side. "Are you ill?"

She opened her eyes and, as the room spun a bit, she took deep breaths to quell the sensation. It was time for her to be honest with her husband. For almost two months she had kept silent. But now she was most certain.

Their time in Calais had left her with a very special memento.

"Aye and nay."

Christian looked puzzled by her answer. " 'Tis either aye or nay, my lady. You cannot be both."

"Then aye, Christian, at this moment I am very ill."

His brow creased with worry as he pressed his hand to her forehead to test its temperature. "I shall fetch a leech."

"Nay, husband, there's no need to waste the good man's time."

"But if you are ill."

"My illness will pass in the next few weeks—at least that is what Renata has told me."

He looked even more confused now. "Who is Renata?"

She forced herself not to smile as she savored the news she was about to give him. But she wanted to play vague a little while longer so that she could torment him. "The large, elderly washwoman who travels with Falcon's men."

"Why would you consult a washwoman about your health?"

"She is midwife to the women who are expecting."

She watched as the full implication of her "illness" dawned on him. His jaw went slack as he stared at her.

"You're with child?"

"Aye. I should deliver this coming summer."

Christian felt the sudden need to sit. His knees were completely weak. Part of him screamed in pride and excitement, while the other part was horrified. That part of himself felt as if it were suffocating.

Adara carried his child.

"Are you not excited?"

He knelt down beside her as her words reverberated through him. "Aye, Adara. The news is most welcomed."

"Then why are you so pale?"

Terror? Abject horror? Panic? Apprehension? She could take her pick of the emotions that caused the color to drain from his face.

"I think I am coming down with Corryn's illness."

She didn't believe him. "You are not happy, then."

He started to lie to her, but to what purpose? "You know that I didn't want children."

Her nostrils flared at that. "Then you should have kept your male piece in your chausses, my lord."

He gaped at her crudity. "Where did you learn such?"

"Have you not seen the women who travel with the men? They are a brazen lot who have taught me much these past few months."

Her face was flushed now as she sat up in the bed. "I told you when we met that I would never expect you to stay with me. I won't need you to play father to my child when 'tis obvious that you have no wish to be near him."

She got up and forced him to stand. "In fact, why don't we start this already? The baby has no need of you at this time. Why don't you spend this night in Ioan's tent?"

"Pardon?"

"You heard me," she snapped in her most imperious tone. "Neither the baby nor I want you near us. So hie yourself from my presence."

He was aghast at her unfounded anger. He had done nothing wrong. "This is my tent."

"Fine!"

He watched in stunned shock as she made her way out of the tent.

Christian went after her. She was making her way quickly down the line of tents.

He pulled her to a stop. "Adara? Where are you going?"

"What do you care? You have wrought your damage. Begone, knave."

He heard the laughter of several men who had paused to watch them. He glared at them, then realized that Adara had left the tent without her cloak. She was standing outside in the freezing cold with nothing on but her gown.

"Come back inside with me, Adara, and warm yourself."

She snorted at that. "I'd sooner sit with the devil himself." She turned and started trudging up the hill to Lutian's tent.

Christian followed her, to find Lutian already offering her a seat as he entered.

"Throw him out, Lutian," she commanded.

He glared at the fool. "Touch me, Lutian, and I will addle your brains for certain this time."

"Fail to touch him, Lutian, and I shall addle something you value much more highly." Her gaze went meaningfully to his groin.

Gaping, Lutian cupped himself. "I think, my prince, that you will understand if I show you the way out. Better to lose my brains than something else."

Christian growled in anger at his wife's unreasonable temper. "Fine, Adara. Whenever you decide to grow up and act responsibly, I shall be in our tent."

"Me, irresponsible? You're the one who wants to run away. So go. Leave. *Creta. Au revior. Bon voyage. Auf Wiedersehen. Vaarwel. Arrivederci . . .*"

Christian glared at her even though she wasn't even looking at him. "I understood you the first time."

"Then why are you still here?"

Ignoring her, he turned to Lutian. "Keep watch on her, Lutian. Don't let her do anything foolish."

"He's too late," she said angrily. "He already let me give myself to you. What could ever be more foolish than that?"

Christian wanted to argue, but knew Adara well enough to know that she would never listen to him while she was in this mood.

So be it.

The best he could do was leave her to it and give her time to cool her temper. Turning on his heel, he left her with Lutian, who looked on him with pity.

Adara seethed as she sat in Lutian's wooden campaign chair. Her husband had to be the most infuriating man to ever live and breathe.

What had you expected?

Truthfully, she had wanted him to be happy. They had spent so many wonderful nights together getting to know each other that she had thought he would welcome this news now. But he hadn't changed. Not even a bit.

"Are you all right, my queen?" Lutian asked as he drew near her.

"I am crushed, Lutian. Crushed. There's nothing to be done for it, I fear. Christian has broken my heart."

"What has he done? Say the word and I shall go and . . . well, he will beat my posterior all the way back to this tent. But I shall muss his clothes for the effort and bleed on him for spite."

Adara smiled at his noble words. "I told him that I'm with child and he wasn't happy to hear my news. Should he not be overjoyed?"

She never expected Lutian to disagree with her. "Perhaps not, my queen."

"Excuse me?"

Lutian looked a bit sheepish. " 'Tis quite a burden to place on any man. Even I would be fretful over it."

"Why should one baby be worth fretting over when he leads hundreds of men? You don't see me fretting, do you?"

"Actually, my queen, I do."

She narrowed her eyes on him. "What is it with you men, that you take up for each other on such a matter? May you roast for eternity, too!"

Adara immediately reversed course and left the tent, only to run headlong into Phantom.

She glared at him. "Out of my way, male, and to the devil with you and all of your ilk."

Phantom arched a single brow as she pushed past him. Completely amused, he watched her walk away.

"My queen!" Lutian said as he left his tent.

She didn't pause.

"So when is she expecting the child?" Phantom asked.

Lutian paused. "How did you know she's pregnant?"

"An emotional outburst for no apparent reason, in which she curses all men? Pregnant, no doubt." He shook his head. "Poor Christian. I pity any man who has a pregnant wife to contend with. They can be most irrational."

"As would you if you had something kicking you every time you moved."

They turned to see Corryn behind them. She gave both men a chiding glare. "You should both be ashamed of yourselves. 'Tis a fearful time when a woman finds herself in such a condition. Know either of you how many women die in childbirth?"

That sobered both men instantly.

Phantom felt his gullet knot over the realization and he wondered if the same thing had occurred to Christian.

Adara had gone and ordered Ioan to have a separate tent erected for her. Part of her knew she was being unreasonable, but the other part of her didn't care.

This should be one of the happiest moments in her life. Christian should have shared her joy. She'd practiced over and over in her mind how she would broach the subject with him, but in all her imagined scenarios, Christian had always been delighted by the news.

How dare he ruin this for her!

Tears gathered in her eyes. Why couldn't they have had the marriage she craved? Nay, Christian had to persist in being impossible.

Fine. It was her turn to be impossible.

The Lord moves in mysterious ways . . .

Christian paused outside the cathedral where he'd gone for absolution and yet had found none. Not from himself anyway. He'd never been really sure why he continued to confess or attend Mass when his faith in God had been utterly destroyed all those years ago.

Habit, mostly. It was all he'd known. He'd ignored the Latin words while standing in the congregation, trying to find something to quell the bitter fury that lived inside him over the injustice that was life.

He'd never found peace. Not until a queen found her way into his room and laid herself bare before him.

In more ways than one.

She had silenced his demons. Her musical laughter drove them completely away.

And now he was terrified of his life even more than he had been before. In truth, he was afraid to be happy. Afraid to let himself know joy again.

How long could it last?

Why can't it last? He hesitated at the voice in his head. *For every thing there is a season, and a time for every purpose under the heaven: A time to kill, and a time to heal; A time to weep, and a time to laugh; A time to mourn, and a time to dance.*

He had wept and mourned. Could this not be his time for joy? A woman to love and a child to protect. Why could they not be his reward for all he'd suffered?

Surely it was possible.

Smiling at the prospect, he turned a corner to head back toward their camp. As he did so, he brushed against a stranger who was dressed as a merchant.

"My apologies," he said. Then all of a sudden he felt a painful sting invade his chest.

It was followed by another that came at his back, then more in quick succession.

Christian's legs buckled as the pain invaded every part of him. He fell to the street to see the men who had stabbed him.

The one he'd brushed up against smiled at the one who had attacked his back. "I told you patience was key. That sooner or later he would leave the others and fall into our clutches."

"Basilli will pay us well."

Christian tried to pull his sword out, but before he could, the "merchant" took it from him. When the man reached for Christian's mother's emblem, Christian tried to fight, only to have the man stab him again.

His entire body convulsed and shook.

"The prince is dead," the man said with a note of glee in his voice. "Long live the King."

Laughing, he wrapped the chain around his hand and smiled at his companion. "Come, let us lay aside Prince Basilli's fear and let him know that the imposter is dead."

Christian struggled to remain conscious. He didn't want to die. Not like this. Not knifed in the street by his enemies.

He wanted . . .

He wanted Adara. He wanted to live to see his baby born. To see his wife round from the life they had created.

Most of all, he wanted to lay his hand against

her precious cheek one last time and hear the gentle sound of her humming while she readied herself for bed.

But what hurt most of all was the knowledge that her last memory of him wouldn't be one of love. It would be one of anger.

Neither she nor his child would ever know how much he'd loved them. How much she had come to mean to his harsh life.

Nay, he couldn't die like this. Not without her knowing.

His anger taking root, he forced himself to roll over and to crawl toward the street so that he could find help. But the wounds were too deep. His entire body burned in agony.

He'd only moved a few inches when everything finally turned black.

Thirteen

"Adara?"

Adara looked up from where she was washing her face to find Phantom entering her tent, with Lutian one step behind him. With his long raven hair secured at his nape with a black cord, Phantom was dressed all in black that was trimmed in silver, while Lutian wore a dark brown surcoat that covered a yellow tunic and brown breeches. The two men looked a bit harried, which would make sense if they were here at Christian's behest. They should be in fear if they dared to mention his name to her. She was in no mood to deal with any man right now.

Luckily they had just missed her last bout with morning sickness that was strangely attacking her at midday instead of in the morning.

She pressed the cool cloth to the back of her neck to ease more of her unsettled stomach.

"Leave me, Phantom, Lutian. I don't feel well at present."

Phantom glanced to Lutian, then back at her. "I assure you, you're about to feel worse."

She gave him a droll stare. "I am in no mood to deal with you and your quips."

"My queen, please," Lutian said as he came forward, "you must come with us immediately."

"Where?"

A tic worked in Phantom's jaw. "Christian's tent."

Anger whipped through her. So she had been right about the purpose of their visit. Well, if her husband wanted her back, he could just come himself and face the wrath that he had wrought.

"You can bloody well forget that! I'd sooner the devil take him and—"

"Well, you're about to get your wish."

Phantom's bland words gave her pause. "What wish is that?"

"The devil is about to take him."

She frowned in confusion. "Pardon?"

It was Lutian who answered. "Your prince lies mortally wounded, my queen. We most likely only have a few more moments before he dies."

Adara's head swam at the news. Her knees felt weak, unstable. "You lie!"

Phantom shook his head grimly. "One of our members headed to town for midday Mass found him. It appears Christian was attacked outside of a cathedral by unknown assailants. By the look of how and where he was attacked, I'd wager it was the Sesari . . . His father's sword was taken from him, as was his mother's emblem."

Grief tore through her at the news. This couldn't be happening.

Christian dead?

She wanted to scream, to rail. And yet that regal sense of bearing came into her. Emotions would get her nowhere. She must be calm. Christian needed her.

Without further comment, she left her tent and rushed to Christian's, which was crowded by the members of the Brotherhood who had been imprisoned with him. They all looked as ill as she felt as they discussed who could have done such a thing to a man who was as capable a fighter as Christian.

"It didn't even look as if he'd tried to protect himself," one man said.

"If he was attacked fast enough, he wouldn't have had time to even draw his sword," another answered.

Ioan was standing closest to the bed, looking down upon it.

Her heart hammered as she followed his line of vision and saw Christian lying there. His skin held a grayish cast to it. His lips were already blue. She could see the bloodied bandages where they had tried to tend him.

There were so many cuts . . .

She walked through the crowd with her head held high, but as she drew closer to him, her bearing shattered under the weight of her grief. She would have fallen had Ioan not caught her as wrenching sobs were torn from her.

"Don't touch me," she screamed, pushing Ioan away from her. She only wanted to feel one man's touch.

And now she would most likely never feel it again.

Sinking to her knees beside the bed, she lay her head down on Christian's arm and wept, stretching her arm over his chest as if to protect him. She didn't care how many were there to witness her common behavior. Nothing mattered to her except her husband who lay so close to death.

"Please, Christian," she sobbed. "Please don't leave me. I promise I shall never speak another angry word to you again."

But he didn't move or respond.

Adara crawled into the bed beside him and lay herself down so that she could hold him for these last few minutes. This might very well be the last time in her life that she would be able to look upon him, to touch him.

And that was enough to cripple her with grief.

She heard Ioan ushering the others out while she brushed her hand through Christian's golden blond hair. His skin was so clammy and cold. He lacked all the vitality, the fire that marked him.

In that moment, she knew she would gladly sell her soul to have him back as he'd been just a few hours ago while they had argued. "I am so sorry that I came here and sought you out," she whispered in his ear. "I should have left you in England where you were safe. What have I done?"

But then she knew. She had killed him. Had it not been for her, he would be in England now with his friends. He would be alive . . .

More agony washed through her as she tried to imagine what her life would be like without him. They had known each other for such a short time, and yet he had come to mean so very much to her.

She loved having his face be the first thing she saw in the morning. Having his touch be the last thing she felt at night.

Now it would all cease.

"Oh, Christian," she sobbed as she buried her face against his biceps. "I don't want to live without you."

She finally understood what he'd meant when he spoke so bitterly about love. Why he refused to love her. There was truly no worse pain than what she felt now. No wonder he'd sought to protect himself from it.

"Adara?" Ioan asked in a quiet tone from behind her.

"Leave us," she said, her voice breaking. "I want to be with him for as long as I can."

He placed a sympathetic hand on her shoulder and gave a light, comforting squeeze. "I will be outside."

She lifted her head from Christian's chest as she felt him withdrawing. "Ioan?"

He paused to look at her. "Aye?"

"I care not what it takes. Find the ones responsible for this and bring them to me."

"I shall have their heads and—"

"Nay," she said from between clenched teeth as a new wave of rage swept through her. "I want them alive so that I myself can have the pleasure of making them pay for this."

"I will send out my men." Ioan made a quick exit.

Her heart broken, she returned to Christian to lay her head on his chest so that she could hear his faint, weak heartbeat. Closing her eyes, she tried to pretend that this was the day before, when all had been right between them.

Christian had spent a full hour in the morning making love to her. He had teased and stroked, and made light of the fact that he was tired of fighting with Ioan over their march to Elgedera.

She had held him in her arms and stroked his hair as they talked about everything and yet nothing of any importance. She'd wanted to tell him then of the baby inside her. But Christian had been in such a good mood that she'd hesitated.

And now this . . .

"I love you, Christian," she breathed against him. "I only wish I had told you that when you could have heard it."

Now, it was too late. He would never know all he was to her, all he meant. Never know the sound of his child's cry or the joy she had felt when she'd realized that she carried this tiny part of him.

"I swear to you, Christian, I won't let our baby die or be used. No one will ever hurt him like they hurt you. I swear it on my immortal soul."

She only wished that she had guarded her husband with the same degree of care.

Days went by as Christian hung on the threshold of death. None of the physicians could understand it. By all rights, given the severity of his wounds, he should be dead.

He wasn't.

That gave Adara hope. "Stay with me, my prince," she whispered, holding his hand and kissing his battle-scarred knuckles.

Adara spent hours singing to him in her language and in Elgederion. She spent even longer praying for him. The days of her vigil blurred together as she waited for him to finally return to her. She would only alternate her watch with Lutian and Phantom.

"He's going to live, Adara," Phantom said as he came to relieve her long enough for her to wash and attend basic needs. "I know it."

She hoped so. The alternative didn't bear thinking on. "I just wish he would open his eyes and look at me. Then I would believe, too."

She brushed his hair back from his forehead. Today his color did seem to be better. It no longer was quite so gray and his fever seemed to have lessened.

But he was so gaunt. His wounds so savage.

If she ever laid hand on the villains responsible, they would know a wrath the likes of which could only be second to the devil's own.

Her heart heavy, she started to rise, only to feel Christian's grip tighten on her hand.

Instantly, she froze. "Christian?"

His grip tightened even more, as if to let her know that he heard her. Tears fell down her cheeks as happiness swelled inside her.

"Phantom, fetch the leech."

He ran without hesitation.

Adara saw Christian's chest rise with the first deep breath he'd taken since they had found him and brought him here. She cried uncontrollably as she held him close.

His breathing turned ragged, no doubt from the pain he was feeling now.

Afraid she might be hurting him, she pulled back.

He blinked open his eyes to look at her, and it was there she saw the confirmation of his physical agony.

"I know, my love," she whispered to him, wanting to comfort his pain. "Lie still and just breathe easily." Adara went to get a cup of wine so that she could dribble tiny drops of it into his mouth to ease the bitter thirst he must have.

The leech came into the tent and paused as he

saw Christian's eyes finally open. " 'Tis unbelievable," he said, crossing himself.

As the leech came forward, she saw Christian reach for his throat where his necklace had rested. The utter grief in his eyes tore through her.

"All will be well," she whispered as she kissed him on his brow, then tried to move aside to allow the leech to tend him. Christian refused to release her as a single tear leaked from the corner of his left eye to run down his temple. He kept her hand in his.

Adara kissed the tear away, wishing she could erase his grief as easily. They had not only savaged his body, they had savaged his spirit. His last ties to his parents were gone now. She only hoped that they found the items . . .

And the thieves.

The leech didn't stay long. Only long enough to check his bandages and proclaim this the most miraculous recovery he'd ever witnessed.

"I'll let the others know," Phantom said.

Adara nodded as she returned to sit on the edge of Christian's bed. He had yet to speak with words. But his loving gaze told her volumes.

"Welcome back to the world of the living, Christian."

He swallowed, then coughed.

"Easy," she said, afraid he might tear the stitches in his chest.

"I'm sorry, Adara," he said, his voice raspy and strained.

His words baffled her. "Sorry for what?"

"That I disappointed you."

Her tears started anew. "You are never a disappointment to me, Christian. Never . . . unless you die on me. That would make me dreadfully disappointed, and then I should have to kill you for it."

The corners of his lips lifted a tiny bit.

Suddenly activity exploded in the tent as Ioan and all the others came pouring in to see for themselves that Christian was awake and living.

But Adara wouldn't let them stay long for fear of weakening him. One by one she shooed them out, until it was just her and Ioan, while Phantom went to find a cup of broth for Christian.

"You scared us all, Abbot," Ioan said sternly. " 'Twould do us no good to win back a throne for a corpse."

Christian snorted at that. "Aye, but it gives us an advantage now, doesn't it?"

Ioan nodded. "They'll think we turned back without you here to lead us."

Adara excused herself to attend her needs.

"Nay!" Christian snapped hoarsely. "They could still be out there, watching for you." He looked to Ioan. "Keep someone with her at all times."

"Consider it done." Ioan paused before they left. "I have a spare sword for you. I know it's not your father's, but it is a fine weapon."

A muscle worked in Christian's jaw, but he said nothing as they left.

Christian lay there in silence as his mind replayed what had happened outside the church. He'd never been angrier over anything.

He would be more vigilant in the future. At no time could any of them afford to let their guard down. He was lucky that he wasn't dead.

Nay, it wasn't luck. He knew why he'd fought so hard to return to consciousness.

Adara.

She was the breath inside him, the strength. How could he deny the truth?

Others need you.

"I need her." It was that easy and that hard. He didn't want to live without her and yet how could he forsake those who needed him to help them?

Unlike the war for Elgedera, he didn't see how he could possibly win in this.

Christian didn't truly breathe again until Adara was back inside his tent where he could watch and make sure she was fine.

"You look tired," he said as she rejoined him.

Ioan snorted. "She's barely rested while you lay ill. We tried to get her to leave you, but it was nigh impossible."

She blushed prettily as she started to take a seat near the bed.

"Come here, wife." He held his hand out to her.

Ioan cleared his throat. "Now that she's returned to you, I'll leave the two of you alone." He inclined his head to them before he took his leave.

"How long have I lain unconscious?" he asked her.

"Just over a sennight."

"I'm sorry if I worried you."

"And well you should be," she said in a stern voice that was belied by her teasing gaze. "I have worn my knees out in prayer for your worthless hide these days past."

"Worthless?"

"Aye. Why I bothered, I have no idea."

Still he could see the relief and the teasing in her dark eyes, and that warmed him more than a raging fire. "I'm glad you bothered."

She smiled, then sobered. "Who attacked you?"

"The Sesari," he said as rage took root in his heart. "No doubt they took my necklace as proof for Selwyn that I'd been slain."

Her gaze narrowed. "I am glad they took that and not your head."

"As am I. I can live without the medallion, but not the head."

Christian heard a disturbance outside. He pushed himself up even while Adara protested his movements.

Suddenly a group of the bishop's knights entered the tent.

"What is this?" Christian demanded.

"We're here to arrest the witch."

Christian felt the color fade from his face. "Then you've come to the wrong place. There is no witch here."

Without hesitation, they moved to take Adara from his side.

Christian came off the bed at the same time Ioan, Lutian, and Phantom entered. He staggered, but refused to fall. "Release her!"

"Nay, we are under the order of the Church. The witch is to be tried for her crimes."

"What has she done?" Christian and Ioan asked at the same time.

"According to her accuser, she summoned the devil to save you. You, by all normal rights, should be dead."

"That is ludicrous!" Christian snarled. "There is no devil here."

"I have done nothing," Adara said.

"Silence, witch." One of the knights drew back his hand to strike her.

Christian grabbed the man and, even while near death, he shoved him away from her. "You lay one hand to my wife, and there's no power on this earth or beyond to save you from my wrath. None. If you want a prisoner, then take me."

"Bishop Innocent wishes to interrogate her himself for the charges against her."

"It will be all right, Christian," Adara said. "I am innocent. You rest and I will be back soon."

But he knew better. He'd studied the Church's laws extensively. He knew firsthand the devices they would use to wrest a confession from her.

"You tell the bishop that he is not to go near her until I speak with him."

The knight laughed at him. "The bishop doesn't speak to heathens who are in league with witches."

Before Christian could move, they had dragged her from the tent.

Christian sat back on the bed, too weak to stop this travesty.

"What do we do?" Ioan asked.

Christian looked to Phantom. It would take too long to get to the pope. By then, Adara would most likely be condemned and executed . . . that is, if she survived interrogation. "Follow them and see where they take her."

Phantom left immediately. Christian went to his trunk to pull out his monk's robe.

Ioan put his hand out to stop him. "You can barely stand, Christian."

He shrugged his friend's hand away. "You know as well as I do what they'll do to her. I cannot allow this."

"If you go to her defense, they could label you a witch as well."

"Then I will die."

Ioan shook his head. "Fine. We die together, then."

Adara stumbled as they shoved her into a small cell and slammed shut the door. Her heart hammered in panic. All around her, she heard echoing screams, cries, and prayers. The sounds of people being beaten. She still couldn't believe the way they had dragged her through the city.

"I am a queen!" she shouted as they locked the door.

The knight laughed at her. "Where's your royal finery, Majesty?" he mocked. "Do you not know the penalty for impersonating nobility is death?"

"I am not impersonating anyone. I am Queen Adara of Taagaria."

"And I'm King David." Laughing, they walked off and left her there.

Adara felt her courage falter as she heard the sound of mice scurrying in the dark corners of her cell. "This can't be happening," she whispered, wrapping her arms around herself as if to protect her from the atrocity.

The walls were damp and cold, the air stale and pungent. Unidentifiable shadows flickered eerily on the walls from the torches that were held in iron sconces. 'Twas truly hell on earth.

And Christian had lived in such a place for years as a youth.

For the first time, she fully understood him. No wonder he hated confined spaces. This was the most terrifying thing she could imagine.

She had done nothing wrong. But then, neither had Christian.

"What am I going to do?"

What if they didn't believe her? She'd heard many stories of the Western church and the madness that at times could possess their clergy. They were known to burn witches and heretics. To torture them until they confessed to any crime just to get the punishment to stop.

I am innocent.

But at the end of the day, would that matter to them?

"God save me," she breathed, hoping for a miracle.

Fourteen

Her miracle didn't come right away. Adara wasn't sure how long she'd been captive. There was no window to judge hour from hour, and the screams of the tortured were endless.

She heard the door rattle on her cell. Getting up, she waited with bated breath, praying it would be Christian come to get her.

It wasn't.

A fat, beady-eyed bishop came in. He was dressed in his black bishop's robes and flanked by two other priests, who wore white. They all had craggy faces that were completely devoid of compassion or kindness.

The bishop curled his lip as he raked a repugnant glare over her. "So you're the witch."

"Nay, Your Grace, I—"

"Silence!"

The queen in her rebelled at his commanding

tone. Bishop he might be, but she, not him, ruled her country. In fact, her country was Orthodox and didn't believe in the authority of the Roman Church to preside over them at all.

But provoking the man would get her nowhere, so she stood there in silence even though what she really wanted to do was give him a piece of her royal mind.

He came forward to stare at her. "She is dark like the devil. Has she been searched for his mark?"

The priest to his right shook his head. "Nay, Your Grace, not yet."

"Nor will I be," she said, stiffening her spine. There was no way she would disrobe and allow these men to prod and search every crevice and part of her body for a mark she knew didn't exist.

He scoffed at her. "Bring her," he said to the guards who were waiting outside her cell.

They immediately came forward to take her by her arms.

Adara rose to her modest height and gave them her haughtiest glare. "In my country, peasants are killed for touching royalty. You so much as breathe on my skin and I shall have your nostrils slit for the affront."

"What claim you?" the bishop asked.

"I am Queen Adara of Taagaria."

"Taagaria?" By his tone of voice, she could tell he had no knowledge of her country or its where-abouts.

"An eastern kingdom, Your Grace," the priest on his left said. "It lies somewhere near Antioch."

The bishop's eyes flashed dangerously as his face flushed with angry color. "Prozymite! You are worse than a witch."

Adara's eyes widened at the derogatory, heretical term that had been applied to many who were Orthodox in their beliefs. To the Roman Church, they were all damned sinners who had no hope of redemption unless they embraced the faith of their "parent" church.

"I am not a heretic!"

"Take her!"

Adara fought the guards, but in the end she was forced to submit for fear of hurting her unborn child. They grabbed her arms roughly and led her behind the bishop and his priests. The hallway was dismal and horrifying.

The screams grew louder.

As soon as the priests opened the door to her new cell, the bishop froze.

Adara didn't know why until she saw knights surrounding them.

"Let her go."

Her knees weakened at the sound of Christian's thundering voice.

She looked past the bishop to see Christian in the room with Phantom and Ioan. Never had he been more welcome or handsome to her.

The bishop glared at him. "You'd best remember your place, brother, as well as who you serve."

"You'd best be warned, Your Grace," Lutian said in his fool's voice. "Lord Christian has a mighty sword beneath his robes. Mighty indeed."

The bishop frowned at Christian. "Monks are forbidden to arm themselves. You should know that."

"I'm not a monk," Christian said as he came forward. "And you will not interrogate my wife for a crime she did not commit."

The man curled his lip as if the idea of any man telling him what to do were the most repugnant action he could imagine. "I have the backing of the Church for what I do."

"And I have the backing of an army who will lay waste to every man here if needs be, should you not heed my words."

The bishop was aghast. "You would threaten me?"

Christian didn't hesitate with his answer. "For her life, aye."

"You would jeopardize your soul for her? She is a heretic and a witch."

"She is a woman. *My* woman."

His words only succeeded in angering the bishop more. "I will have you excommunicated for this."

Christian pulled the black monk's robe from over his head and balled it up. "Then excommunicate me. If I am in the wrong for protecting an innocent woman, then God can judge me as He will."

He handed the robe to the bishop, then pushed

past him to Adara's side. "I'm sorry I couldn't come for you sooner," he said to her.

"I will have you killed for this!" the bishop screamed.

Christian gave him an angry glare. "Then I will see you in hell."

The men vacated the cell, then locked the bishop, his priests, and the guards in the room. Christian and the men led her from the dungeon, up to the aboveground hallway where she could see the light from outside.

She half expected someone to stop them, but they walked as if there were no fear in any of them. As if they knew no one in Venice could keep them from leaving.

"I hope you're ready to ride, my lady," Christian said earnestly. "I fear Venice is no longer welcoming to us."

True enough. They had risked much to save her, and for that she would always be grateful. "What of the others? All of you will be excommunicated for this."

Phantom laughed at that. "Too late for me. I was damned long ago by both churches."

"As for the rest of us," Ioan said, "the bishop would have to know our names and nationalities to implement his excommunication. We'll just make sure that when we return this way, we bypass this city."

She gave a nervous laugh at his nonchalance. At

all of them for their actions. There were few men in this world who would dare so much to help another person.

"I can't believe you would all do this for me."

Ioan stopped to look at her. "You are one of us now, Adara. Queen, heretic, and beautiful lady. We, as brothers, have marched through the fires of hell together already. What's a little papal damnation compared to that?"

Christian threw open the door that led to the street outside so that she could see the whole of their army waiting for them. She was free.

It was the most spectacular thing she had ever seen. And she owed it all to the man beside her.

She looked about for her horse, but didn't see it. Before she could ask about it, and in a manner that belied his grave words, Christian swung her up onto the back of his white stallion, then mounted behind her.

"What is it you do, my lord?"

He surrounded her in his embrace as he took the reins into his hands. "I just damned my eternal soul for you, my lady. Therefore I think it best that I keep you in close proximity before anything worse happens."

"I doubt there is anything worse than damning your soul, Christian."

"Aye, there is."

She could think of nothing else. "And what would that be?"

"Losing you."

His words washed over her like a silken caress that touched her all the way to her soul. This man who had lived his life so nobly had forsaken all to protect her. Surely no one had ever sacrificed more.

Not caring who saw them, she leaned her head against his chest and held him to her. "I love you, Christian, more than anything else in this world."

Christian's entire being burned with her words. He wanted to tell her that he loved her as well, but the words choked him. He didn't dare utter them for fear of losing her.

He'd come so close already that it scared him all the more. It didn't seem to be God's will that he should have hearth or home. In truth, he was scared to even hope for it.

But with her . . . a tiny part of him wanted to believe that there was hope for them.

Unable to tell her what he felt, he held her to him and kissed her soundly.

Ioan loudly cleared his throat. "You know, Christian, that bishop is most likely calling for aid even as we sit here and do nothing. I would suggest we set heel to flank before we find ourselves brothers-in-hell once more."

Reluctantly, he pulled back and gave a quick nibble to her lips. "Aye, let us leave this cursed place."

Ioan gave the call to ride that resonated through their ranks as they began their trip that would take them far away from this city.

As they galloped, Christian had never been

more unsure of himself. Everything about him had changed and he was riding to his new fate, to become king of a country he'd never seen. A country whose soldiers had tried repeatedly to kill him.

He didn't know what the future held, but so long as he faced it with his wife, he knew he could tolerate it.

His only fear was that something might happen to her.

They rode for hours without stopping. Adara was amazed by Christian's strength, given that he hadn't had adequate time to recuperate from his injuries.

It was long after dusk before Ioan gave the command to stop for the night. Too tired to lay a large camp, they pitched light tents and cots.

Lutian and Phantom pitched one for Adara and Christian while she sat next to a stream, looking over Christian's injuries.

"They didn't hurt you, did they?" he asked her while she held a cloth to cleanse some of the new bleeding from his ribs.

"Nay, Christian. For that I have you to thank."

"Good."

As they were chatting, she felt someone draw near. She turned her head to find Phantom approaching them.

He seemed reserved and, if she didn't know better . . . nervous. He clutched a blue bundle of cloth as he watched them.

"It was impressive what you did today, Christian," he said quietly. "Damn impressive. Very few men in this world would jeopardize so much for a woman, even their own wife."

Christian inclined his head to Phantom respectfully. "I would never seek to save my life at the cost of someone else's."

"I know. It is what I admire most about you." Phantom looked down at the royal blue cloth in his hands. Adara frowned. There was something very stilted and unsure about Phantom. It wasn't in his nature to be like this.

He took a deep breath and expelled it before he spoke again. "Since you no longer have the robes of a monk to wear, I thought you might want this."

Phantom stepped forward and handed it to Christian, then turned quickly and walked away.

She exchanged a puzzled look with her husband as he unrolled the cloth to show that it was a knight's surcoat. The center of the blue fabric was embroidered with three golden crowned passant dragons bend sinister.

Gasping, Adara covered her mouth with her hand as she recognized it.

"What is it?" he asked.

" 'Tis the royal coat of arms for Elgedera."

Christian was completely shocked by her disclosure. "How does Phantom have this?"

He saw the uncertainty in her eyes before she answered. "That is a question best left to him."

Even though his body protested it, Christian

pushed himself to his feet to find him. By the time he made his less-than-agile way into camp, Phantom was helping to pitch Corryn's tent.

He stopped hammering in a stake the moment he saw Christian.

Christian inclined his head in a direction away from the hearing of others. "May I have a word with you?"

Phantom looked less than pleased and it was obvious the man didn't want to join him. "I would say nay, but I have a feeling you wouldn't allow me that exit, would you?"

"Nay."

Sighing, Phantom left the group and led him to where they could be alone. There was a small clearing to the west end of camp. Phantom drew up short and folded his arms over his chest as he turned to confront Christian.

"Where did you get this?" Christian asked.

"My father gave it to me for safekeeping."

Christian frowned. In all the years he'd known the man, Phantom had never spoken of his father, except to say he was a devil who had died during Phantom's youth.

"Who was your father, that he would have this?"

He saw pain flit across Phantom's eyes before Phantom banished it. His face was solemn and angry. "Tristoph bon Aurelius."

Christian had no idea who that was.

"Your uncle," Phantom reminded him, his voice

defensive and cold. "The eldest who murdered your grandfather, who was then slain by his brothers. I am his bastard seed that he spawned on a village whore."

Christian was incredulous at the news. "Why did you never tell me this?"

"Why should I? What would it have mattered?"

"It would have mattered much to me to know this. We are family."

"We were brothers before you knew this of me. It changes nothing between us now."

"Aye, Phantom, it does."

Phantom looked agitated by Christian's declaration. "I knew I shouldn't have given it to you. I didn't want you to know that about me."

"Then why did you give me this?"

War raged on the man's face. Christian saw his anger and bitterness.

When he spoke, his tone was feral. "Because they took your emblem from your neck so that no one in Elgedera would believe your claim." He picked up a corner of the surcoat. "This is proof of who you are. It will mark you as the son of Princess Barratina the same way my eyes mark me as the son of my father. It is time that things were set right."

Christian couldn't agree more.

Phantom released the cloth and pinned him with a tormented stare. "My father was no traitor. Selwyn lied to him. He got my father drunk and told him that our grandfather had raped my mother, who was then my father's mistress. For all his faults, my father loved my mother, and when he heard the story, he went to confront his father. They fought and my father killed him. Our uncles were then told by Selwyn that my father had killed him to be king. Grief-stricken, they attacked and slew him while he was passed out from drink, unaware of what he'd done. In the days that followed, Selwyn turned them against each other until they were afraid of their own shadows."

"Why would they believe him?"

"He is an evil bastard. He knows how to play on your fears and to manipulate your mind. Truly, if Satan were ever to wear a human face, he would be Selwyn."

Christian had no doubt that Phantom would know all about that. "And you? How do you fit into this? Why did Selwyn try to kill you?"

"I may have been bastard born, but without you there to take the throne, I was the closest blood link to it. It was a chance Selwyn and Basilli decided they couldn't take. Basilli had his men dress as Moors and then attack my dormitory."

"As he attacked my monastery?"

"Aye. And before you ask the question of how I came to be in your prison . . . Selwyn sent me there to kill you."

Christian was stunned by that. "What?"

He nodded. "After the death of my father, I was turned out by my mother, who feared what would befall her if anyone found me in her home. With no other option, I became a thief and a hired dagger. One night, I had decided that the time had come to pay retribution for my father's death. I snuck into Selwyn's chambers intending to cut his throat as his men had cut mine. Unfortunately, they caught me and I was imprisoned. He tortured me for weeks, wanting to know who I had told about my father's murder and his part in it. In the end, after I had lied and convinced him that I knew nothing and had tried to kill him only because someone had paid me to, he offered me a pardon from my crimes provided I kill you."

"But you didn't. Why?"

Phantom laughed bitterly. "I wouldn't give Selwyn the satisfaction of having you slain. I knew we would escape eventually. I never had a doubt. And I figured that one of us would return at last and pay our debt to him in full."

Now everything made sense. Phantom turning up all these years whenever Christian was in trouble. He'd always suspected that the man followed him.

Now he knew for certain and he finally knew why.

They were family.

"So that is why you have haunted me all these years."

He nodded. "I wanted to make sure that you would live to take his coveted throne from him." Phantom's pale gaze bored into him. "My father was a good and decent man who loved me and my mother the way your parents loved you. I don't want to see one man destroy that and get away with it."

"Neither do I." Christian held his hand up before Phantom. "I hope that this means you will stay in the light, by my side, cousin. You have lived far too long in the darkness that he relegated you to."

"I make no promises to that. I personally like the feel of shadows on my face. But I will stand by your side, Christian. Always." He took his hand and squeezed it.

Christian pulled him into a quick hug, then released him. "Thank you, Phantom, for everything."

He inclined his head to him.

Christian stepped away, then pulled the surcoat over his head and settled it into place over his armor. It was a perfect fit.

Belting his girdle around his waist, he started back for camp.

"Christian?"

He paused at Phantom's call. "Aye?"

"You have been blessed with a good wife. Better than I think even you know. Don't let the past blind you to the future you could have."

"It's not that easy, cousin."

"I know. Believe me, I do. But you two have made great strides together. I have seen something inside you change with her presence and I would hate to see you cast that away."

Phantom's words confused him. "Why would you care, Phantom?"

"Because if a man as good as you doesn't deserve a blessed life with a woman like her, then what hope is there for someone like me?"

Fifteen

With Phantom's words ringing in his head, Christian paused as he entered his tent. Adara was already there, unpacking a few of their things, making their spartan tent more welcoming. But then, her presence alone accomplished that. There was truly nothing more soothing than the gentle visage of his wife doing the simplest of things.

As always, she was humming.

Her long black hair hung in an intricate design of braids woven with red ribbons that matched the red of her gown. Something about the style reminded him of a delicate rose. Her body bore no sign yet of their child. Still, he could just imagine what she would look like in a few weeks as her body grew to accommodate the new life. How even more lovely she would be to him.

In spite of what Phantom had said, Christian

didn't think of himself as a particularly good man. He was just as guilty of sins and crimes as Phantom had been. How many men had fallen to his sword over the years? But he had always tried to live his life nobly. To honor his word and never fail his brothers-in-arms.

Just as he prayed he would never fail his wife and child . . .

Child. That one word echoed through his soul. He would now be responsible for another life, one of his own making. That child would turn to him for advice and for care and protection in a way no one ever had before.

And that child would be devastated to find itself alone in the harsh world that had raised Christian.

What did he know of children? Not since his own boyhood had he been near one, and even then his association with other children had been sparse at best. He knew only that they smelled badly, cried loudly, and were oft grimy with sticky fingers and moist noses. Truly, they were a horror on earth.

"Christian?"

He focused his gaze to find Adara watching him. "Aye?"

"Are you well? You look uncertain."

He was, but he would sooner die than ever let her know it. "Nay, I was only thinking of something Phantom said." He crossed the floor to help her lay out their blankets. "It's been a long day. You should rest."

She paused to look up at him. "What of you?"

Her gentle brown eyes searched his, but it was the concern he saw there that touched him deep in his heart. Christian reached out to lay his hand against the flush of her cheek. The softness of her skin never failed to amaze or to warm him. She was a part of him in a way no one had ever been before. Deep. Integral.

He'd almost lost her this day. The rage and pain he'd felt still simmered inside him. He didn't want to feel this. Didn't want to know that one person held so much power over him that by simply leaving or dying she could utterly destroy him.

It was humbling.

And it was wonderful. Being with her . . . feeling her . . . there was nothing else like this. Her presence gave him strength and made him deliriously happy.

Adara covered his hand with hers. He watched her so intently that it made her throat tight. There was so much emotion in those blue eyes. So much love and adoration, and at the same time she saw his fear, his torment. How she wished she could take that from him.

All she could do was offer him whatever solace was humanly possible. Rising up on her tiptoes, she laid a gentle kiss to his well-shaped mouth.

She was completely unprepared for his reaction to her kiss. He crushed her to him with a groan as he raided her mouth. His tongue spiked against hers as if he wanted to completely devour her. The ferocity of his passion left her breathless. He teased and nibbled her lips, before he deepened his kiss even more.

He pulled back to stare down at her with his eyes glazed and probing before he buried his lips against her neck. Adara hissed as chills spread over her while he loosened the laces for her gown.

She unbuckled his belt, then let it fall to the floor before she seized his surcoat and pulled it over his head. He removed his mail hauberk just as quickly.

Her heart hammering, Adara started unlacing his aketon.

"Bugger it," he snarled. "I can't wait."

Adara frowned, not quite understanding until he unlaced his chausses and let them fall to the floor. He seized her then and pulled up the hem of her gown. Two heartbeats later, he pinned her to the stake in the center of the tent and was deep inside her.

Her head spinning, she wrapped one leg around his hips as he thrust himself into her over and over again. He was raw and fierce with his need, letting her know just how much he craved her touch.

Christian ground his teeth as the pleasure of her body assaulted and eased him. He needed this physical connection to her in a way that defied his best abilities to understand. She was his soul. A part of him that he had long ago forsaken.

In her arms, he found the sanctuary he'd been

searching for. But for how long could he stay here? Sooner or later, all men had to forsake sanctuary. It was the nature of the beast. Somehow it always turned on its master.

He pressed his cheek to hers and inhaled the fragrant scent of her dark hair. "You are mine," he whispered against her ear as he thrust himself deep.

"I am yours, Christian," she breathed. "I have always been yours."

He pulled back to stare at her in wonderment as he eased the ache in his body with hers. Her face was creased by pleasure as she watched him carefully. All these years she had waited for him.

If only she'd come for him sooner.

Or maybe she shouldn't have come for him at all. His indecision tore through him, and yet how could this be wrong? How could what he felt for her be the end of him? Surely something this confusing and wonderful had to be divinely inspired.

"I want you to stay with me, Adara. Always."

She reached up to touch his lips. "I'm not the one who threatens to leave."

Nay, she wasn't. Christian drove himself in deep and held himself there so that he could feel the sweetness of her body wrapped around his, feel the warmth of her arms clutching him in the heat of this moment.

"I know nothing of this life you offer me, Adara. I know nothing of riches or ruling. Nothing of a woman's love or her heart. I only know warfare and cruelty."

Adara's heart clenched at his whispered, grief-laden words, but it was the tormented look in his eyes that seared her.

"I know not how to be your king . . ."

She held her breath as he stayed completely still, his body still inside hers. She expected him to withdraw, expected him to run away from her.

Instead, he continued to stare at her as he lifted his hand to touch her cheek. "But God help me, I want to be your husband. I want nothing more than to see you in my bed every night before I lay myself down to sleep."

She choked as joy consumed her. She took his hand into hers and kissed his callused fingers. "I love you, Christian. I will never leave you."

He closed his eyes as if to savor her words. She ached to hear him repeat loving words back to her, but he didn't. Still, he had committed himself to her. It was more than he'd ever done before.

They had come far these weeks past. Not just in distance, they had traveled leagues in their relationship. Mayhap by the time they reached Taagaria, he would be ready to travel that last step that would bring him completely into the shelter of her heart.

He started moving against her again, swift and strong. Adara held him close as she let his strength wash over her. There was nothing she wanted more than to have her husband in her arms.

To have and to hold . . .

Aye, that was what she wanted. Her heart aching for it, she came, crying out his name.

Christian kissed her gently as he felt her body spasm. His breathing ragged, he joined her in paradise. His body shook from the force of his ecstasy. Adara alone had the ability to sate him on this level. To make him feel complete and wanted.

"What have you done to me, my lady?" he whispered as he nuzzled his face against hers. The softness of her . . . the smell of her flesh . . .

She weakened and strengthened him.

"I seek only to make you happy, my lord."

He smiled, then kissed her soundly. "You definitely do that."

Reluctantly, he withdrew himself from her and let her gown settle back around her body.

Adara pressed her lips together as her gaze dipped to take in the length of him. Against her will, she started laughing.

Christian frowned. "What has possessed you?"

"The sight of you," she said as she realized that in his haste to take her, he still wore his unlaced aketon. His mail chausses had fallen to his ankles, but were held to his knees by his boots. It was quite comical, really, especially given the fact that her husband normally looked so composed and somber.

Christian glanced down and joined her laughter. "I fear my rose has turned me into a buffoon to match her fool."

"Your rose?"

"Aye," he said, pulling his chausses back up,

then tying them at his waist. "There is no other word to better describe your prickly beauty."

She sensed he was teasing her and she enjoyed the novelty of it. "Prickly?"

He nodded. "You do have a surly nature about yourself. Stubborn, too."

The light in his pale eyes was so playful that she couldn't resist teasing him back. "Why, sir, I do believe you have me confused with you."

"Do I?" He tried to pull her close.

Adara refused. She traced the line of his jaw with her fingernail, letting it gently scrape his whiskers. "Aye. You are the only prickly thing I see in this tent."

The smile on his face warmed her. "You didn't mind my prickliness a moment ago."

He pulled her flush to his chest. Adara sighed involuntarily at the hard feel of him. There was something about Christian that was overwhelmingly masculine. The manly scent of his skin, his sleek muscles. He was all sinewy strength.

His hungry gaze dipped to her lips before he took possession of her mouth again. Adara surrendered herself to him, content to taste the only man she'd ever wanted. His tongue teased hers while she tasted his warm passion. At times like this, she knew he loved her even if he didn't say the words. It was only in the darkness that she doubted him.

He said he would stay with her, but she wasn't

so sure. At night he oft left her so that he could visit with Ioan and the others. It was then that she saw her husband's true nature and his ease with the men.

He was a soldier at heart.

How long could such a man be content with home and hearth? The last thing she wanted was to make him miserable. Christian meant everything to her. What good would it do to keep him if he died in captivity?

He pulled back from his kiss with a frown. "Is something amiss?"

"Nay," she said sweetly. "I was only trying to imagine what tomorrow might bring our way."

Christian tightened his hold on her as his own doubts assailed him. "Let us not think on that. Tomorrow will come no matter what we plan. Tonight I've no wish to think of it. I only want to feel you with me."

She kissed his hand, then released him. "Very well, all my thoughts are banished."

If only his were. Now that she had broached the matter, his thoughts spun with concerns.

But the most immediate was the one that wanted him to abandon everything in the world for the woman in his arms.

However, it was time to lay aside his fears. His decision was made and there was no choice except to march forward with it and trust that fate would see him through.

Adara was his wife . . .

Nay, Adara was his life. *Lives are taken every day . . .*

The ominous voice in his head was haunting. It was debilitating. He'd delivered enough Last Rites to know firsthand how fragile life was. They had men out to kill them and she was pregnant. Women died every day of childbirth.

A man could go mad with such thoughts.

Christian laughed in spite of himself.

Adara scowled at him. "What has possessed you?"

"I am merely thinking that Lutian must have been quite sane until the day he fell at your feet. Indeed, I wonder how soon before I find myself his intellectual equal."

She bristled under his humor. "Are you saying I made him daft?"

"Nay, I say only that you are making me lose all sense whenever you are near."

"Addled you, have I?"

"Completely."

She placed a kiss to his cheek. "And you have captured me, Christian."

Christian smiled at that as she excused herself for a few moments to attend her needs. "I love you, Adara," he said beneath his breath.

He only wished he could find the courage to say it aloud to her face without the fear that something would then come along and steal her away from him.

Sixteen

Adara and Christian settled into an easy camaraderie as they traveled over the next few months. With every day that ended, Adara found herself ever more hopeful that Christian might be content being king and husband, and that he was learning to need her, at least as much as a man so strong could need another person.

He seemed excited about the baby, and even Ioan had finally started to slow the army's movement in regard to Christian's constant nagging over her tender condition.

They were only about a week from the border of Taagaria. The heat of summer was upon them now, making her snappish from the discomfort of it. According to the midwife and her own calculations, the baby still had two more months before he or she joined them.

But honestly, Adara was more than ready either to have the baby born or to be home where she could rest comfortably. The endless traveling was grueling and hard on her. To help ease some of her discomfort, Christian and Lutian had made a cozy wagon filled with pillows and a feather tick for her to ride on during the day. However, she wasn't sure if it was any better than riding a horse. The cart jostled constantly and left her having to hold on for dear life at times. Still, it was so sweet of them that she didn't have the heart to complain.

She lay in her wagon, watching the men around her. Over the last few days, as they drew nearer to the Elgederion and Taagarian borders, they had become more sober. Watchful. It was as if they expected an attack at any moment.

The men had long come to the conclusion that Selwyn would not suffer the army to enter either country without battle. He would have too much to lose. They fully expected him to attack them before they had a chance to cross the borders.

Christian rode just to her left so that he could watch over her. Phantom and Lutian were with him, but no one spoke.

Sighing, Adara wiped at her damp brow.

"Do you need to rest?" Christian asked immediately.

Adara smiled at him. "If you stop this army one more time, I fear, husband dearest, that Ioan will sacrifice you to the buzzards."

"Aye, he would," Phantom said. He cast a teasing look to Christian. "So should we stop?"

Christian gave him a droll stare. "I don't want you to stress yourself unduly, my lady. You have enough of a burden upon you."

"Aye," she teased lovingly. "Putting up with you is truly the most insufferable of fates."

Christian's face lightened instantly. How she adored it when he looked like that.

Phantom made a choking noise. "Come, Lutian, they're about to get sickeningly sweet again. I feel a bellyache coming on should we stay to witness it."

"True," Lutian agreed. "My teeth ache with it already."

Adara rolled her eyes as the two of them drifted back out of hearing range. "They're only jealous, my lord."

"Indeed." He reached his hand down to her.

Adara took it and smiled at him as they rode hand in hand for a bit. But with every step that brought them closer to her borders, fear and uncertainty shredded her. Part of her wished she had never insisted they return. She had found in Christian so much more than she had ever hoped for. In truth, she'd been happy without the burdens of her people. For these past months, it had only been the two of them.

And she liked it.

You are being ridiculous. You are queen.

Aye, and she was Christian's wife.

Ioan called out for Christian's attention as one of their scouts came riding into the group from the south. Excusing himself, Christian released her hand and kicked his horse forward.

Adara sat up in the wagon to watch the two of them talking while they rode. She couldn't hear anything, but by their faces she could see the news was dire.

"Lutian?" she called, waving for her fool to join her.

"Aye, my queen?"

"Please go and tell me what it is they discuss."

He nodded, then moved to obey.

Adara fretted incessantly until his return. He, too, looked less than pleased, while Christian and Ioan continued to speak to each other at the front of their troops.

"Well?" she asked.

"Ioan's scout has found an area about a day's ride south where he believes Selwyn might attack us. 'Tis the narrowing in the road between the Yador Mountains . . . Killer's Ridge."

Adara's heart stilled at his words. She knew the pass well. It was oft an area where thieves chose to raid traveling caravans and merchants. The hills provided cover and the pass was so narrow that no more than two men or a single wagon could traverse it at a time. An army could lie in wait above the pass and easily pick them off with archers as they came through it.

Aye, that was exactly what Selwyn would do.

Ioan called for the army to halt.

Christian rode back to her side. "We are breaking camp for the night so that we can plan a strategy," he told her.

Adara nodded in understanding as she, too, tried to think of an alternate route. "We can travel southwest and skirt around the mountains."

"That would take us into Irovar," Lutian reminded her. He then directed his attention to Christian to explain the problem with that. "They are allies to Elgedera and most loyal to Selwyn."

A tic started in Christian's jaw. "Not to mention I am sure they wouldn't think highly of having an army march through their borders."

Adara sighed in frustration. "You're correct about that. We haven't had the best of relations with them since I refused to allow their king to court me."

Fire sparked in Christian's eyes. "Did he press his suit?"

"Nay, my love. He only made a few arguments as to why I should consider him over you. They were paltry and weak reasons indeed."

Christian grew quiet at the reminder of his wife's loyalty to him even when he hadn't deserved it. He dismounted and helped her from her wagon. "I am glad you waited for me, Adara."

"Not nearly as much as I am, I assure you. The Irovian king is fat, bald, and highly rude. He's little better than a tyrant who is renowned for overtaxing his people."

Christian pulled her into his arms with her back to his chest. He wrapped his arms around her shoulders and held her there with his chin resting atop her head. He loved holding her like this. She was a perfect fit to his body. The scent of her hair filled his head while she lightly stroked his hand with hers.

Closing his eyes, he drew strength from her even though he knew she would soon be angry with him. One of the possible plans he'd discussed with Ioan had been to leave her here while the majority of the army rode forward to meet the trap they were sure Selwyn was planning.

By now Selwyn had to have received word of their army coming toward his country. It wouldn't take much for him to learn who they were and why they were coming.

Christian's first priority was to protect the woman in his arms.

One life should never take precedence over the many.

It shouldn't. But in the case of Adara, he would sacrifice them all to keep her from harm. Sighing at the realization, he kissed the top of her head and released her.

"We have much to do tonight."

She looked at him suspiciously. "Why do I have the feeling that something isn't right with you, Christian?"

He forced himself to betray nothing about what was to come. "How so?"

Her dark eyes were probing. "I know not. But I

sense that there is something you are hiding from me."

She was a woman of high intuition. Nay, he corrected. She was a woman who knew him far too well.

He cupped her tender face in his hand. "Fret not. I am only concerned about the men I am sure are waiting in the mountains to ambush us."

"Ah, is that all? For a moment I thought you might actually have something of great importance troubling you. But what's a few hundred maniacal zealots out to kill us for their treacherous usurper? Nothing, truly. I now wonder what could have possibly had me concerned."

He laughed at her humor. She was spectacular and brave in a way very few women were. How he had been fortunate enough to have her for wife, he didn't know, but he was eternally grateful for it.

Lutian was headed for them. Christian turned her loose with her fool while he went to speak more to Ioan and Corryn about their plan.

If Adara ever learned what he intended to do, he had no doubt she would be calling for his head on a pike. It was why he must plan carefully and quietly.

Come the morrow, she most likely would never forgive him.

Adara couldn't get rid of the feeling that something wasn't quite right. Christian spent most of the night plotting with Phantom and Ioan.

It was long after dark while she lay in bed, waiting for Christian. She could hear the reserved sounds of the men outside as they made ready for their beds. All any of them could speak about was the battle they expected on the morrow.

It left her terrified. What would happen? All these months, the idea of war had been a vague one. Now it was all too real to her. In her mind, she saw the faces of the men she had grown attached to. Tomorrow any one of them could be dead.

And it would be all her fault.

That thought was sobering and frightening. She was asking all of them for a sacrifice none of them should have to make.

"Damn you, Selwyn," she said under her breath, hating the man who had forced them to this.

"You're still awake?"

She turned her head to find Christian drawing near. "Aye. I was wondering if you would retire this night."

"We had much to discuss."

Adara didn't say anything more while he disrobed, then joined her in the bed. As was his custom, he lay beside her and kept his hand on her stomach so that he could feel their baby moving.

"He's active tonight."

"Aye," she said with a smile. "He's much like his father and ever on the move. He has been tossing about for hours now."

Christian stroked her distended stomach with the tenderest of touches. "I can feel his foot against my hand."

"I can feel his foot against my bladder."

He laughed. "Does he hurt you much?"

"Nay, not at all."

Christian leaned forward at that and placed a light kiss to her stomach before he settled down to sleep.

Adara took his hand into hers and held it close while she listened to his breathing become steady and deep. Many times she would lie awake and listen to him while she wondered what he dreamed of. Tonight more than ever before, she was curious. Did he dream of a future with her or of a time when he would leave to help his brothers-in-arms?

He continually told her that he intended to stay, but part of her refused to believe it. His family was his Brotherhood. How could she hope to compete against their loyalty?

Letting out a deep breath, she closed her eyes and forced herself to join him in the arms of Morpheus. Tomorrow would be a long day and both of them would need their strength.

Adara came awake slowly. As she'd done many times over the last few months, she scooted across the mattress, seeking the warmth of Christian's body.

He wasn't there.

Opening her eyes, she realized her bed was empty. His armor gone. But more than that was the quiet from outside. There was no armorer hammering. No people chatting. It was ominously silent.

Her heart pounding, she got up without dressing and rushed to the flap of her tent wearing nothing but her chemise. She threw the thick canvas back to see a small group of men outside with Lutian.

There was no one else around.

"Lutian?" she called as a sense of dread consumed her. "Where is Christian?"

He passed a sheepish look to the other soldiers before he headed toward her. He didn't speak until he stood directly before her. "He's gone, my queen."

"Gone where?" But in her heart she already knew.

"They rode ahead to fight. We are to take you on to Taagaria so that you will be safe."

Her head spun. Nay! How could they have left her like this without any word? "He didn't say good-bye to me."

She saw the guilt on Lutian's face. "He thought it best."

Tears filled her eyes. "Best for whom? I had a right to know what he had planned."

"My queen—"

"Nay!" she snapped. "Do not try and placate me when you are ever as guilty of this as he is. How dare the lot of you decide something like this for me? I had a right to know and I had a right to see him off to battle."

"I know, my queen, but—"

"There are no buts in this, Lutian. None. Should he die this day, I shall never forgive either of you!" Angry at the lot of them for treating her as a child, Adara took a step back intending to return to her tent and to refuse to leave it until Christian returned. But no sooner had she moved than she heard the sound of hooves approaching.

Could it be Christian and the army?

The thought had barely completed itself before she heard a strange sound. It was an odd whirring noise.

"Arrows!" one of the knights shouted an instant before one embedded itself into his heart.

Hissing, Lutian grabbed her and pushed her into the tent, then onto the floor.

"What is happening?" she asked him.

"I know not, my queen. I know not."

She heard the sound of the men calling orders to each other outside as more arrows rained down upon their camp. Three fell into her tent, landing far too close to them.

Still the hooves came closer until she knew their attackers were in the camp. The arrows stopped and were replaced by the sound of men fighting with swords. Her stomach knotted in fear.

"We have to escape," she told Lutian. It was their only hope.

She grabbed the dagger from his waist and cut a slit in the back of the tent to see that they were surrounded.

Biting her lip, she realized she had no choice. They needed to get to a horse and ride away from here. With Lutian right behind her, she rushed from the tent as quickly as she could, given her condition. Men battled and fell all around.

As she approached the makeshift corral, she realized that all the horses had been freed. Angry and scared, she turned, only to come face to face with a man on a large black stallion.

She looked up at his face, then felt her heart sink.

It was Selwyn. His beady black eyes stared out from the slits of his helm as he laughed at her. He removed the helm so that she could see the sneer he raked over her body.

"So you found your prince," he said coldly. "Good. We'll make sure to have him present when we carve his seed from your belly. Take her!"

Seventeen

"Something's amiss," Christian said as he surveyed the rising mountains around them and saw no trace of the army they had suspected would be waiting for them. By now there should have been a call, a glint of sun on armor . . .

Something.

But nothing gave away the enemy's position. It was as if they weren't there.

"Do you see something?" Ioan asked.

Christian shook his head. "And therein is my problem. There's . . ." He let his voice trail off as a sense of doom possessed him. Why had he not thought of *that* earlier?

"Phantom?" he called, then waited for the man to ride apace of him. "How well do you know Selwyn?"

He shrugged. "Since he murdered my father

and tried to kill me, we were never overly friendly. Why?"

Christian ignored his question and sarcasm. "Is there any other place where they could be waiting for us? Another position that would be more advantageous to them?"

Phantom shook his head. "This would be the most likely."

"Aye, the most likely. The *only* likely place." Christian cursed at their stupidity.

"Why are you upset?" Ioan asked.

Christian felt a muscle in his jaw begin to tic. "Because he knew this was the only place to attack us."

Falcon looked bemused. "And how is it bad that he's not here to slay us?"

Phantom's face mirrored the dread Christian felt. "You don't think he . . . ?"

"Aye, cousin, I do."

"What?" Ioan and Falcon asked at the same time.

"How do you win a chess match?" Christian asked them.

"You capture the queen," Falcon said at the same time Ioan cursed as he finally understood Christian's fear.

Ioan looked ill. "You don't think they waited for us to leave, then marched on Adara?"

Christian didn't bother answering. He wheeled his horse about and spurred it toward their camp.

He knew to the depth of his soul that that was exactly what they'd done. His heart pounded as fear took root inside him and grew to titanic proportions.

He had to get back to Adara.

"Please let me be wrong," he whispered over and over again as he raced back to camp.

For the first time since he was a boy, he prayed. He breathed every prayer he'd ever been taught while he urged his horse to fly over the rocky terrain.

But those prayers caught in his throat as he drew near the camp and saw the bodies of his fallen men. They lay scattered about the ground like abandoned dolls. Christian threw his head back and bellowed in agony and rage at the sight of them.

He jumped from the back of his horse even before it stopped, and rushed toward the tent where he'd left his wife sleeping just a short time before.

It was empty. There was no trace of Adara anywhere.

"Damn you!" he shouted as pain ripped through him. How could he have been so stupid?

He left the tent to see Ioan, Corryn, and Phantom reining to a stop in the center of the carnage before they dismounted.

"She's gone?" Phantom asked, his tone angry.

"Aye." Sick to his stomach, Christian's gaze fell to the sight of a man wearing a bright yellow jerkin.

Lutian.

He rushed to the fool's side, aching over the fact

that he had been loyal to his queen unto the end. Poor Lutian. His face was covered in blood from a beating, and it was obvious from his injuries that he had fought valiantly to save her.

Christian fully expected him to be dead.

He wasn't.

"Fetch water!" he called to Corryn as he realized the fool was still breathing, although very shallowly.

Corryn ran to obey while Christian carefully lifted the fool up and took him into his tent. He lay him on his cot so that he could rest comfortably. Lutian coughed as his eyes blinked open.

"Christian?" It was the first time Lutian had ever called him by name.

"Aye, my friend. Rest easy."

Lutian's gaze was filled with agony. "They took her. I tried to stop them, but—"

"I know, Lutian. It's not your fault. I'm the one who left her here unprotected."

Corryn joined them with a skin of water for the fool. Christian helped him to drink a bit, then turned to Ioan, who stood behind him. "Regroup the army. We'll march on them—"

"Nay!" Lutian sputtered as he choked on the water. He pushed the skin away from his lips. "Selwyn left me alive only so that I could tell you that if your army doesn't retreat immediately, he will kill Adara."

Phantom scoffed. "If you retreat, he will kill her anyway," he said ominously.

Christian's mind whirled as he considered his

options. "Did he say anything else, Lutian?"

"He wants you to give yourself up to him. Your army is to withdraw and in three days hence you are to go alone to St. Sebastian's Abbey to turn yourself over to him. He has left men behind to watch and if by nightfall you fail to set off toward the abbey and the army fails to withdraw from their borders, Adara dies."

Phantom and Ioan erupted into curses while Christian thought the matter over. There had to be a solution to this.

"I say we march onward," Phantom growled. "What guarantee do we have that she lives? He's a sneaky bastard who is just as likely to have already killed her."

Christian wasn't so sure. "He needs Adara to control her people and to add legitimacy to his son's claim for the throne. Given that, I doubt he's killed her yet."

"Then what do we do?" Ioan asked. "It sits ill with me to be held hostage by any man."

Christian stood up and let his thoughts whirl as an idea began to take form. "Our options are few. We either need to get to Adara before she reaches the city or we need to be able to break her out before they hurt her."

"The land here is too flat and open to march for long," Ioan said. "There's nowhere to ride in secrecy. They'll see us coming after them."

Lutian sighed. "We are still a week from either Elgedera or Taagaria."

"Nay," Phantom said as he stroked his beard thoughtfully. "We are week out for a thousand men. For a small group of a dozen or less—"

"We could be there in a few days," Christian said as he followed Phantom's line of thought. "What are you thinking, exactly?"

One corner of Phantom's mouth quirked up as he exchanged a knowing look with Lutian. "I was merely thinking that what we need to do is *steal* our lady away from them."

Christian frowned. "Steal?"

Lutian smiled, then winced as if pain had cut through him from his damaged ribs. "Aye, there are many in Elgedera who hate Selwyn and who know the back alleyways of the city better than the rats who live there."

Phantom looked to Lutian. "Is the Grand Vizier still in charge of the alleyways?"

Lutian nodded.

Christian was completely confused. "Grand Vizier?"

Phantom gave a light laugh. "He rules the thieves of Elgedera and he owes me favors still."

"So what's your plan?"

"Retribution, Brother Christian, grand retribution."

"They withdraw."

Adara stopped trying to work the ropes free from her hands as she overheard a messenger speaking to Selwyn. On the back of a white mare, she rode with her hands tied before her, between Selwyn and his general.

Selwyn laughed. "So the prince is craven after all." He looked at her and sneered. "Or mayhap you're not worth fighting for."

She scoffed at him. "If you truly believed that, you wouldn't have threatened him. He only does what you said because he has no wish to see me harmed."

Selwyn curled his lip at her before he turned back to his messenger. "What of the bastard imposter? Does he ride with the army?"

"Nay. We saw him head out toward the abbey alone just as you instructed."

Selwyn's smile turned insidious. "Are the assassins in place?"

"Aye, my lord. They will kill him the moment he enters the abbey's gates."

Selwyn looked about with pride and delight beaming on his oafish face. "I want his head delivered to me after they sever it from his body."

"I shall see it done."

Adara's heart hammered at their words. Surely Christian wouldn't be so foolish as to fall for such a trap. Nay, she had faith in him. Even so, there was a part of her that didn't trust Selwyn not to have more treachery lying in wait for all of them. God have mercy on them all.

Terrified for her husband and child, Adara forced herself not to show her fear to her enemy. She would be strong for Christian.

"Have you nothing to say, Majesty?" Selwyn asked her.

She feigned supreme nonchalance. "What would you have me say?"

"I would expect you to beg for the life of your husband."

She gave him an arch stare. "I would rather die than beg anything from you. Besides, I know you better. There is nothing on this earth that could make you spare his life."

"You are an intelligent wench and would have made a fine match for my son. Too bad you refused to see our cause."

"I might have seen your cause, had I not seen your heart first. I have faith in God that no one as foul as you will remain in power."

He drew back as if to strike her, then hesitated. Adara knew he didn't dare such an affront under the watchful stare of his men. Even though they were Elgederion soldiers, they were still aware of her power and position as the Taagarian queen. As the Elgederion queen. She might not be able to command them, but they were honor-bound to make sure no harm befell her in the absence of their king.

She looked at Selwyn smugly. "Aye, Selwyn, I carry the next Elgederion king inside me. Strike me and your men will revolt."

He scoffed at her. "We have no proof of your word. For all we know 'tis a bastard you carry."

"I am the queen of two nations and as such my

word is above contestation by you. I am legally married to Christian and this is the child he claims. It must gall you to know you have failed."

He gave her a sinister glare. "The game isn't over yet, my lady. Children are stillborn every day. Women widowed. You will learn your place soon enough."

He spurred his horse and rode ahead of her.

Adara curled her lip at him. Learn her place indeed. 'Twould be he who learned his, and she would be the one to teach it to him.

The next three days were horrifying for Adara, who had no idea what was to become of her. Selwyn had ridden her into Kricha, the Elgederion capital, under the cover of darkness. They had whisked her up the back halls of the palace and ensconced her in a small room in the northernmost tower under the careful watch of four guards.

Her room was pleasant enough if it weren't for the fact that she was a prisoner. Neither Selwyn nor Basilli had come to visit her. All she knew was that Ioan's army was heading back toward Europe and that Christian was headed for a monastery.

Since the messenger had left Selwyn three days ago, no one had told her anything else. She wasn't even sure why Selwyn was keeping her alive. Perhaps he was waiting for word of Christian's death.

She had tried many times since her arrival to invoke a riot amongst Selwyn's soldiers. As their queen, she should have command of them. But Selwyn had reminded them that it was her husband, not her, who commanded them, and in her husband's absence, Selwyn was the regent. Their duty was to protect her and their future heir, which meant she was locked in this room with no hope of escape.

Damn him for this.

How could one man so evil continue to thrive? It disturbed her sense of rightness. But she forced herself to have faith. Christian would come for her. She knew it.

Christian was exhausted as Phantom led their small party through the dark streets of Kricha. They had literally crawled up through the drainage trenches like rats to enter the city, which was still active even hours after sundown.

They wore the garb of peasants over their armor as they moved silently. There were only ten of them: Lutian, Phantom, five archers, two knights, and himself. It was a small number, but it should be sufficient to get to Adara and smuggle her out to safety.

He only hoped that Jerome had fooled Selwyn's spies into believing that he was Christian. With any luck, they had followed the knight to the abbey while Ioan led the army away from the borders.

Fear and anger had been his constant companion these days past as he thought of how frightened Adara must be, worried over how they were treating and caring for her. So help him, he would kill Selwyn yet.

None of them spoke as Phantom led them toward the seedier area of town. The streets here weren't clean and smelled of offal. Several of the men pressed their hands to their noses to help block the stench.

It made it easy to know which of them were members of the Brotherhood. Christian remembered a time when such a smell was as commonplace as breathing.

Phantom paused before a tawdry stew. There were several prostitutes hovering at the entrance who turned a speculative gaze toward them.

"Looking for a bit of entertainment?" one said to Phantom. She was a petite woman with long black hair and painted eyes.

Phantom dropped his cowl.

The woman immediately crossed herself as if she were facing a ghost. "You're dead."

Phantom shrugged as he replaced his cowl. "Interesting greeting, Romany. Where's your father?"

She immediately turned suspicious, worried. "Why do you seek him?"

"He owes me a debt and I'm here to collect it. Now lead me, woman. I've no time to dabble with you."

Fretful, she swept them all with her gaze before she turned to lead them into the stew.

Christian cringed at the filth. There were half-dressed prostitutes lounging about, many of whom were servicing clients in full view of anyone who happened by. "Interesting friends you have, Phantom," he mumbled.

"They kept me alive, Abbot. Trust me, that's not something easy to do in this kingdom."

Romany led them to a small room in the rear of the building, where she pushed open a door, then hesitated.

Through the opening, Christian could see a group of men playing dice and drinking. They were a loud group that appeared to be made up of three peasants, two lords, and the man he assumed by his coarse nature and expensive clothing to be the one they sought.

"Father?" Romany said, gaining the man's attention.

He was large and bald, with bulging eyes that reflected cruelty. "I told you not to disturb me, girl. Go tend to your whores." He tossed a cup at her, which Phantom deftly caught and launched back at him.

The man sputtered as the wine soaked him. Enraged, he shot to his feet at the same time Phantom pulled a dagger out and angled his head in warning. Once more, Phantom lowered his cowl so that all the men there would know him.

"Velizarii." The man breathed the name with reverence and fear. "I was told you were dead."

"That seems to be the consensus, Azral. But as you can see, I am alive and well and thoroughly enraged by my current situation." Phantom entered the room as if he owned it. He surveyed the men who were there.

"Leave," he snapped at the men who'd been playing dice.

As they got up to obey, he buried his dagger into the sleeve of one of the noblemen. "Not you."

Christian and the others stepped back to give the men room to leave. They didn't speak, but allowed Phantom to take the lead. This was his domain and he knew the rules here.

Phantom waited until they were alone.

Christian and the rest of their guard entered the room and shut the door, then locked it.

The thin, well-dressed nobleman began to sweat. "I didn't know they were going to kill you, Velizarii. I swear I didn't. Had I known they were raiding your dormitory that night, I would have warned you."

Phantom looked less than convinced by his words. "Silence, Petr. I've no desire to hear of your innocence, especially not while I can see for myself just how far your family has risen through your father's treachery. How many of the guard were slain that night? I know my dormitory wasn't the only one that they attacked."

The man gulped audibly. "All of them died."

Pain went through Phantom's eyes before he masked it. "Your father? What position does he hold?"

"Minor vizier to Selwyn."

Azral watched the two of them as if Petr's fear

and Phantom's intimidation entertained him greatly. "Should we take his head and send it to his father?"

Phantom didn't respond to his question, but rather asked one of his own. "Is the Circle still intact?"

Azral shrugged. "I was never a part of them. Even after you were captured, they refused to follow me."

"Are they still intact?"

"Aye. Darian leads them now."

"Summon them."

Azral started for the door, but paused as Phantom added, "Betray me to Selwyn, Azral, and my wrath will be such that I will gut you like a squealing pig and roast your entrails in your own fire."

Azral's face lost color. "I would never be so foolish."

"Good."

Once they were alone, Phantom turned back to Petr. "Has anything changed in the palace since I've been away?"

Petr shook his head.

"What is this Circle?" Christian asked.

Phantom let out a long, slow breath. "They were my family. After Selwyn left me for dead, their leader took me in and trained me to work with them. They are assassins and thieves for hire."

"Phantom used to be their leader," Lutian said. "It was well known by all that no one could touch the Circle so long as he led it."

"And this Darian?"

"He was just a boy when I left. His mother died at his birth, his father from illness."

Christian felt for Phantom's past. "Do you trust them?"

"Aye. You guarantee them amnesty and they will be an even more potent army than Ioan's."

"They are few," Lutian said.

Phantom gave him a dry stare. "And the greatest fires are set by the smallest sparks. Darian and his men will gladly rid us of those loyal to Selwyn. Mark my words, Selwyn has sat his last upon our grandfather's throne."

Petr's face blanched as he looked up at Christian. "You are the uncrowned king?"

Christian lowered his cowl. "Aye."

Before anyone knew what he was doing, Petr grabbed the dagger from the table and tossed it with deadly precision at Christian.

Eighteen

"The imposter's dead."

Adara froze as she heard the unfamiliar male voice through her prison's door.

"Are you sure?" her guard asked.

"Aye. Lord Selwyn identified him himself. He was stabbed straight through his heart."

Adara felt her world shift at those words. Christian dead? Nay. It couldn't be.

The men outside laughed and began to celebrate.

"Christian," she breathed, her heart shattering in waves of bitter agony. He couldn't be gone. He couldn't.

"Open the door. Lord Selwyn wishes to have the queen join him so that they can set a date for her new wedding."

Never!

Adara struggled to breathe as she glanced about

for a weapon. There was nothing. But when the door opened, her rage took hold of her.

"Damn you!" she shouted, then commenced to throwing every object toward the soldiers who entered.

She couldn't see clearly through her tears. All she knew was that she wanted vengeance on all of them. How dare they kill her Christian!

How dare they!

Sobs assailed her. She wanted to crumple from the excruciating weight of her grief. But she refused. So instead, she vented by pelting them with everything she could lift and launch.

"Adara, cease!"

She froze at the sound of a voice she hadn't expected to hear. For a moment she thought she might be dreaming, until she blinked to look up into the most handsome face she'd ever known. She stared at the same blue eyes that made the tenderest of love to her.

Christian.

Her grip went lax and the candlestick in her hand fell to the floor. He was alive!

She threw herself into his arms and held him close as giddy tears replaced her grief-induced ones. At least until her rage took hold again. "Damn you, you worthless, heartless son of a dog!" she snarled, pulling back to strike at his chest. "How dare you make me think you were dead! Don't you ever do such a thing to me again."

Christian was stunned by her language and actions. "I didn't know you could hear us through the door."

She struck him again on his armor, a blow that no doubt he felt not at all, but it gave her some degree of satisfaction. "Well, think better next time."

Her untoward anger amused him. Wiping the tears from her face, he kissed her tenderly.

Phantom cleared his throat. "Need I remind the two of you that we still need to get out of this place before the guards regain consciousness?"

"We are coming," Christian said, pulling back from her and taking her hand into his.

Two men brought the guards into her room and dumped them by her bed before they tied them securely.

"How did you know where to find me?" she asked them.

"Phantom has many unsavory friends who know every machination of Selwyn's."

For some reason she didn't doubt that.

Looking uncertain, Lutian came forward. Royal protocol aside, Adara hugged him close in relief of seeing him whole and hearty. "Thank the Lord that you are unharmed. I was terrified of what they'd done to you."

"Methinks they unaddled my noggin, my queen. For the first time in years, I seem to be thinking right again."

She smiled at him, then placed a chaste kiss to

his cheek. "We both know there was never anything really wrong with your noggin, Lutian," she whispered in his ear.

"Aye, but 'tis more fun to pretend that there is."

She laughed at that before Christian placed her hand into the crook of his arm and led her from her prison. They moved quickly through the palace's corridors. She was actually amazed at how well Phantom remembered a place he hadn't been in since his childhood.

"Just a little farther," Phantom said as they entered the civil chambers.

They were halfway across the waiting antechamber when Christian drew to a sudden stop.

Adara paused to frown at him. "Christian?"

He didn't seem to hear her as he stared up at the wall with a scowl on his handsome face.

She turned to see what held his interest, then swallowed. It was a painting of his family. His grandfather sat on his throne in full royal regalia with his grandmother on the throne beside him. Christian's mother sat at their feet with two of her brothers on each side of her.

The likenesses were poor, but enough that even Christian must realize who they were.

He looked around the antechamber then as if seeing it with new eyes. "What is this room?" he asked Phantom.

"The waiting antechamber for the throne room."

"And the throne room? Where is it?"

Phantom indicated a pair of doors to his left with a jerk of his chin. "Through yon doors."

Without another word, Christian headed toward them.

"Christian?" she asked, following after him.

What was he doing?

He opened the door to the gilded room, which was completely empty. Adara hadn't been inside it since she was a small girl. The room was large and open, and trimmed in green. At the far end was a golden dais that held a pair of ornately crafted thrones. Behind them was the royal banner that bore the symbol of the three dragons of Elgedera.

Since time immemorial, Christian's family had reigned here. Like her own family, his had never been overthrown. Not until Selwyn.

Christian turned to look at her. "Come, my lady," he said, holding his arm out to her.

"Come where?"

"Take my arm, Adara."

Uncertain, she did. He led her toward the thrones, then placed her on the queen's.

Confused, she watched as Lutian, Phantom, and the other seven men came forward, into the room. Without a word, Christian removed his peasant garb to reveal his royal surcoat. He picked up the royal scepter that was lying on a pillar between the thrones, then took a seat on his own throne.

"What is it you do?" Phantom asked.

He looked at Phantom, his eyes haunted. "Our fathers died for this. You and I have risked everything to return here. I say we send for Selwyn and let him know that the true king has returned and that his days of usurpation are over."

Phantom laughed darkly. "Only a fool would do such a thing."

"Nay," Lutian said from his right. "Not even a fool would be so foolish. 'Tis suicide."

Phantom took a long, deep breath, then expelled it slowly before he crossed the room to stand before Christian. "My father died here in this room." His gaze turned stormy as he looked to the corner where it must have happened. "What more fitting place for me to be when I, too, am sent to hell? I am with you, brother, until the very end."

Adara started to rise.

"Stay, my queen," Christian said. "This is your throne and it is the throne that will one day belong to our child."

Now he wanted his throne? She could strangle him for his timing. "They will kill us, Christian."

He took her hand into his and held it. "We shall see."

Selwyn was preparing himself for bed when a knock on his door disturbed him.

"What can it be at this hour?" he snapped at his valet. "Open the damned door and send them away."

But as the door opened to show him his grand

marshal, a bad feeling went through him. The man looked scared and unsure.

"What is it?" he asked.

The marshal swallowed audibly. "There is . . . The king demands your presence."

Selwyn frowned at his nonsensical words. "King? What king?"

"The one who sits on the throne and claims to be Prince Christian, grandson of King Alonzo the Great."

Selwyn's stomach sank at his words. Nay, it couldn't be. There was no way Christian could be here. His spies had seen him heading for the abbey, not toward the city.

"Ready my guard," he snarled as he pulled on his red surcoat. "Send for my son."

The marshal hesitated. "Only the true king can command me, Lord Selwyn. You know our laws."

"He is an imposter!"

"Perhaps, but he does favor his grandfather, whom I served for many years. He has his bearing and form . . . and bears the royal coat of arms. I believe him to be who he claims, and as such, I am his servant."

Selwyn hissed at the man. He grabbed his sword, then went to rouse his guards himself.

"Was the hall always this melancholy?" Christian asked Phantom. "I think we should add more windows."

Adara sat there in shock as the two of them continued to speak of inconsequential matters while the grand marshal had gone to fetch Selwyn, who would most likely muster an army.

She still couldn't believe Christian's audacity. When the marshal had come in, she had expected total anarchy, but the man had looked at Christian and seen the family resemblance.

Even so, she had expected him to balk. He hadn't. But one old man's loyalty wouldn't win this throne.

They heard the sound of many footsteps outside.

Adara crossed herself and prayed as the doors to the throne room were slung open to show her Selwyn and a large group of guards.

Christian and Phantom continued to chat about redecorating the throne room.

"I think we should remove that set of swords," Christian said, indicating a display over the hearth. "Rather morbid, I think."

"Aye," Phantom concurred. "My father never cared for it, either."

"Hmm," Christian said. With a regal wave of his hand that was completely out of character for him, he motioned to the grand marshal. "Can you read and write, Marshal?"

"Aye, Majesty."

"Good, then. Fetch a ledger and make notes."

"What is this?" Selwyn demanded as he stormed into the room.

"Silence!" Christian roared in an imperious tone that left Adara wide-eyed. "No one has addressed you, servant. My new vizier and I are discussing grave matters."

Christian rose from his throne and stepped down toward the wall opposite the hearth. "This entire room needs to be redone. My queen doesn't care for green." He looked to her. "What color pleases you most, my love?"

She exchanged a nervous look with Lutian while Selwyn sputtered in indignation. "Blue."

"Then let us redo this room in blue. *Royal* blue."

"Seize him!" Selwyn snarled.

The guards looked to the marshal, who appeared sheepish.

Christian gave an exaggerated sigh. "You forget, servant, that the guard serves the king. You are—or should I say *were*—the regent ruling only until the king returned." He smiled evilly. "Well, the king has come home. You are relieved of all your duties."

"He's not the king," Selwyn snapped. "Prince Christian is dead."

Without a single comment, Christian walked to the wall where Selwyn's painting rested. He looked at it coldly, then knocked it from the wall. It landed with an echoing clatter. "Marshal, I want this burned."

Selwyn started for Christian, only to stop the instant an arrow embedded itself beside him. He froze.

"I came with my own guard," Christian said coldly.

Selwyn looked to the balcony overhead, where three of the archers were visible. The others were hiding with arrows at ready, and while they had been waiting there for his appearance, their number had grown to twenty from the thieves who had joined their ranks.

Christian turned to face the guards. "Take him."

As they moved to obey Christian, Adara heard a loud cry from the antechamber. "Attack!"

She came to her feet as complete chaos erupted in the doorway of the antechamber. A large group of men came in, with Basilli leading them.

"Protect the queen," Christian snarled, unsheathing his sword to join the fray.

Lutian rushed to pull her to safety. The two knights who had come with Christian pushed her into a corner so that they could form a barrier between her and the fighting.

Adara pressed her hand to her lips as she watched the fighting from over the knights' shoulders.

Christian didn't expect his people to fight with him, but to his surprise the guards Selwyn had brought immediately turned on the newcomers who were being led by a man not much older than Christian.

"Basilli!" Selwyn snapped. "They must be killed."

"Must we?" Phantom asked with a laugh.

Selwyn ran for him. Phantom jerked and moved so fast that it wasn't until the dagger embedded itself into Selwyn's heart that Christian realized Phantom had thrown it.

"That's for my father, you bastard," Phantom snarled as Selwyn fell to the floor on his knees and pulled the dagger free. By his actions it was obvious he intended to use it against Phantom.

Phantom gave him no quarter. His eyes blazing hell's wrath, he unsheathed his sword and drove it deep into Selwyn's body. "And that is for my grandfather, who trusted you."

Basilli cried out as he saw his father fall. Enraged, he lunged for Christian, who fought him back. Basilli's men retreated as they realized Selwyn was dead.

Christian's guards moved forward.

"Nay," Christian growled. "This matter ends here and now. There will be no one left to threaten my child or my queen."

Basilli sneered at that. "I will see both your whore and your whoreson skewered beside you."

Christian parried his attack and countered it. He would give the man credit, Basilli was an accomplished swordsman.

But not accomplished enough. Christian caught his next stroke and disarmed him. "Take him," he said to his guards.

Before they could, Basilli rushed forward, dagger drawn. He caught Christian off guard as he unbalanced him and sent them both to the floor. The impact knocked the sword from Christian's hand.

Christian grabbed the man and punched him hard before he grabbed Basilli's hand that held the dagger.

The guards moved forward again.

"Nay," Phantom snapped. "Your king can handle himself."

Christian lifted his leg and kicked Basilli in the back, lurching him forward. Basilli hissed loudly, his eyes flaring an instant before they widened.

It was then Christian realized that Basilli's wrist had been turned during his lurch. The dagger in his hand was now embedded in his chest.

Basilli panted in pain as he let loose his hold. Christian pulled the dagger free as the man slid from him to fall back against the floor. Rising to his feet, Christian felt for the man and for the greed that had led father and son to such a fate.

He should hate them. Part of him did and always would. But the other part of him that had been raised in the Church knew his hatred would destroy no one but himself.

And he had far too much to lose now.

Christian made the sign of the cross over Basilli as the life seeped out of him. *"Pax vobiscum, frater.* May God be with you, and may He show you the mercy you never showed anyone else."

"Mercy is for the weak," Phantom snarled as he moved to stand over Basilli's body.

Christian shook his head at his cousin. "That kind of thinking is what led them to this end,

Phantom. Don't let your hatred destroy you, too. They are dead now. Let the past go with them."

If he didn't know better, he'd swear he almost saw admiration in Phantom's eyes. "You're a bloody damned fool, Christian of Acre." He looked over to where Adara was moving away from her protectors. "But you're a damned lucky one."

"And I thank God every day for that."

He really did. Adara had given him more than he had ever hoped to have. She had given him his life, his purpose, and now she'd restored his faith.

There was nothing he wouldn't do for her. Nothing he wouldn't sacrifice.

Taking her hand into his, he placed a loving kiss onto her palm, then looked up to see the men watching him. They were looking to him for leadership.

And he was their prince and soon-to-be king.

At least in theory. In his heart he knew the truth. He might rule this land and these people, but the tiny woman before him ruled his heart. In her hands she held the only real power, and it wasn't one of destruction. It was one of healing and of love. For that he owed her more than he could ever repay, and he looked forward to the years ahead of them.

Epilogue

The last two months had moved far too swiftly for Christian's tastes. Everything about his life had completely changed. With Adara's help, they had merged their two kingdoms into a force to be reckoned with.

After a few minor skirmishes with rebel lords who weren't ready to give up the power Selwyn had allowed them to wield, Ioan and Corryn and their army had bade them adieu to return to Europe. To Christian's shock, Phantom had stayed even though every day he asked Christian why he was still there.

Christian had no answer, but he was eternally grateful for his cousin's ill-bred humor.

With every day that passed, Christian settled more into his role as king. If not for Adara, it would be unbearable to him. He still hated the feeling of stone walls around him, but there in the shelter of her arms, he could somehow forget about them.

Now he was in the throne room with Phantom. True to his word, it was completely redecorated. There were no remnants of Selwyn and it was a perfect blue to please Adara. He again wore his mother's emblem, which had been found in Selwyn's room.

The doors to the throne room opened to admit Adara's cousin Thera, who had done well on the Taagarian throne during Adara's absence. As always, she looked to Phantom and blushed, then bowed low before Christian. "Your queen bade me to tell you that she is in labor, Majesty."

Christian's heart stopped at the words he'd been waiting for these months past with an equal share of dread and excitement. He couldn't seem to do anything more than stare at the woman who bore a striking resemblance to his wife.

Phantom snapped his fingers before his face. "Baby, Abbot. Your child?"

Christian bolted from his throne. With no thought of how it looked for the king to be running as if the devil himself were in pursuit, he raced down the hallways until he reached their bedchambers.

He threw open the doors to see his wife lying in their bed with a circle of women around her. There was one surgeon waiting off to the side while the women offered comfort and advice to Adara.

The surgeon came forward as soon as he saw

Christian. "'Tis unseemly for you to be here, Majesty," the man said. "I will present the baby to you when he is born."

"Nay," Christian growled as he pushed past him. "I was there when my child was conceived, and by God, I shall be here when he or she is born." He went to Adara's side. Her beautiful face was strained, her eyes filled with pain.

Even so, she managed a smile for him, then she cursed him as she screamed out in obvious agony. Honestly, he hadn't known his queen knew such an insult existed.

"Methinks we traveled far too long with Ioan's men," he said as he took the cloth from her maid's hand and wiped her brow.

She glared at him as she panted. "I choose that you have this child." She cried out again.

Christian kissed her brow as guilt consumed him. "I wish that I could, Adara."

But she didn't hear him as more pain shook her slight frame. Christian wasn't sure what to do, so there he remained by her side as she struggled for hours.

It was just before dark when their son finally joined them. Adara fell back in relief while the surgeon examined the baby.

Christian felt the tears stinging his eyes as he looked back and forth between his wife and his son.

His son.

It hadn't seemed truly real until this moment. He was a father and he owed it all to the exhausted woman lying in his bed. He kissed her gently and wiped at her own tears of joy.

"He's beautiful, my lady," he whispered to her.

The surgeon brought the baby to them and placed him in Adara's arms. Christian stared in awe at the tiny infant who squalled angrily at them. He ran his finger down the side of the red, soft skin.

"What shall we call him?"

She looked thoughtful. "Lutian."

Christian choked on the name. "Pardon?"

Her dark eyes teased him. " 'Twould only be fair, given your treatment of him when he volunteered to donate himself for my cause."

He growled at her.

"Then let us call him Josyn."

"Josyn?"

"It means 'Son of the Valiant' in Taagarian. I can think of no better name for your child."

He leaned down and nuzzled his face against hers so that he could inhale her sweet skin. "Then Josyn it shall be, but not for me. Rather he be named for his fearless mother, who crossed the known world to find a lost soul and bring him home again. Thank you, Adara, for everything you have brought me."

Adara's eyes teared up again at her husband's words. She knew how hard it was for Christian to say such tender things and she savored every syllable.

"You were more than worth the journey, Christian. I would traverse hell itself for you."

His gaze was tender and adoring. "I love you, Adara."

A single tear fell as she finally heard those longed-for words. Not that she had really doubted his love. But it was nice to hear the words from his lips.

"I love you, too."

Christian kissed her, then moved back so that she could feed their son.

Her maids congratulated her one by one, then left. The surgeon looked over the baby one last time before he, too, left them alone.

It was so intimate to be with her family. The three of them. She watched her husband closely while he said nothing. He merely sat on the bed, watching his son suckle her.

Adara finished feeding Josyn.

Christian reached for the baby. "I'll take him so that you can rest."

She looked at him suspiciously. "What do you know of babies?"

"Truly nothing more than how to create them. But I should say that is only slightly less than you yourself know."

He had a point with that. Laughing at him, she released her son to his father and watched as Christian's large hands all but swallowed up the size of the baby. Christian snuggled the baby close to his chest and went to sit near the window.

The corners of her mouth twitched up as she listened to him telling his son all about the future Christian had planned for him.

Closing her eyes, she had just settled back when a knock sounded on her door. Adara wasn't paying much attention as she heard Lutian come in to see the baby.

At least not until the word "Brotherhood" was spoken.

"What was that?" she asked, immediately sitting up.

Lutian looked at her sheepishly. "There is a call for their members."

Adara's chest tightened as tears gathered in her eyes. But she refused to let them fall. She had known this day would come. She'd only hoped it wouldn't come so soon.

Christian looked away from her, his brow creased by indecision.

"You must go to them, husband," she said quietly, even though her heart was breaking. She had seen the men's love and devotion to each other firsthand. "I told you that I would never interfere with your vows."

He came forward and placed Josyn beside her. "And I vowed to stand by your side as king and husband for the rest of my life." He looked over his shoulder to Lutian. "Have Phantom take as many men as he needs and lead them. He will see to it that my honor is held."

Her tears fell silently. "Are you certain? I don't

ever want you to think that I have interfered with your choices."

He scoffed at that. "You are my life. My heart. My soul. I cannot survive without any of those. Besides, every time I have ever left you alone, you have found trouble of epic proportions."

She gaped at his teasing words, which sparked her ire. "Me? You were the one who—"

He broke her words off with a kiss. "Aye, Adara, I am the one who loves you and who will never leave you."

Her outrage fled before the wealth of love she felt for this man. For there was one thing she knew in this life that was true . . . Christian was, and would always be, a man of his word.

And nothing born of this world would ever take him away from her.

"I need a hero!"

Imagine that you are the heroine
of your favorite romance. You are
resilient, strong, intrepid.
You rule a country, own a business,
or, perhaps, run a drafty country house
on a shoestring budget. You *can* do it all . . .
and, usually, you do.

But every now and then a gal needs
some help—someone to vanquish
the enemy soldiers,
keep your business afloat . . .
or just plain offer to keep
the servants in line.

Sometimes you need a hero.

Now, in three spectacular new romances by
Kinley MacGregor, Samantha James and
Christie Ridgway—
and one delicious anthology
by Stephanie Laurens, Christina Dodd
and Elizabeth Boyle—
we meet heroines who can
do it all . . . and the sexy,
irresistible heroes who stand
by their side every step
of the way.

**Experience the passion of
Kinley MacGregor's**

Return of the Warrior

**The unforgettable second installment
of the "Brotherhood of the Sword"**

Queen Adara has one mission: to find her wayward
husband and save their throne! But handsome warrior
Christian of Acre doesn't seem to care much about
ruling his kingdom; he clearly doesn't even consider
himself married! All he wants to do is travel the countryside, helping the poor and downtrodden. But it's
Adara who needs his help right now, and she'll do
anything—even appear in his bedroom naked and
alluring—to get him to rule with her . . . forever.

"Well?" Queen Adara asked in nervous anticipation as her
senior advisor drew near her throne.

Xerus had been her father's most trusted man. At almost
three score years in age, he still held the sharpness of a man in
the prime of his life. His once-black hair was now streaked
with gray and his beard was whiter than the stone walls that
surrounded their capital city, Garzi.

Since her father's death two years past, Adara had turned

to Xerus for everything. There was no one alive she trusted more, which didn't say much, since, as a queen, her first lesson had been that spies and traitors abounded in her court. Most thought that a woman had no business as the leader of their small kingdom.

Adara had other thoughts on that matter. As her father's only surviving child, she refused to see anyone not of their royal bloodline on this throne. Her family had held the royal seat since before the time of Moses.

No one would take her precious Taagaria from her. Not so long as she breathed.

Xerus shook his head and sighed wearily. "Nay, my queen, they refuse to allow you to divorce their king. In their minds you are married and should you try to sever ties to their throne by divorce or annulment they will attack with the sanction of the Church. After all, in their eyes they already own our kingdom. In fact, Selwyn thinks it best that you move into his custody for your own welfare so that they can protect you . . . as their queen."

Adara clenched her fists in frustration.

Xerus glanced over his shoulder toward her two guards who flanked her door before he drew closer to her throne so that he could whisper privately into her ear.

Lutian, her fool, crept nearer to them as well and angled his head so that he wouldn't miss a single word. He even cupped his ear forward.

Xerus glared at the fool.

Dropping his hand, Lutian glared back. A short, lean man, Lutian had straight brown hair and wore a well-trimmed beard. Possessed of average looks, his face was pleasant enough, but it was his kind brown eyes that endeared him to her.

"Speak openly," she said to her advisor. "There is no one I trust more than Lutian."

"He's a half-wit, my queen."

Lutian snorted. "Half-wit, whole-wit, I have enough of them to know to keep silent. So speak, good counselor, and let the queen judge which of the two of us is the greater fool present."

Adara pressed her lips together to keep from smiling at Lutian. Two years younger than she, Lutian had been seriously injured as a youth when he'd tumbled from their walls and landed on his head. Ever since that day, she had watched over him and kept him close lest anyone make his life even more difficult.

She placed a hand on his shoulder to silence him. Xerus couldn't abide being made fun of. Unlike her, he didn't value Lutian's friendship and service.

With a warning glare to the fool, Xerus finally spoke. "Their prince-regent said that if you would finally like to declare Prince Christian dead, then he might be persuaded toward your cause . . . at a price."

Closing her eyes, she ground her teeth furiously. The Elgederion regent had made his position on that matter more than clear. Selwyn wanted her in his son's bed as his bride to secure their tenuous claim to the throne, and the devil would freeze solid before she ever gave herself over to him and allowed those soulless men to rule her people.

How she wished she commanded a larger nation with enough soldiers to pound the arrogant prince-regent into nothing more than a bad memory. Unfortunately, a war would be far too costly to her people and her kingdom. They couldn't fight the Elgederions alone and none of their other allies would help, since to them it was a family squabble between her and her husband's kingdom.

If only her husband would return home and claim his throne, but every time they had sent a man for him, the messenger was slain. To her knowledge none of them had ever reached Christian and she was tired of sending men to their deaths.

Nay, 'twas time to see this matter closed once and for all.

"Send for Thera," she whispered to Xerus.

He scowled at her. "For what purpose?"

"I intend to take a lengthy trip and I can't afford to let anyone know that I am not here to guard my throne."

"Your cousin is not you, Your Grace. Should anyone learn—"

"I trust you alone to keep her and my crown safe until I return. Have her confined to my quarters and tell everyone that I am ill."

Xerus looked even more confused by her orders. "Where are you going?"

"To find my wayward husband and to bring him home."

It's a special treat

Hero, Come Back

Three unforgettable original tales
Three amazing storytellers:
Stephanie Laurens, Christina Dodd, Elizabeth Boyle

Imagine, the return of three of the characters you love best—Reggie from Stephanie Laurens's *On a Wild Night* (and *On a Wicked Dawn*)! Jemmy Finch from Elizabeth Boyle's *Once Tempted* (and *It Takes a Hero*)! And Harry Chamberlain, the Earl of Granville, from Christina Dodd's *Lost in Your Arms*!

Now you get to meet them all over again in this delicious anthology of heroes who were just too good *not* to have stories of their own.

Lost and Found
Stephanie Laurens

Releasing Benjamin, Reggie looked at Anne. He'd recognized her soft voice and all notion of politely retreating had vanished. Anne was Amelia's sister-in-law, Luc Ashford's second sister, known to all family and close friends as highly nervous in crowds.

They hadn't met for some years; he suspected she avoided tonnish gatherings. Rapid calculation revealed she must be twenty-six. She seemed . . . perhaps an inch taller, more assured, more definite, certainly more striking than he recalled, but then she wasn't shrinking against any wall at the moment. She was elegantly turned out in a dark green walking dress. Her expression was open, decided, her face framed by lustrous brown hair caught up in a top knot, then allowed to cascade about her head in lush waves. Her eyes were light brown, the color of caramel, large and set under delicately arched brows. Her lips were blush rose, sensuously curved, decidedly vulnerable.

Intensely feminine.

As were the curves of breast and waist revealed by the tightly-fitting bodice . . .

Jerking his mind from the unexpected track, he frowned. "Now cut line—what is this about?"

A frown lit her eyes, a warning one. "I'll explain once we've returned Benjy to the house." Retaking Benjy's hand, she turned back along the path.

Reggie pivoted and fell in beside her. "Which house? Is Luc in town?"

"No. Not Calverton House." Anne hesitated, then added, more softly, "The Foundling House."

Pieces of the puzzle fell, jigsawlike, into place, but the picture in his mind was incomplete. His long strides relaxed, he retook her arm, wound it with his, forcing her to slow. "Much better to stroll without a care, rather than rush off so purposefully. No need for the ignorant to wonder what your purpose is."

The Matchmaker's Bargain
Elizabeth Boyle

"Oh, this cannot be!" Esme said, bounding up from her chair. "I can't get married."

"Whyever not? You aren't already engaged, are you?" Jemmy didn't know why, but for some reason he didn't like the idea of her being another man's betrothed. Besides, what the devil was the fellow thinking, letting such a pretty little chit wander lost about the countryside?

But his concerns about another man in her life were for naught, for she told him very tartly, "I am not engaged, sir, and I assure you, I'm not destined for marriage."

"I don't see that there is anything wrong with you," he said without thinking. Demmit, this is what came of living the life of a recluse—he'd forgotten every bit of his town bronze. "I mean to say, it's not like you couldn't be here seeking a husband."

The disbelief on her face struck him to the core.

Was she really so unaware of the pretty picture she presented? That her green eyes, bright and full of sparkles, and soft brown hair, still tumbled from her slumbers and hanging in long tangled curls, was an enticing picture—one that might persuade many a man to get fitted for a pair of leg-shackles.

Even Jemmy found himself susceptible to her charms—she had an air of familiarity about her that whispered of strength and warmth and sensibility, capable of drawing a man toward her like a beggar to a warm hearth.

Not to mention the parts, that as a gentleman, he shouldn't know she possessed, but in their short, albeit rather noteworthy acquaintance, had discovered with the familiarity that one usually had only with a mistress . . . or a hastily gained betrothed.

He shook that idea right out of his head. Whatever was he thinking? She wasn't interested in marriage, and neither was he. Not than any lady *would* have him . . . lame and scarred as he was.

"I hardly see that any of this is your concern," she was saying, once again bustling about the room, gathering up her belongings. She plucked her stockings—gauzy, French sort of things—from the line by the fire.

He could imagine what they would look like on her, and more importantly what it would feel like sliding them off her long, elegant legs.

When she saw him staring at her unmentionables, she blushed and shoved them into her valise. "I really must be away."

The Third Suitor
Christina Dodd

Leaning over the high porch railing, Harry Chamberlain looked down into the flowering shrubbery surrounding his oceanfront cottage and asked, "Young woman, what are you doing down there?"

The girl flinched, stopped crawling through the collection of moss, dirt and faded pink blossoms, and turned a smudged face up to his. "Shh." She glanced behind her, as if someone were creeping after her. "I'm trying to avoid one of my suitors."

Harry glanced behind her, too. No one was there.

"Can you see him?" she asked.

"There's not a soul in sight." A smart man would have let her go on her way. Harry was on holiday, a holiday he desperately needed, and he had vowed to avoid trouble at all costs. Now a girl of perhaps eighteen years, dressed in a modish blue flowered gown, came crawling through the bushes, armed with nothing more than a ridiculous tale, and he was tempted to help. Tempted because of a thin, tanned face, wide brown eyes, a kissable mouth, a crooked blue bonnet and, from this angle, the finest pair of breasts he'd ever had the good fortune to gaze upon.

Such unruliness in his own character surprised him. He was, in truth, Edmund Kennard Henry Chamberlain, earl of Granville, the owner of a great estate in Somerset, and because of the weight of his responsibilities there, and the additional responsibilities he had taken on, he tended to do his duty without capriciousness. Indeed, it was that trait which had set him, eight years ago, to serve England in various countries and capacities. Now he gazed at a female intent on some silliness and discovered in himself the urge to find out more about her. Perhaps he had at last relaxed from the tension of his last job. Or perhaps she *was* the relaxation he sought.

In a trembling voice, she pleaded, "Please, sir, if he appears, don't tell him I'm here."

"I wouldn't dream of interfering."

"Oh, thank you!" A smile transformed that quivering mouth into one that was naturally merry, with soft peach lips and a dimple. "Because I thought that's what you were doing."

**Be swept away by the
passion of Samantha James's**

A Perfect Hero

The third in her Sterling Family trilogy

When Lady Julianna Sterling is left standing at the altar, she heaves a sigh and reminds herself that the Sterlings never had much luck. But one fateful night, Julianna's luck changes in a most unexpected way, and her staid, steady life is turned upside down. Her coach is attacked by the Magpie—a mysterious and enticing highwayman who audaciously kidnaps her, plunging Julianna into a life of seductive excitement.

Julianna felt herself tumbling to the floor. Jarred into wakefulness, she opened her eyes, rubbing her shoulder where she'd landed. What the deuce . . . ? Panic enveloped her; it was pitch black inside the coach.

And outside as well.

She was just about to heave herself back onto the cushions when the sound of male voices punctuated the air outside. The coachman . . . and someone else.

"Put it down, I s-say!" the coachman stuttered. "There's nothing of value aboard, I swear! Mercy," the man blubbered. "I beg of you, have mercy!"

Even as a decidedly prickly unease slid down her spine, the door was wrenched open. She found herself staring at the gleaming barrel of a pistol. In terror she lifted her gaze to the man who possessed it.

Garbed in black he was, from the enveloping folds of his cloak to the kerchief that obscured the lower half of his face. A silk mask was tied around his eyes; they were all that was visible of his features. Even in the dark, there was no mistaking their color. They glimmered like clear golden fire, pale and unearthly.

The devil's eyes.

"Nothing of value aboard, eh?"

A gust of chill night air funneled in. Yet it was like nothing compared to the chill she felt in hearing that voice . . . So softly querulous, like steel tearing through tightly stretched silk, she decided dazedly.

She had always despised silly, weak, helpless females. Yet when his gaze raked over her—*through* her, bold and ever so irreverent!—she felt stripped to the bone.

Goose bumps rose on her flesh. She couldn't move. She most certainly couldn't speak. She could not even swallow past the knot lodged deep in her throat. Fear numbed her mind. Her mouth was dry with a sickly dread such as she had never experienced. All she could think was that if Mrs. Chadwick were here, she might take great delight in knowing she'd been right to be so fearful. For somehow Julianna knew with a mind-chilling certainty that it was he . . .

The Magpie.

Dane Quincy Granville did not count on the coachman's reaction—nor his rashness. There was a crack of the whip, a frenzied shout. The horses bolted. Instinctively, Dane leaped back, very nearly knocked to the ground. The vehicle jolted forward, speeding toward a bend in the road.

The stupid fool! Christ, the coachman would never make the turn. The bend was too sharp. He was going too fast—

The night exploded. There was an excruciating crash, the sound of wood splintering and cracking . . . the high-pitched neighs of the horses.

Then there was nothing.

Galvanized into action, Dane sprang for Percival. Leaping from the stallion's back, he hurtled himself down the steep embankment where the coach had disappeared. Scrambling over the brush, he spied it. It was overturned, resting against the trunk of an ancient tree.

One wheel was still spinning as he reached it.

The horses were already gone. So was the driver. His neck was broken, twisted at an odd angle from his body. Dane had seen enough of death to know there was nothing he could do to help him.

Miraculously, the door to the main compartment had remained on its hinges. In fury and fear, Dane tore it off and lunged into the compartment.

The girl was still inside, coiled in a heap on the roof. His heart in his throat, he reached for her, easing her into his arms and outside.

His heart pounding, he knelt in the damp earth and stared down at her. "Wake up!" he commanded. As if because he willed it, as if it would be so . . . He gritted his teeth, as if to instill his very will—his very life—inside her.

Her head fell limply over his arm.

"Dammit, girl, wake up!"

He was sick in the pit of his belly, in his very soul. If only the driver hadn't been so blasted skittish. So hasty! He wouldn't have harmed them, either of them. On a field near Brussels, he'd seen enough death and dying to last a lifetime. God knew it had changed him. Shaped him for all eternity. And for now, all he wanted was—

She moaned.

An odd little laugh broke from his chest, the sound almost brittle. After all his careful planning that *this* should occur . . . But he couldn't ascertain her injuries. Not here. Not in the dark. He must leave. Now. He couldn't afford to linger, else all might be for naught.

The girl did not wake as he rifled through the boot, retrieving a bulging sack and a valise. Seconds later, he whistled for Percival. Cradling the girl carefully against his chest, he lifted the reins and rode into the night.

As suddenly as he had appeared, the Magpie was gone.

**We're going to make you
an offer you can't refuse in
Christie Ridgway's**

An Offer He Can't Refuse

The first in her delicious new Wisegirls series

Téa Caruso knows what everyone thinks about her
family . . . her very large, very powerful family. After
all, she grew up in the shadow of her grandfather—
The Sun Dried Tomato King—and her uncles, with
their mysterious "business." And, of course, there
are her aunts, who don't ask too many questions.
She's spent a lifetime going legit, and now her past
comes back to haunt her when she falls for John
Magee. He's a professional gambler, the worse kind
of man, one who'd make the family proud . . . or
is he?

Téa Caruso had once been very, very bad and she wondered
if today was the day she started paying for it. After spend-
ing the morning closeted in the perfume-saturated powder
room of Mr. and Mrs. William Duncan's Spanish-Italian-
Renaissance-inspired Palm Springs home, discussing baby
Jesus and the Holy Mother, she emerged from the clouds—
both heavenly and olfactory—with a Chanel No. 5 hang-

over and fingernail creases in her palms as deep as the Duncan's quarter-mile lap pool.

Standing on the pillowed limestone terrace outside, she allowed herself a sixty-second pause for fresh air, but multitasked the moment by completing a quick appearance check as well. Even someone with less artistic training than Téa would know that her Mediterranean coloring and generous curves were made for low necklines and sassy flounces in gypsy shades, but her Mandarin-collared, dove gray linen dress was devised to button up, smooth out, and tuck away. Though she could never feel innocent, she preferred to at least look that way.

The reflection in her hand mirror presented no jarring surprises. The sun lent an apricot cast to her olive skin. Tilted brown eyes, a slightly patrician nose, cheekbones and jawline now defined after years of counting calories instead of chowing down on cookies. Assured that her buttons were tight, her mascara unsmudged, and her hair still controlled in its long, dark sweep, she snapped the compact shut. Then, hurrying in the direction of her car, she swapped mirror for cell phone and speed dialed her interior design firm.

"She's still insisting on Him," she told her assistant when she answered. "Find out who can hand paint a Rembrandt-styled infant Jesus in the bottom of a porcelain sink."

Glancing over at the Madonna blue water of the pool, Téa was reminded of the morning's single success. "The good news is I talked her out of the Virgin Mary in the bidet bowl." Surely the Mother of God would appreciate that fact.

Still on forward march, she checked her watch. "Quick, any messages? I have lunch with my sisters up next."

"Nikki O'Neal phoned and mentioned a redo of her dining room," her assistant replied. "Something about a mural depicting the Ascension."

The Ascension?

Téa's steps faltered, slowed. "No," she groaned. "That means Mrs. D. has spilled her plans. Now we'll be hearing from every one of her group at Our Lady of Mink."

A segment of Téa's client list—members of the St. Brigit's Guild at the posh Our Lady of Mercy Catholic Church—cultivated their competitive spirits as well as their Holy Spirit during their weekly meetings. One woman would share a new idea for home decor, prompting the next to take the same theme to even greater—more ostentatious—heights.

Three years before it had been everything vineyard, then after that sea life turned all the rage, and now . . . good God.

"The *Ascension*?" Téa muttered. "These women must be out of their minds."

But could she really blame them? Palm Springs had a grand tradition of the grandiose, after all. Walt Disney had owned a home here. Elvis. Liberace.

It was just that when she'd opened her business, filled with high artistic aspirations and a zealous determination to make over the notorious Caruso name, she hadn't foreseen the pitfalls. Like how the ceaseless influx of rent and utility bills and the unsteady trickle and occasional torrent that was her cash flow meant she couldn't be picky when it came to choosing design jobs.

Like how *that* could result in gaining woeful renown as designer of all things overdone. She groaned again.

"Oh, and Téa . . ." Her assistant's voice rose in an expectant lilt. "His Huskiness called."

Her stomach lurched, pity party forgotten. "What? *Who*?"

"Johnny Magee."

Of course, Johnny Magee. Her assistant referred to the man they'd never met by an ever-expanding lexicon of nicknames that ranged from the overrated to the out-and-out ridiculous. To Téa, he was simply her One Chance, her Answered Prayers, her Belief in Miracles.

Varian walks a fine line between the forces of good and evil. Born of the Adoni who serve Morgen, he's chosen the path of nobility even though the lure of the darkest part of himself is ever at odds with the part of him that wants to do what's right. It's a battle he can't always win.

Merewyn was born of light, and through an ill-conceived bargain to save herself, she damned herself completely. Now she's been given one last task. Bring Varian over to le Cercle du Damne or lose her soul forever to Morgen and her whims. It's a race against time and it's one she's determined to win.

But Varian isn't always what he seems and though he was born of the darkest powers, his is an iron will that can withstand any temptation that Merewyn throws at him. Until she accidentally discovers the one weakness that can break him completely. Now she has to choose between saving herself or damning the entire world to Morgen's clutches.

www.LordsofAvalon.com